NIGHT MOVES

NIGHTHAWK SECURITY - BOOK FOUR

SUSAN SLEEMAN

D1073339

Published by Edge of Your Seat Books, Inc.

Contact the publisher at contact@edgeofyourseatbooks.com

1

———

Sympathize with a serial killer? No way. Natalie Dunn could never tolerate one, much less empathize with him. Especially not with the man she suspected of killing her sister. Her sister, for goodness' sake! But when Kirk Gentry was released from the hospital and walked through his front door, dredging up her usual professional smile was the only way she might escape his house alive. If he had even a hint of the fact that she suspected him, he could end her life too.

"Please don't tell." His eight-year-old daughter, Willow, leaned back against her headboard in her frilly bedroom and splayed out her fingers. Her brown eyes darkened with fear as she stared at the polished nails. She'd just shared a horrifying tale.

One that Natalie was struggling to comprehend.

Natalie swallowed. Once. Twice. Dug deep for a smile for this curly redhead with apple cheeks, a pudgy nose covered in freckles, and a gap in her upper teeth. The child had no idea what her father might have done, even considering his bizarre behavior.

Could be because he was a police officer. Sure, she would trust him as her father, but as an officer, she probably held additional respect for him, and it would be hard to believe someone in law enforcement could be a serial killer.

Willow locked eyes with Natalie. "Dad will be mad that I told you he paints my nails. He said not to. I didn't mean to tell you."

Willow tucked her arms under her pajamaed legs as if hiding them could change the fact that she'd blurted out that her dad got his kicks from polishing her nails.

"It just came out. Honest." She lifted her face to Natalie. "You said you're safe to tell my secrets to, and you won't tell anyone else. That's what you told me. That social workers want to help kids, not hurt them."

"And I meant that." Natalie rested her hand on Willow's knee, thankful her younger siblings were tucked into their beds and not listening to this conversation. "It's safe to talk to me. But sometimes I have to put things in my reports for my supervisors because it's my job to make sure you and your little brother and sister are safe and that your dad is providing you with a stable home."

"But you won't have to say about the fingernails, right? They don't have anything to do with stable or safe."

"Probably not," Natalie said, knowing she was lying to this poor child.

Not that the manicuring of a child's nails by her father didn't happen in other households. But behaving as if the act turned him on while doing it was unusual. And disturbing.

Very.

Especially when Kirk's wife, Tracey, had gone missing under suspicious circumstances just over a month ago. A neighbor called the police to report Tracey as a missing person. The neighbor said Kirk and Tracey had been fighting like crazy for days. Then it suddenly stopped, and Tracey hadn't been seen since then. The police had found a bloody blouse in Kirk's closet, but he explained it away, and they found no evidence of foul play on his part. Natalie wondered if the detective gave Kirk the benefit of the doubt because he was a fellow officer.

Still, in the absence of the mother, Natalie had been assigned to the family to be sure Willow and her siblings were safe and cared for. Natalie had been monitoring them for over a month, and little hints and actions by Kirk led her to question if he'd killed his wife. Nothing overt. The guy was charming and personable. It was just a gut feeling on Natalie's part.

And now this? Polishing his daughter's nails and acting weird in doing so? Forbidding her to mention it?

Too freaky, especially with law enforcement hunting a local serial killer who manicured his victims' nails after he killed them. The lunatic who had murdered Natalie's sister. The press had nicknamed him The Clipper. Now it was looking like Kirk not only could have killed his wife but Natalie's sister and three other women.

Natalie had nothing concrete to go on and needed additional information, but she couldn't alert Willow to the problem. Natalie would do everything within her power to protect this child from harm and mental distress.

Natalie leaned back, trying to act casual, but her heart was thumping hard. "Does your dad do Sadie's nails too?"

"Nuh-uh. She's only a baby." Willow lifted her chin. "'Sides, she wouldn't sit still. She wiggles too much, and Dad gets mad when you wiggle."

"What does he do when he gets mad?"

Willow grimaced. "He pinches my fingers hard, just to keep me still. But it hurts."

Natalie swallowed down her anger over this man's actions. "Do you and your dad spend a lot of time together doing other things?"

Willow shook her head. "He likes to be by himself. Says he has to be kind to people all day at work and it's hard. So he has to 'cuperate."

"You mean recuperate?"

"Yeah. He said he used to be able to go out at night 'cause Mom watched us. But now he makes me watch Sadie and Logan, and he fixes up the house. He calls it remodeling."

"What has he fixed up?" Natalie asked, curious now because she'd seen no signs of recent renovation.

"He got rid of the basement. He said we didn't need it anymore so he closed up the window and door."

He what? He'd recently inherited family money, and unless he'd blown all of it already, he could easily have afforded to hire a contractor to do the work. Could he have killed his wife and closed off the basement to hide her body?

"When did he do that?" Natalie held her breath waiting for the answer.

"Right after Mom left. He likes pounding a hammer. Makes him feel better." Willow gnawed hard on her lip, a habit Natalie had frequently seen Willow engage in, and her lip and the skin below remained red and raw. "I was mad and wanted to hammer too. Dad wouldn't let me. Said it was just for him."

"What else did he do?" Natalie asked.

"Built a new deck. He said the patio was too small. So he dug it out and put a huge deck over it."

Natalie's sixth sense never failed her when she worked with troubled children, and it was humming like a high-speed fan.

"I wish Mom would come home. She would like the deck in the summer. She liked sunshine." Willow worried that lip again. "But she can't come home. Dad said a bad man musta taken her."

Natalie wanted to punch the pillow. What a terrible thing this was to tell a child. He'd told Willow this story, but not the detective. As the family social worker, Natalie had access to the police reports that said Kirk claimed Tracey had taken off on her own. That she'd had enough of being a wife and mother. He even described the jacket she was wearing and the purse and tote bag she was carrying as she walked out the door and slammed it in his face.

So Natalie needed to dig deeper, but she made sure her tone was gentle. "Why does he think that?"

"'Cause she never would've left us. She loved us too much." Willow drew her legs up to wrap her arms around them. "I miss her."

Natalie squeezed Willow's knee. "I'm so sorry she's not here, sweetie."

Willow frowned.

"Did I say something wrong?"

"Mom called me sweetie."

"Oh, sorry."

"No. I kinda liked it. Dad's not like that." Willow's eyes glistened with unshed tears. "Except when he does my nails. Then he gets weird like I told you." Willow sighed. "He said when I get older, I'm gonna replace Mom if she doesn't come home. I already have to help take care of Sadie and Logan. I don't want to do more. Like cooking. I don't like to cook. Or wash dirty clothes. They're stinky."

Natalie didn't want this eight-year-old to have to raise her siblings either. Natalie had to care for her sister at a similar age, and she'd resented it. "Do you want me to have a talk with your dad about that?"

"No!" Willow screeched. "No. Please don't. I'll get in big trouble."

"Shh, it's okay." Natalie held Willow's hand to calm her.

"I won't say a word." *But I will go looking for that hidden basement.* "Where was the door to your basement?"

Willow raised her right eyebrow, just like her father did when he was suspicious of something Natalie had said.

Natalie waved a hand. "Just curious to see if I can tell if it was once there."

"You can't. Dad did a good job."

"Mind if I look for myself?"

"By the back door. There's a bookshelf there now." Willow yawned.

"Time for lights out, sweetie." Natalie stood. "I shouldn't have kept you up so late as it is."

"I like talking to you." Willow snuggled down under her Princess Barbie comforter. "It's like talking to Mom. Not Dad. Dads just aren't the same. They have too much to think about and can't pay attention. But moms don't work all the time, and they can think about you. At least sometimes."

Natalie tugged the covers up to Willow's chin, wanting to give her rosy cheek a kiss, but that would cross the professional line Natalie had to draw with clients. She shouldn't even have agreed to bring the children home tonight, but Kirk had been injured in a car accident, the children's nanny, his emergency contact, was unavailable, and he didn't have anyone else to pick the children up. If Natalie hadn't gotten them, someone else in social services would've taken the call and put them in emergency foster care, likely splitting them up. Natalie had spared them additional trauma by bringing them here until Kirk was released from the ER.

Natalie forced a smile for the girl. "Sleep tight, Willow."

"I wish you could babysit us all the time. You're nicer than our nanny." She turned over and tugged a well-worn Curious George plush monkey to her chest and closed her eyes.

6

Natalie closed the door and charged down the stairs. Those poor children. They needed her. Maybe more than she'd first thought. Still, it was only a gut feeling. She had no grounds to remove them from the home. Yet.

Sure, Kirk's inability to pick them up tonight and a failure of his backup plan was a red flag, but still not reason to remove them. Just a reason to counsel him and help him find a backup to his backup.

Polishing Willow's nails was another red flag. A big one. But again, it wasn't abusive. Could even be construed as sweet—if the creep factor didn't go along with it. There was no way Natalie could take the children from Kirk, not unless she found the basement and located proof of wrongdoing there. Or even located Tracey down there.

A shudder raced over Natalie as she hurried through the tidy family room, perfectly decorated in warm beiges and browns with a hint of flashy orange that fit with the way Kirk had described Tracey's flamboyant personality.

Natalie stopped at the bookcase where the family cat, Tabitha, was crunching dry food from her nearby bowl. She paused to glance up, the black rings around her eyes looking like a mask in her otherwise sleek tan fur. If she were a human, Natalie could see her shrugging as she went back to eating, not caring that Natalie was present.

Natalie turned her attention back to the shelf filled with decorative items and family photos. She leaned closer to inspect it for a hidden opening, but Tabitha scooted past Natalie's feet, nearly upending her. She grabbed onto the shelf to balance. The shelf gave way, and the whole unit popped out.

The opening was still there. A hidden passage. Willow was right. Her dad had done a great job making the door look like a simple bookshelf.

Natalie pulled the bookcase wide open and flipped on

the light switch. The single bulb revealed rough wooden steps leading down to gray cinder block walls. She started down, careful not to trip with her high heels, but paused on the third step.

Did she have time to check out the basement before Kirk's tests were finalized and he was released? Was it safe to do so? He said he would call before he left, but he could forget.

It didn't matter. She had to go.

Her suspicions weren't enough to go to the police. Not nearly enough. She'd brought leads to the detective after her sister's murder only for him to patronize her and send her on her way. She wouldn't make the same mistake here. If concrete evidence of Kirk's guilt existed in this basement, she would locate it so when she *did* call the police, they could finally take action.

She felt her pocket to confirm she had her phone and started down the stairs.

One at time. Careful. Slow. Listening. Her heart pounded hard, each beat sounding like an explosion in her head.

She reached the stained concrete floor. A strong musty odor greeted her. She moved ahead, inching toward a worn door with flaking white paint. She pulled it open. Another odor, sharp and caustic, swept out. Bleach. Yes, it was bleach.

Was she right? Had Kirk killed Tracey here and cleaned up after he murdered her?

Natalie swallowed hard. Dreaded going into the dark room with low ceilings. Dreaded seeing what was in there, but she would continue on for her sister's sake.

She tugged on the string hanging from a florescent fixture, and light flooded the room. She blinked a few times. Looked around. A rugged workbench filled one wall. It was

8

scarred and chipped from years of use. It had probably been in this basement since the house was built in the twenties. Ahead she found large plywood cabinets painted white but grayed over time. She was half afraid to open the doors, but she'd come this far. She had to look.

She crossed the room, stepping over a rusty floor drain. She used the hem of her blouse to keep from destroying evidence and jerked open the first cabinet. One quick look and she gasped.

A tote bag with the name Tracey embroidered on the pink canvas sat on the shelf. Next to it was the navy blue rain jacket Kirk had described her wearing the last time he'd seen her, along with a small Gucci purse.

Oh my gosh. Tracey didn't take off like Kirk claimed. He killed his wife. He really did.

Was her body in one of the other cabinets?

No. Please, God. No.

Natalie's stomach churned with acid, but she forced herself to pull open the next door.

She jerked it wide. Looked.

Empty.

Thank you. Thank you. Thank you.

But wait. She had the lower cabinets to look in yet.

She bent down. Jerked open the first door. Found boxes stacked neatly on top of each other. The next cabinet held totes marked *camping supplies*.

She opened the bins to confirm the contents then closed the doors and gulped in deep breaths.

Clearly Tracey didn't take off. Or if she did, she'd left her belongings behind. And why would that be? She had to be fleeing in a hurry. Maybe a serial killer right behind her.

Natalie could easily imagine it. Kirk with the knife in hand that he'd used on his other victims. Rage contorting his face. Tracey terrified, racing out the door with just the

9

clothes on her back. Did she get away? Did he grab her? Drag her down here and kill her? Did that explain the scent of bleach?

A shiver ran down Natalie's body. She reached for her phone to call the police.

No. No. He *was* the police. He could talk his way out of this or get whoever responded to cover up for him. But Natalie couldn't just grab all these items and take them with her.

Pictures. She needed to take pictures of Tracey's things. He couldn't get someone to cover up Natalie's pictures. She fumbled to get out her phone and snapped several shots. Her hands shook so badly that she took the time to check the photos.

One by one. They were clear and sharp. *Good. Good.*

She charged across the room, but the tool laden workbench caught her eye and stopped her. Did it hold the murder weapon?

He'd used a sharp object to kill her sister, Gina. Drugged her first then stabbed her in the heart. Brutally. Viciously. Same for the other three women The Clipper had killed. Likely a knife, but the ME couldn't be one hundred percent positive.

Had Kirk left the murder weapon behind for his next kill? *If* he had one planned. She ran her gaze over the tools. Sets of screwdrivers. A hammer. A battery operated drill and circular saw. Being careful not to touch anything and leave prints, she checked the metal ends. The bits. Blades. Saw no blood.

A metal storage container with small plastic compartments like you'd store nails or screws in caught her attention. The bins were numbered one through twenty-four with neat white labels. Each row held four compartments and there were six rows. She tugged down her sleeve to keep from contaminating the evidence and pulled out the first drawer.

No. Oh no.

She jerked her hand back. Stared. Gasped for air. Her heart fluttered like hummingbird wings.

A bottle of nail polish lay in the drawer. Pink. Pale Pink. *Angelic*. The name and brand of polish The Clipper used on Gina after he'd stabbed her to death.

Natalie gulped in a breath. She didn't want to look in the other drawers. She wanted to flee like she hoped Tracey had done. Maybe she discovered this bin too, and that's why Kirk killed her.

Natalie stepped back. *No. No.* She had to look. For Gina. For the other women. For Tracey.

One at a time across the top, she pulled them out.

Angelic. Chameleon. Bewitching. Vixen.

The same colors The Clipper had applied to his victims, arranged in the order in which he'd killed them. Not information released to the public, but when she'd visited a detective to talk about a client, she'd overheard another detective on the phone discussing if the polish names meant anything.

Angelic. Chameleon. Bewitching. Vixen. The right names. The right order. Four women dead.

Oh my gosh. Natalie was right.

Her phone rang. She jumped, and it almost went flying. Shocked to get a signal down here, she glanced at the screen.

Kirk's name burned on her screen.

No. Oh no. No. No. No.

She stared. Frozen. Deciding. She had to answer. To know where he was and when he'd be home.

The serial killer. Coming here.

She tapped the screen, forced calm into her tone. "How are things going at the ER?"

Her voice shook only a little, but her hand was trembling like a frightened kitten.

"Just finished." His booming voice held his usual confidence, not the uncertainty of his earlier call. "I'll grab a cab and be home in twenty minutes."

Twenty minutes. She shot a look around the room. Twenty minutes until a brutal killer of women showed up at the door—her sister's killer showed up at the door.

"The children are all asleep, so no need to rush." She tried to act cheerful, but her voice came out sounding like Minnie Mouse. "I'm just watching a show on my phone."

"Okay." He sounded confused, and it wasn't surprising. Why would she tell him what she was doing?

"See you soon." She disconnected the call before she said anything else that might make him suspicious.

Now what?

"Think, Nat," she said. "Think. Think. Think."

Take more pictures, grab the children, and flee.

She snapped a shot of the top row of polish then opened the remaining drawers. Each bin held a different color of polish all leading to a blatant red. Was he planning to kill twenty-four women?

Hopefully her pictures could stop him. Save lives.

She carefully took them. Checked the quality.

She slid the drawers closed and started for the stairs, turning to make sure she didn't leave any trace of her visit.

Perfect. Everything looked the same. She tugged on the light string and rushed up the stairs, flipping off the switch at the top. She secured the door and drew in deep breaths.

Now what? The children. She couldn't leave them with him. No. Never. She had to flee with them. Where to?

She couldn't go to the police. With Kirk's inside connection, he could convince someone to hand his children over to him. She couldn't let that happen.

So what?

Malone. Malone Rice. She dialed her friend and attorney who worked with runaway teens and abused women and children. Malone had given Natalie an emergency number to call if an abusive spouse or father threatened one of her clients.

"It's Natalie. One of my clients is a serial killer. I'm at his house. With his children. He's coming home in twenty minutes, but before you tell me to call the police, I can't." Natalie quickly relayed her story. "I've got to take the children and run. Please tell me you have a place I can go."

Malone didn't speak for a moment. "I have a team of investigators who can help you. Nighthawk Security. They're Sierra's brothers. You know—my brother Reed's wife. She's the evidence expert at the Veritas Center. She has five brothers, and they're all former law enforcement officers."

Natalie hated to involve anyone else in this mess. "Why not just send us to one of the shelters you use?"

"No can do. You'll be illegally taking the children, and I can't send you to a reputable shelter under those conditions. And if Gentry is indeed a serial killer, it's too dangerous to mix you with other women and children. Plus, you'll need special protection from him."

Right. Natalie hadn't thought of that. "Protection sounds good. Give me Nighthawk's phone number, and I'll call them once I get out of here."

"I'll make the call, and I'll call a detective I can trust to recover the evidence. You get the kids and go. Drive straight to this address and wait for them." She rattled off a location in Portland. "This's a safe zone. CCTV camera free. I check it on a regular basis to make sure none have been added. Once you get off the freeway at that location, you can't be tracked."

Natalie let out a long sigh and made a mental note to find a way to repay Malone for her help.

"And Natalie," Malone continued. "Ditch your phone as soon as possible. If you can take out the SIM card, do it. Then smash the phone."

"But the pictures I took of the evidence—"

"Is your phone set up to upload photos to the cloud as you take them?"

"Oh, yeah. Yeah. It is."

"Then get out of there and destroy the phone."

"How will I recognize the guys you're sending?"

"I'm not sure which brother will respond at this time of night, but he'll be wearing a red armband. And whatever you do, don't put this address in your car's navigation system."

"Thanks, Malone."

"Sure thing. The Byrd brothers will have a secure way to contact me when you're safe. We'll talk more then. Praying for you."

They would need all the prayers they could get.

Natalie shoved her phone into her pocket and charged toward the stairway to get three young children ready to go and in her car before this brutal killer of women walked through the front door.

2

Drake Byrd stretched as he strode from the Veritas Center's parking garage to the elevator for the residence tower where he and his brothers lived, letting the blustery night air wake him. He'd just come off eight hours of boring surveillance, and he wanted a pepperoni pizza and a night of watching sports. Any sports. And, after the silence on his latest work shift, some human companionship.

His brother Erik had just ended his shift too. He would definitely provide a break from the silence, probably blabbering on and on. But Drake had been feeling kind of lonely lately. Why? He had no idea. And he would never admit it to anyone. Was hard enough to admit to himself.

Feelings. Right. Like he was going to spend time analyzing them. He probably just needed a long weekend hang gliding. *Yeah.* He would ask for time off. Aiden and Brendan were just finishing up the last night of surveillance on the tedious divorce investigation they'd all worked for two weeks, and Drake deserved a break from the boredom. He could ski the slopes or hang glide for a day and not be tired, but sitting around? Man. That exhausted him.

In the elevator on the sixth floor garage entrance, he

punched the number two, and his stomach grumbled. Erik was on his way to pick up their pizza. Drake's mouth was already watering, and he could almost smell the tangy sauce from their favorite pizza place just down the road. A mom-and-pop place with authentic Chicago-style pizza.

The elevator stopped on the fifth floor, and the doors split open. His sister's husband, Reed, stepped partway in and blocked the door. "Man, am I glad to see you. My sister's on the phone"—he lifted his cell—"and she needs to talk to one of you guys."

Well, dang. Drake was all for helping Malone out, but the pizza was coming, and he was starving.

"Can't she leave a message on the office phone?" he asked, perhaps sounding cranky, but he got that way when he was hungry. And he was hun-gry!

"It's an emergency. A woman in immediate danger."

That changed things. Big time.

"Let me talk to her." Drake took Reed's phone and lifted it to his ear. "Malone, it's Drake Byrd."

"Good. Glad I caught you. I have a social worker, Natalie Dunn, who was babysitting a man's children at his house and had to flee with the children. She believes he's a killer."

"Say what? Killed who?" Drake stared at Reed as if he could give more information. He shrugged.

"I can't waste time on the story now," Malone said. "You need to get going. They're vulnerable."

Drake didn't like being in the dark, but he disliked having a woman and children in danger far more. "What do you need me to do?"

"I've sent them to the usual rendezvous spot." She shared the address, but he didn't need it. He and his brothers had transported women and children from this location to local shelters.

"Which shelter do you want us to take her to?"

"That's the thing. She can't go to a shelter, not with kids who aren't her own. So I need a safe place for them. Somewhere off-grid until this is properly investigated, and he can't hurt her or the kids."

"Has he tried?"

"No, but seems like he's grooming the oldest girl for something unsavory."

Drake didn't want to let this father near the kids. "I'll take them to—"

"No. Don't tell me. And don't call me from the secure location. Just in case."

"You think he could connect her to you and come after you?"

"He's a police officer and works in internet crimes so he has tech skills and more resources at his disposal than a civilian. Plus he recently came into some family money so he has plenty to spend on it."

Drake's gut clenched. He hated hearing that a law enforcement officer sworn to protect others might be a killer. "This guy being a cop changes things big-time."

"It could," Malone admitted reluctantly. "But we were careful. I use burner phones for my clients in danger. Natalie called on one of those numbers. So I should be fine."

Sounded like she knew how to take precautions. Reed, an FBI agent, had probably schooled her on the very subject.

"Okay," he said. "I'll go get them."

"I'll be calling a detective I can trust to get officers out to the house to preserve the evidence, but then it will take time to get a warrant to search the basement. Since the father is a police officer, I'd feel better if you also had someone watch him. He was injured in a car accident, and his car is out of commission, but there's a minivan in his garage. He's in a cab, on the way home from the hospital now."

"We'll have someone there as soon as possible. What's his name and address?"

"Kirk Gentry." She added the address.

He dug a pen from his pocket and wrote the information on his palm. "I'll need you to update me on the detective's progress. I don't want to use phones as there's no such thing as an untraceable phone. But I can access email via a secure network so go ahead and communicate updates that way." He shared the secure company email address. "And if you find yourself in any danger, or even a hint of danger, you contact me. Don't hesitate. Just do it."

"I—"

"Give me the phone," Reed demanded.

Drake would normally finish his call, but with the thunderous look on Reed's face, Drake handed it over. He didn't want to get between this guy and his sister any more than he would want anyone to interfere with him and Sierra. Plus, Reed was totally capable of holding his own, and Drake didn't want to peeve him off.

"What's this about you being in danger?" Reed demanded.

Drake couldn't hear Malone's answer, but she was a headstrong, independent woman, and he had to figure she was arguing with her brother.

"That's it, then." Reed widened his stance. "You're staying with us until this is over." He paused and gnawed on his cheek. "This isn't up for discussion, Malone. If you're not here within an hour, I'll come get you." Reed shoved his phone into his pocket.

"I take it she agreed," Drake said.

"Reluctantly." He gritted his teeth. "We'll see if she follows through."

"Would you really go drag her over here?"

"What would you do if there was any hint of danger to Sierra? Especially from a potential killer?"

"Exactly what you're doing." Drake firmed his stance. "Let me know if you need our help with Malone."

"You do your thing, and I'll take care of my sister."

Figuring Malone was still going to give Reed a run for his money, Drake nodded and headed for the stairway. Not only would it be faster than the elevator to go up one floor to their office where he would gather needed supplies, but the exercise would wake him up too. He texted Erik to meet him at the office and took the stairs two at a time to the sixth floor, where he crossed the skybridge to their office tower.

He used his fingerprints to unlock the door. Once inside, he dialed his brother Clay, who also should've just gotten off shift.

"Yo," Clay answered.

"I need you to get eyes on a suspect." Drake relayed Kirk Gentry's details, including his address and that he was a police officer, as he headed to their gear closet. "How soon can you get over there?"

"Just finishing up here, so I'd say I could be there in ten minutes or so."

"Book it and get there in less." Drake tossed his and Erik's Kevlar vests onto a table.

"Can do."

"And, bro. When this guy finds his children are missing, he could get the whole police force looking for them. Means you best—"

"Lie low so they don't think I'm involved in their disappearance. Yeah. I got this. I'll text you when I have the guy in sight."

The call went dead.

Perfect. His brothers readily took on an assignment like

this without question. Sure, they'd ask them later, but in the moment, they knew when to act and did so. Their parents were the same way, though their mom usually didn't even need to be asked. She somehow sensed when one of them needed her and was already waiting by the time they got to her.

Erik stepped through the door as Drake grabbed extra ammo for his sidearm and a rifle with the corresponding ammo. Probably overkill, but he never knew what he'd run into on this assignment.

"Pizza will have to be to-go." Drake slipped into his vest and shared the details with his younger brother. "Gearing up now, and then we'll head out."

Erik grabbed his vest. "Just you and me?"

"Clay's on his way to get eyes on Gentry, and Aiden and Brendan are still winding down our current surveillance. Besides, we can handle a transport."

"We're talking a potential murderer here and a police officer who knows how to evade capture."

Drake grabbed the rifle and met his brother's gaze. "Then let's pray this social worker took off before he got home, and he has no idea where she went with his children."

Natalie's hands were still shaking, and she couldn't quit checking her rearview mirror. She'd gotten on the road before Kirk stepped through the door, but she'd passed a cab with a backseat passenger heading into the subdivision.

Could it have been Kirk? Did he know his children were gone?

So what? Even if it had been him, it would take time to pay the cabbie. Discover they weren't there. Jump in his minivan. By the time he accomplished all of that, she would be long gone. And Malone could have a police officer there by now too, though Natalie figured it might take longer as she would want to get someone on scene who wouldn't put the police brotherhood ahead of doing their job the right way.

Even if she didn't think Kirk was coming after her, she looked in the mirror. Plus, she wanted to check on the children.

Thankfully, Willow was the only one who'd woken up. Natalie had tucked two-year-old Sadie and four-year-old Logan into seats she'd checked out from her department for her earlier pickup, and they snoozed away. And when Natalie had gotten on the highway and headed into the city, Willow dropped off in her booster seat, George clutched in her arms. Until that point, she was full of questions, but Natalie told her she had an errand to run.

A lie, but what could Natalie say? *I'm abducting you from your serial-killer father.*

Man, oh, man. She could imagine it—the day the children learned about him. Only Willow would really understand now, but they would live their lives with this horror as part of it. And without parents.

Natalie looked in the mirror again at the three precious children in the back seat. Asleep. Innocent. Smelling of baby shampoo and sweet dreams.

A defensive instinct raced through Natalie. She was going to do everything she could to protect those children right now, even giving of her life if needed. In the future, she was going to make sure they found good homes and got the counseling they needed. No matter what she had to do, these children would not only survive, they would thrive.

$\sim$

Drake polished off the pizza slices he'd grabbed on the way out of the office and opened the windows in the company SUV. Wouldn't do to pick up a client and have the smell of pepperoni oozing from the leather upholstery. But he'd had to eat something or he might've gotten testy with this social worker. That would be even worse.

His vehicle's infotainment center alerted him to a text from Clay, and he told it to read the text.

Eyes on suspect. At home. Pacing his office.

Good. Right where they wanted him to be. Not in the basement destroying evidence and not coming for his kids.

Drake replied, *Keep me updated.*

He turned onto the street in the warehouse district, streetlights so sparse the area was cloaked in darkness, and thought ahead to the rendezvous. He'd worked with plenty of social workers in his prior job with the U.S. Marshals and could just imagine the woman waiting for him. Middle-aged. Ill-fitting pant suit. Serviceable shoes. Harried and exhausted.

Okay, so he was stereotyping, but based on his past experiences, he had a good chance of being right on target. One thing this particular social worker had going for her before they even met was her willingness to break the rules to protect these children. He suspected if it turned out that this father wasn't a killer, this little stunt was going to cost her job.

He spotted her car ahead, sitting under one of the few streetlights. A large family kind of car, just the kind his social worker stereotype would drive. Except it was a sporty red color that glinted in the light. Didn't fit his preconceived notions, so maybe she wasn't quite what he expected.

He parked behind the vehicle and put on his red armband. Erik drove up in his pickup. He would remain in his vehicle and act as cover.

Drake checked the clip on his gun, left the headlights shining on the car, and got out, leaving the SUV running for a potential fast getaway should Clay report Gentry was on the move.

Hand on his sidearm, a flashlight in the other, Drake approached the driver's side door, a sharp May wind making it feel colder than the fifty degree temps. The same hint of unease that made him cautious when he'd served as a deputy crawled up his back now. This woman was supposedly on the up-and-up, but he could never be too careful on the job.

Ever.

Not if he wanted to stay alive. Taking risks was reserved for off-duty time.

He was about to knock on the window when it whirred down. He shined his light inside and did a double take. The matronly social worker he expected was a gorgeous blond with flawless skin and brown eyes that held a world-weary fatigue.

"Ms. Dunn?" he asked, sure he'd gotten the wrong car.

"You have the red armband," she said. "Means Malone sent you, right?"

He nodded and took a second to stop all the crazy thoughts and questions just looking at this woman was raising. He shined the light into the back seat, revealing three young children strapped into safety seats.

Yeah, he had the right person, all right, and his boring night had just gotten very interesting.

"Shouldn't we get going?" she asked. "Kirk could be right behind me."

"He's at home. The police haven't arrived yet, but my brother Clay has eyes on Gentry."

"Good. Good. I..." She let out a long breath and sagged in her seat. "Good for us, I mean. But I don't like the fact that the police haven't gotten there yet. Hopefully Malone isn't running into any problems."

"She's going to update me via email when she knows anything, but I'm not surprised that I haven't heard from her. With Gentry being a police officer, this isn't like any other investigation. Malone has to get the right officer out there who's willing to forget the police officers' code if needed." From Drake's past experience in law-enforcement, he knew she would have a hard time finding such a person. "We should get the kids moved to my vehicle."

"What about my car?"

"We'll arrange to have it taken to a safe location."

"And where are we going?"

"Let's get on the road, and then we'll talk about it. I'm assuming Malone told you to disable your phone or destroy it."

Natalie nodded. "I smashed it then threw it out the window on the highway."

"Then let's move." He stepped back, hoping she wouldn't insist on knowing the destination. His rustic hunting cabin probably wouldn't be tops on her list of places to visit.

She closed her window and opened her door. Long shapely legs capped with a short black skirt slid out, and he had to work hard not to stare at them. Or at the sky-high heels with a shiny black finish she was wearing. They were open in the front, her toes peeking out. They might be stylish and professional, but the wrong kind of shoe if she needed to run. And not at all friendly with his wooded property.

It was his job to keep her out of any situations where she had to run. Traversing his property? That would be up to her.

He glanced back at Erik to make sure he was still there and had their backs. His truck sat at the curb, his lights beaming into the night. Gentry couldn't be nearby. Clay was watching the guy at his house, but the man could've somehow tracked Natalie and sent someone else to deal with her. Not likely, but possible, and Drake worked on possibilities.

"Which one are you?" She straightened the short suit jacket that covered a silky pale pink blouse. "Of the brothers, I mean."

Well, shoot. An introduction would've been the logical thing, but he let the surprise of a beautiful woman get to him. Something he would call out his brothers on, and here he was gawking at her. "I'm Drake. My brother Erik's in the truck."

She opened the back door and bent in. He kept his focus on the roof of the vehicle and not on how well her skirt fit. She backed out holding a small female child sporting a thick head of curly red hair and dressed in pink footie pajamas. Natalie held the little girl out to him.

He flashed up a hand. "I don't know anything about kids."

"Which means you probably know far less about installing car seats."

"Well, yes, but..."

"Take Sadie, and I'll move the seat."

"I—"

"She's asleep, for goodness' sake. She won't hurt you." She lifted the child to him.

He clasped the toddler under the arms and held her out, feeling like a fool for letting the child dangle in the air. That wouldn't do for long. He hefted her into his arms, and she snuggled close to his chin and settled in next to his neck. She smelled like honey and something else sweet that he couldn't identify, and her hair was soft and feathery against his skin. He'd never been charged with protecting a child this young before and didn't know what to expect. He sure wouldn't have guessed his heart would melt as some primal need to keep this child safe raged inside his body.

Natalie pulled out a car seat and lugged it to his SUV her heels clicking on the asphalt. She hefted it up and struggled to get it to his vehicle. He should be the one carrying the heavy seat, not letting a woman do it. His mother would have a fit if she saw this. She'd instilled manners of bygone days in them, and he and his brothers always held doors and chairs for women unless they protested. Natalie had protested. Made this fine, right?

No. No, it wasn't fine with him. He marched over to the SUV. "I'll do the next seat."

She glanced back, a cute grin on her face. "A two-year-old too much for you, huh? I mean, she's really giving you a run for your money there with the way she's sound asleep on your shoulder." She chuckled, and the sound of her voice lightened the mood.

But he didn't know how to respond to her comment and felt his face flush. Good thing it was dark. He wasn't coming across as the professional he'd hoped to portray.

She took Sadie, lifting the child as if she'd had many years of practice. Maybe she was a mother. He glanced at her ring finger. No ring or dent where one had been. Didn't mean anything.

She put Sadie in the seat. He couldn't see what she was doing, but she had to be buckling straps as he heard clicks like a seatbelt might make. He had to admit he wouldn't know what to do, and the children's safety came first. Still, he could carry the next seat to his vehicle and let her install it.

They returned to her car, and she lifted a larger boy out of the backseat.

"Logan," she said. "He's four."

Drake didn't know if the child or the safety seat weighed more, but after a few tries, he figured out how to release the vehicle strap.

He took it to his SUV and located the latch system, which he knew existed because Clay had used them on the investigation when he'd met his fiancée. Drake got the seat connected and beamed with pride at the major accomplishment.

"All yours," he said, embarrassed by the ridiculous satisfaction in his tone.

She cocked her head and looked at him. Her hair fell back, revealing the angular bent to her square jaw and the streetlight emphasized her high cheekbones. "Then I'll just get Logan in the seat, wake Willow up, and we're good to go."

She settled the boy inside then Drake followed her back to the car. She gently woke Willow and led the sleepy young girl out of the car as the child clutched a well-worn monkey.

Willow rubbed her eyes and peered up at Drake. "Who is he?"

"A friend named Drake who's going to drive us the rest of the way in his car."

"Did yours break?"

"Something like that."

Willow eyed him suspiciously, but Natalie steered her toward the SUV. Drake got the booster seat disconnected and carried it to his vehicle.

"Just let me grab my purse, and the children's backpacks, and I'll be right back." Natalie took off for her car, those heels breaking the silence with each step and leaving him alone with the kids.

Willow continued to eye him suspiciously as she climbed into the seat.

"How old are you?" he asked.

"Eight." Willow looked up at him. "How old are you?"

He worked hard not to laugh at her earnest question and buckled her seatbelt. "I just turned thirty."

"That's old. Not as old as my dad, but still old."

"It is indeed."

"He was in a car accident tonight. That's why we're with Natalie. She's our social worker. She checks on us since Mom went missing. I like her. Natalie, I mean. I like my mom too. I just wish she didn't have to leave." Willow let out a long breath and drew in another one as if she planned to launch into another speech, but Natalie joined them, and Willow's attention shifted.

"Ready to go." Natalie opened the front door before Drake could do it for her.

He closed the back door and ran around to the driver's side. He nodded at Erik and climbed in. Resting his hand on the wheel, he glanced back at Willow. Her eyes were narrowed, confusion clear on her face.

Drake couldn't blame her. She'd been hauled out of bed by her social worker and didn't know her destination.

And what about her mother taking off? Malone hadn't mentioned that. Something Drake needed to know more about. He might not possess much information about Natalie or the kids, but learning everything he could about them was priority number two. Right behind their safety. If he was going to provide the level of protection they all deserved, he had to know every detail. Every single one, even if she didn't want to share them.

3

Heading down I-5 toward his hunting cabin in Linn County, Drake adjusted the heat flowing from the vents and glanced at Natalie, who'd been staring out the window since they'd gotten on the highway. The dashboard light reflected against her creamy skin, and he was distracted by her impossibly long lashes, which brushed her cheeks when she blinked. And highlighted large eyes a very unique color of brown. He was looking forward to seeing them in the light other than a street light or the dash lights.

Oh. Man, Come on. Focus.

He glanced in the mirror to make sure Erik tailed them and no one else. They had several hours to go yet, but as the miles rolled under the vehicle, he kept checking the mirror for a tail and to see if Willow remained awake. She'd fought sleep hard but finally nodded off.

He took a quick look at Natalie. "Care to tell me what evidence you located at Gentry's house?"

She swiveled and glanced over her shoulder.

"Don't worry," he said. "Willow's asleep."

"No." Natalie shook her head. "No, I won't talk about it until I'm sure the children can't possibly overhear me."

"But they—"

"No!" She lurched forward.

"It's that bad? I mean whatever you found at the house."

She gave a sharp nod, and her chin trembled.

That gut-wrenching need to protect her, very similar to the one he'd felt for the children, had Drake tightening his fingers on the wheel. "Does it have something to do with the missing mother?"

"Maybe." Natalie sat back again, but he saw the tremor in her hands as she clutched her suit jacket closed. "Sorry I snapped at you like that. I'm a little stressed."

"That's to be expected."

"Let's talk about something else."

Not his first choice, but he'd let it go for now. "You're safe now, you know? Gentry is under surveillance, and Erik and I have everything under control in your transport."

She nodded, but her wary gaze gave away her true feelings. "Tell me about your family. Your business."

Okay, so maybe she needed to know they were capable and discover if she could trust them. He got that and even respected it. "We were all once law enforcement officers. Now we have an investigations and protection agency. We've handled a lot of investigations and protection details, even for celebrities."

She clasped her trembling hands together in her lap. "Which law enforcement agency did you serve with?"

"U.S. Marshals."

"So you brought in bad guys who didn't want to be found."

He nodded.

"What was that like?" She swiveled to face him.

He felt her gaze digging, searching for something he couldn't quite place. For some reason, what she thought

30

about him felt important when he rarely cared about other people's opinions of him.

"I worked the fugitive task force," he said. "We concentrated on only the most violent offenders. Murderers, armed robbers. At first, the target is usually pretty predictable. Going to his family and friends to hide out. But when the felon gets wind that you're after them and learn they're wanted, they panic. That makes them unpredictable and hard to find. Takes foot work, and honestly, a lot of luck."

"Is your current job anything like that?" she asked, her attention still riveted to him.

"Some of the time, but mostly it's the exact opposite."

"How so?"

"We have two basic roles. The first and most common is to provide protection for a client who's in danger, like we're doing for you and the kids tonight. Our job is to keep the bad guys like the ones I used to hunt down away from our client. So it's helpful that I once chased down these kinds of offenders because I know how they think."

She shuddered. "I would hate to think like they do."

"Someone's got to do it, or they would all go free and innocent lives could be lost."

"Yeah, I suppose." A hint of unease deepened her voice. "And the other role you fill?"

"Investigation. Sometimes it's investigating a cheating spouse. Or maybe our clients have been threatened but don't know who's after them. We investigate and provide the information for law enforcement to arrest the perpetrator and bring them to justice."

"Sounds like you enjoy it."

"It's hard to see people suffering, but I enjoy helping the people who need us." He glanced at her again, as he couldn't seem to quit looking at her. "What about you? I can't imagine a kid wanting to be a social worker when they grow up, so what made you choose your profession?"

"Actually I *did* choose it as a kid. On my ninth birthday to be exact." She frowned and laced her fingers together, resting them on the short skirt that drew his attention to those amazing legs again.

"Mind sharing why?" he asked for the job, but also because he wanted to know on a personal level.

"My early years were all messed up," she said, looking down and pressing her hands flat. "My mom and dad fought a lot. Big, huge, ugly fights. And they were consumed with themselves, so my younger sister and I were often left to fend for ourselves. I looked after my sister. Made meals a lot of the time. Got both of us off to bed and off to school. Did laundry. Dishes."

She drew in a huge breath then let it out slowly. "When I turned eight, my dad decided he'd had enough, and he walked out. My mom didn't turn to drugs or alcohol for comfort like a lot of the clients I work with. She just got mad. And then bitter. Ugly bitter. And didn't remember my sister and I existed except to complain to us. She quit her job, and we lived on the child support from Dad. It wasn't enough, but we survived okay for a year. Then Dad called social services. Told them Mom was neglecting us. Not that he wanted custody of us. He just wanted to get back at her."

She paused for another breath, and he had to say something. Maybe find a way to make her feel better.

"That must've been rough," he said, and instantly knew it wasn't nearly enough or in any way the right words to convey how badly he felt for her having to endure such a difficult time.

"It was and it wasn't," she said matter-of-factly. "The first social worker told Mom to do a better job at feeding us and said she'd visit regularly to make sure we were getting the minimum nutrition requirements. But she never came back. Four months later, a really sour woman arrived. She was even more bitter than Mom, if you can believe that. She wrote Mom up for a ton of things, and she also said she would be back in a month to make sure Mom complied. This woman scared my mom, and Mom took an interest in us until after that social worker's return visit. Mom got a good report, and then she let things slide again."

He tightened his fingers on the wheel when what he really wanted to do was punch something for the way Natalie and her sister were treated. But his anger, even righteous anger, wouldn't help her. "And this made you want to do their job?"

"On my ninth birthday, Ms. Abernathy showed up. She apologized right off the bat for the changes in caseworkers and promised she wouldn't let us fall through the cracks again." A fond smile crossed Natalie's face. "Something about her made me believe her. She was sweet and kind and smiled a lot."

A flash of a smile brightened Natalie's expression. "And she took me aside and asked about my life. Asked me what I needed. None of the other caseworkers had ever even talked to me or my sister. They had a list to check off, and they rushed through it. But Ms. Abernathy spent time with both of us. And she came back. Over and over until Mom got it all right and continued to be a better mother. Then Ms. A finally released us from supervision."

Natalie crossed her arms. "Things went downhill again, but by that time I'd learned the importance of a social worker and how a good caseworker could make a difference in children's lives. Adults too, but most often it's the children who bear the brunt of the issues. So I worked hard in school to get scholarships and ended up with a Ph.D. in psychology specializing in children and youth."

"Most impressive degree," Drake said and meant it. "But I'm sorry you had to go through such a tough childhood."

She waved a hand. "My childhood formed me and made me want to help others. Good from bad. What's better than that?"

"Maybe you could want to help others without all the suffering."

"But the suffering is what really lets me understand what these children and families are going through. Nothing like firsthand experience to know. God gave me that experience. It was hard at the time, but I'm grateful for it now."

He was more than impressed. Not only was she easy on the eyes, but there was a depth and maturity to her that he admired. She could've chosen bitterness, but instead she'd chosen to allow her past to make her a better person and devote herself to helping others. "You obviously didn't inherit your mother's attitude."

Natalie shook her head hard. "I make sure to find the positives every day and embrace them. It's far easier to be negative, but being bitter is just as bad for a person as an illness. Or at least I think it is. My mom died in her forties. A stroke. It doesn't run in our family and surprised her doctor. I think her attitude had something to do with it, but of course, I can't prove that."

"You sound a lot like my brother Clay. He's the most even-keel guy in the family. Usually doesn't get upset over anything."

"And you?"

"Me?" He slowed at a four-way stop near the cabin and met her gaze. "I guess I'm perceived as being negative, but that's really just because I question pretty much everything. When other people don't like my questions, they see it as negative."

"Otherwise you're pretty content?"

Good question. "Content? Hmm. Not sure I'd say that. I like excitement and adventure, and I'm always looking for new and challenging experiences. So maybe restless is a better description."

She frowned, why, he didn't know, but it bothered him. He got them moving again and kept his attention on the road. When the driveway to his twenty acres came into view, he cleared his brain and shifted into protective mode.

She leaned forward and watched out the windows. "Wow, this really *is* out in the boonies."

"I suppose you live in the city," he said.

She nodded.

"Is there a Mr. Dunn?" he asked, hoping she said no.

"Too busy with work to even think about dating." She glanced at him. "You like all this wilderness stuff, huh?"

He nodded. He loved his thickly forested land, but she seemed less than thrilled, another thing that bothered him. What was his deal? Why did he care what she thought of him or his land? He had a job to do here. Protect her and the kids. Period. Nothing else.

So stick to that.

He parked in the small clearing, leaving the vehicle running and his headlights on, and waited for Erik to park behind him and get out. The beams illuminated the log exterior, and a fondness for the first property he'd ever owned came over him. Man, he loved this place.

Natalie released her seatbelt and scooted even closer to the window. "It's pretty rustic, isn't it?"

"It's a step up from most hunting cabins," he said to try to alleviate some of the apprehension in her tone and body language. "I'm going to check things out. Stay here until I tell you it's safe to get out."

"Safe, but..." She swung her head to stare at him, her

eyes wide. "Kirk can't possibly be here, right? Your brother would've told us if he'd left the house."

"I'm not thinking of two-legged danger but four-legged. Bears are waking up from hibernation and looking for food. They're known to break into and trash cabins in their search. I haven't been here in a while so I want to be sure one hasn't moved in."

"Oh, right. Bears." She shuddered.

He watched her for a second. She seemed nervous now, not afraid. Maybe uncomfortable. "You're not big on the outdoors."

"Nope. Give me a book and a cozy fire inside an adorable little cottage on the beach, and I'm a happy girl."

Now it was Drake's turn to frown. He was attracted to her. Big time. And he admired her and liked her personality. She might be a woman he could date when this was all over. But she didn't seem to like any of the things he did. Dating would never work.

Stop thinking about that, doofus. Get your mind on work and keep it there.

He grabbed a flashlight from the bin between the seats. "Erik will join you while I'm gone."

"Thanks." She smiled, but it was strained.

He got out and scanned the area while Erik marched past him and slid into the car. One final look at Natalie and the kids, and Drake started up a flagstone path he'd put in this past fall. He could just imagine Natalie trying to navigate it in the heels. He would offer to help her, but he suspected she would refuse.

He swung the light over the shrubs and undergrowth along the path, his pulse just a bit faster than normal. He wasn't afraid of the dark or what lurked beyond the clearing he worked hard to maintain. But he had a healthy respect for bears and for adversaries. He planted his hand on his weapon and searched for a bear's beady eyes looking back at him. Nothing but dark and fog.

Drake knew what to do if a five-hundred-pound bear showed itself. But if Natalie felt a need to break the law by abducting Gentry's children and running, the guy had to be bad news, and Drake didn't know enough yet to be fully confident in making sure Natalie and the kids were safe.

He reached his small porch, the steps creaking underfoot, and unlocked the door. As soon as the kids were settled, he'd question Natalie about Gentry. But answers or not, with her terror, Drake suspected he was facing a very worthy foe, and he'd have to bring his A-game to keep the two-legged danger at bay.

4

Natalie hardly jumped when Erik slid into the SUV, the sharp night wind coming in with him as he locked eyes with her. His jaw, covered in a thick five-o'clock shadow, dropped. "Oh...hi. I didn't expect..." He shook his head.

"Expect what?"

"You." He rubbed a hand over his face. "Drake didn't mention you were so young and well...nice looking."

She didn't know what to make of his comment. "I guess that was a compliment, so thank you."

He shook his head. "Sorry. You took me by surprise. Let's start over." He shoved out his hand. "Erik Byrd, in case my brother didn't say."

"He did." She took hold of his hand. "Natalie Dunn."

He released her hand and stared out the front window.

She took in his profile illuminated by the dashboard lights. He didn't look like she'd expected either. He had light brown eyes and dishwater blond hair in a buzz cut. Nothing like Drake's dark coloring. His wide shoulders and trim body spoke to many hours working out in a gym.

He turned and caught her watching him.

"You don't resemble Drake at all," she said bluntly, as she couldn't very well hide the fact that she'd been staring.

"He takes after our dad. I look like Mom. So does our sister, Sierra."

"She's the one who works at the Veritas Center."

He nodded. "Forensic expert and darn good at her job."

"Any other siblings?"

"Three more brothers. Aiden, Brendan, Clay, Drake, and then me."

"Alphabetical order."

"Our parents thought it would be cute to do that." He rolled his eyes. "It was a pain growing up, but it does help people remember our names."

"I think it's cute."

He groaned. "Maybe when we were kids, but we're all adults now. And we own a business where the last thing you want is for your clients to think you're cute."

Natalie laughed. "Drake said you all worked in law enforcement. What branch were you in?"

"Portland Police Bureau. Patrol officer for five years until I had to join the company business."

"Had to join?"

"I guess *had to* is the wrong way of saying it. Our dad needed a kidney transplant. Aiden donated one of his. He was ATF at the time. Meant he went on a lot of dangerous raids. We all worried that he might lose the remaining kidney on one of them. We agreed forming an agency together would keep him safer."

She loved learning about this family, not only to take her mind off Kirk, but because they seemed to really care about each other. "Sounds like your family is very close."

"Yeah." He stared out the front window.

If she knew him better, she might ask what was putting

the pensive look on his face, but that was too personal. Odd, when she would've asked Drake if he were sitting there.

Erik didn't move a muscle but continued to stare ahead. Maybe he was thinking about his family. She might've declared them a normal family at one point in her life, but normal wasn't a concept she embraced anymore. Not with so many families that she dealt with who didn't have the traditional two-parent home. Many were working through their problems, and, with a little help, were starting to thrive.

The closest she'd come to understanding family was with her sister, Gina, but her brutal murder four years ago ended that. When Gina died, so did Natalie. Inside. And along with her concept of family, every ounce of her ability to love disappeared. Now she sought vengeance for Gina. That's what kept her going outside of her work.

Should she tell Drake about her connection to Gina? Seemed like the right thing to do, but the detective she'd talked to and brought leads to regarding Gina's murder discounted her because she was a relative. He said she was too close. Clutching at straws, he said, and he dismissed her.

Now that she knew The Clipper's identity, she wouldn't let this team dismiss her. She'd found a strong lead tonight, very strong, and she had to pursue it. How, she didn't know, but she would. After she got the children settled in bed, she'd talk to Drake, see what he was thinking, and decide what she would do.

Eric's phone chimed, and he grabbed it from his pocket. "Email from Clay. Police are at Gentry's House."

"Oh, good." She let out a long breath of relief. "Does he say if they arrested him?"

"No. They just arrived."

The lights flickered on inside the cabin and glowed steadily through the windows. An outside security light on the corner of the cabin burned bright, but from this distance, she still had to squint to make out the building. The log cabin had a front porch and a green metal roof. She thought it might be something even more rustic, maybe in a state of disrepair, but the building looked inviting.

Listen to her, thinking about a cabin in the woods as inviting. What was she going to think next? There were animals, mosquitos, and critters out here, for crying out loud. Just the kinds of things she avoided, mostly because she had no experience in the wilderness, and the creepy darkness left her feeling unsettled.

"Looks like Drake is about ready for us," Erik said, his focus now pinned to the building.

Drake bounded down the steps to march across the clearing, his flashlight swinging side to side. He had a sure stride and confidence in his step. Man, oh man, she found that attractive. She had no idea why, but she'd always had a thing for the bad-boy type. The opposite of her in every way. Not that she knew he fit the bad boy stereotype, but his comment about calling others out on things made her think he might be one.

They say opposites attract. Maybe that was why she kept her gaze pinned to Drake's every move as he closed the distance. She certainly found him intriguing.

Erik opened his door, and Drake bent down to look at her. "We're good to go. I want all of us to head in at the same time."

"No problem." She made sure to not stare at the way the fabric of his shirt pulled tight against his biceps.

"Three adults means a kid per person," she said.

Drake frowned. "Not quite that easy. I want my hands free. Might need to go for my gun."

"No worries," Natalie said, though his comment brought up all kinds of worries. "I'll wake Willow up. She can take my hand and walk, and I'll carry Sadie. That leaves Erik free to carry Logan."

"Works for me. Let's move." Drake stepped back and looked at his brother. "I'll get Logan for you. Kid's car seat takes an engineering expert to figure out."

Natalie smiled at his exaggeration, slid out, and opened the back door. She stifled a shudder at the cooler temperature and released Willow's seatbelt. "We're here, kiddo. Can you hop down so I can reach Sadie?"

Willow rubbed her eyes and looked around. "Where's here?"

"Drake's cabin. You'll like it."

"Okay," she said warily and slid from her seat.

"Stay close to me, Willow." Natalie undid Sadie's straps and lifted the sweet child into her arms. She didn't wake and was twenty-five pounds of dead weight. Natalie hefted her higher, and the adorable child with red hair and chubby cheeks like Willow's rested her head on Natalie's shoulder. Natalie took Willow's hand and joined the brothers at the front of the SUV with the headlights still burning bright.

She looked at Willow. "You met Drake, and this is his brother Erik."

Willow gave him a long look then faced the cabin. "Don't like being out here."

"Think of it as an adventure," Natalie said, trying her best not to let her own dislike of the great outdoors influence her tone.

"Don't like adventures."

"Sure you do. It'll be fun."

Willow narrowed her eyes, and her very expressive face declared her lack of trust in Natalie's opinion. Still, Natalie clutched the child's hand and followed Erik. She wobbled in her heels and had to pick her way carefully among the scrub. No way she would faceplant due to her stupid shoes.

Okay, not stupid. One of her favorite pairs. Just the wrong choice for the woods.

Drake stayed by her side, his gaze roving over the area. His hyperalert behavior raised Natalie's concern even more.

She searched the shadowed shrubs and trees just out of reach of the warm glow from the porch light. What was lurking out there? Would she let her fear win out, or would she trust this man?

Trust. Ha. That was a word that got stuck in Natalie's mouth and mind. She'd never really trusted anyone other than Gina. At least not fully. Natalie had come close with Mrs. A, but that was it.

The wooden steps groaned under their feet as they climbed to the porch and entered the cabin. A soaring vaulted ceiling made the room that served as a living and dining room feel larger than it was. A small kitchen took up the back wall, but a massive stone fireplace at the far side of the room was the showstopper.

Drake closed and locked the door. "I'll get a fire going while you put the kids to bed."

Natalie looked around the large space with log walls. She spotted two doors. A bedroom and bathroom? And on the other wall a stairway leading up to what appeared to be an enclosed loft.

"The loft has several beds where they can all bunk together." Drake grabbed a large piece of wood from a stack by the hearth. "There's a bathroom up there too."

"Follow me." Erik crossed the room to the wooden staircase with a rustic log railing.

She released Willow to go ahead of her, and they trailed him up the stairs.

Willow slipped out of her hoodie but gripped George tightly to her chest. "I'm not sleepy anymore."

"It's not even midnight. You need to go back to sleep."

43

Natalie hoped Willow would fall asleep the moment her head hit the pillow. Not only because she needed sleep, but because Natalie needed to form a game plan with Drake for protecting these children. The loft had a door, so she would be able to talk freely once Willow was settled.

Erik flipped back the covers on a twin bed near a window and laid Logan down. Natalie tucked Sadie into a nearby matching bed.

"See you downstairs." Erik glanced at her but looked uneasy and took off.

He passed Willow, who stood by the door, and Natalie wasn't surprised by the deep frown on her face. She'd suffered the most with their mother's disappearance and having a social worker interfering in their lives. The other two missed their mother but were adapting fairly well. Maybe thanks to having a familiar caregiver in their nanny who'd been with the family for over a year.

Natalie planned to suggest they interview the nanny, see if she knew anything about the basement or noticed anything odd in Kirk's behavior. But now, getting the children to bed was her top priority.

Willow looked around the room, George dangling from her hand, and stifled a yawn. She looked like little Orphan Annie—lost and bewildered. One side of her curly red hair was matted against her head, and her freckled cheek was rosy from sleeping against the SUV door. She looked sad and adorable at the same time.

Oh, gosh. Just the sight of Willow's dejected body melted Natalie's heart. Add what Natalie had learned about Willow's dad tonight, and Natalie's heart shattered. She'd worked so hard to maintain her professionalism at work, to keep a certain detachment from her clients. At some point tonight, her professional separation had disappeared with these children.

Natalie wanted to take them into her own home and make sure they had a wonderful life.

Seriously. How could she even think that way? She was single and no prospective husband. She wasn't even dating anyone. Didn't want to be dating anyone.

No. That wasn't right. She wouldn't allow herself to date. She had no time for dates, not with her demanding job. Sure, she was lonely at times, but she focused on how much she was helping families. Helping kids like the Gentry children. She swallowed away her longing for a family.

"You're looking at me funny," Willow said.

Natalie snapped out of her thoughts. "Sorry. Do you need to use the restroom?"

Willow shook her head.

"Then you and George hop into bed."

She glanced around. "Which bed?"

Natalie pointed to two double beds on the opposite wall. "Choose either one."

Willow walked slowly to the closest, dropped her pink hoodie on the end, pulled back the camo bedspread and crisp green sheets, and climbed in. She tugged the covers and peered up at Natalie. "I'm afraid."

Natalie offered a silent prayer and sat on the edge of the bed. "Of what, sweetie?"

"Everything. Like why are we here? Where's Dad? Did he die in the car accident? Is that why you brought us here because he's not coming back?"

"Oh, sweetie, no. He didn't die." Natalie didn't want to frighten the girl so she would carefully choose her words. "His treatment just took longer than they thought."

"Then why are we here?"

"I had to come here, and because I was watching you, you had to come along." Sort of the truth. "Now don't worry about a thing. Get a good night's sleep, and tomorrow we

45

can explore the area. Maybe see deer and rabbits and other wildlife."

"Like a bear?" Her eyes widened.

Natalie had learned over the past month that Willow's first instincts were negative. Just the way Natalie had felt as a child. Maybe that was why God brought the child into Natalie's life, so she could help Willow adjust and learn to see the positive in her life. As a kid, Natalie had needed to force herself to think positive just to survive, and then it became a habit.

"We could see a bear, I suppose. Not likely though. And Drake will come with us. He knows this area and can keep us safe, so you have nothing to worry about. And if you don't want to go hiking, you don't have to."

"I want to." She nibbled on her raw lip.

Poor little sweetheart was trying to be brave, but her chin trembled. Natalie couldn't stand seeing her hurting any longer and not do anything about it. So what if her job frowned on personal contact? They didn't forbid it, just made sure that the social workers didn't put themselves in a situation that could be misconstrued. But this child needed to be held.

Natalie scooped her into a hug. Her warm little body molded to Natalie, and her fiery red curls tickled Natalie's cheek. She held her warm body tightly and hummed, "My God Is So Big," a song she'd learned in Sunday School.

She felt Willow relaxing and wished she could sing the chorus to her—and that Willow would believe that God was so big that He could do anything. Even take away Willow's fears.

Show us that. Please.

Natalie gave Willow a squeeze and then pulled back. "I'm here for you, sweetie. Always. You can count on me."

"I'm glad." Willow turned on her side and drew George

close, then pulled the covers up to her eyes. "Can you stay with me until I fall asleep?"

"I don't think so, sweetie."

She grabbed Natalie's hand. "Please. Please. I'm afraid."

"There's a nightlight in the corner." Natalie stood. "Do you want me to turn it on?"

"Yes." The precious high voice sounded from under the covers. "But I still want you to stay."

Natalie didn't want to leave the child, but Willow needed to sleep, and Natalie feared if she stayed in the room, Willow would keep asking questions instead of resting.

Natalie flicked on the nightlight and turned back. She was about to say good-night and head to the door, but then she thought about what was waiting for her downstairs. A man who wanted her to recount what she'd seen in the basement. With the police at Kirk's house, she didn't mind putting that off. Not at all.

Not when Willow needed her. Her loyalty had to be to the children. They had to come first. Always.

5

Drake paced the knotty pine cabin floor, waiting for Natalie to come back down. The fireplace blazed with warmth and he'd had to shed his jacket and overshirt but he wanted to be sure the kids were warm enough up in the loft. He paused by the stairway and looked at his watch. He didn't want to rush Natalie but maybe he should go after her.

"How long does it take to put kids to bed?" he muttered under his breath.

"Not something I can answer," Erik said from where he sat at the dining table, his laptop open in front of him.

"I didn't really expect an answer."

"Just messing with you." Erik grinned, a broad smile that was often on his face.

"You finding any information on this Gentry guy?"

"Not a lot. No social media accounts. Not at all unusual for a cop. As you already know, he has a wife and three kids. No criminal record, not even a speeding ticket. Not surprising for a police officer. From what I've found, he seems like an upstanding guy. Decorated as an officer several times."

"Any pictures of him?"

"Not yet, but maybe when I do my deep dive, I'll find something."

"I want a check on Natalie too."

Erik didn't respond for the longest time but finally raised a brow.

"What? It's the right thing to do."

"Yeah, but..."

"But nothing. You guys don't call me the devil's advocate for nothing. And just because I'm the one who took lead on this detail, doesn't mean I'm going to change my MO."

"Thought I picked up on vibes between the two of you."

"So what." Drake shoved his hands into his pockets. Maybe the vibe was keeping him from marching up to the loft and demanding to talk to her.

That ended now.

He spun and charged up the stairs two at a time. He might be ready to insist she come down with him, but he gently opened the door so he didn't wake the kids. His hand froze on the knob. Natalie was lying in bed next to Willow, the child snuggled up to Natalie, both of them sound asleep.

He let his gaze run the length of her body. Lingering on the slender legs below the short skirt. Definitely one of her assets, as was the thick head of hair that looked glossy in the nearby nightlight. He expected that wave of attraction to rush over him. Didn't happen. The desire to make sure her and these children didn't come to any harm nearly overwhelmed him.

They were vulnerable. To what, he still didn't know. He'd only just met Natalie, but he instinctually knew she wasn't the kind of person who would take a man's children and run unless it was a big deal. She was a Christian, and she seemed ethical.

So what did he do? Wake her up? Let her sleep?

The adrenaline from her fright had likely taken her down, and she wouldn't wake up soon. He might want answers, but he didn't have the heart to wake her.

She was probably cold without a blanket. And she still had those crazy high heels on. From the closet, he grabbed a warm quilt his mom had stitched and crossed the room. The floor groaned under his weight, and he hoped the sound didn't disturb any of them.

He set down the quilt and took hold of one of her shoes to slip if off and place it on the floor. She didn't move. Not a bit. He took off the second one and noticed that the pale pink polish on her toes matched her fingernails. Fit what he knew of her. Utterly feminine.

He'd usually be attracted to a woman who liked the outdoors. Why she was flipping his switch, he didn't know.

He tucked the quilt near her shoulders and resisted the urge to give the top of her head a kiss. She stirred, a smile crossing her face, and he had a flash of what it might be like to wake up next to her. Wouldn't be a hardship, that was for sure.

He glanced at the children. Their faces were flushed with innocence. Hers was too. He had to guard against that vulnerability. It was the one thing in a woman that he could never resist. But in the past, when any danger was removed, so was his interest. He didn't want to give this woman signals only to disappoint her.

Listen to him, thinking she would even pick up on his signals.

He stifled a groan and backed out of the room.

On the landing, he took several deep breaths to clear his mind so he wouldn't transmit his crazy feelings for his brother to pick up on.

He jogged down the stairs.

Erik looked up. "She coming down?"

Drake shook his head. "She's out for the count."

"And you're not going to wake her up?"

"Likely an adrenaline crash, and she needs to sleep it off."

Erik arched a brow, looking like their mother when she was grilling them for misbehaving. Drake had rarely caved under their mom's scrutiny, and he wouldn't cave for his little brother.

Erik tipped his chair back. "So how do you want to proceed?"

"Let me check in with Clay and Malone to see what's happening at Gentry's place." Drake went to his iPad to send an encrypted message using their Virtual Private Network, which masked his location, and asked for an update from Clay.

Clay's reply came right away, and he read it aloud for Erik.

Subject inside. Police knocking but no answer. Seems like they're waiting for direction to proceed.

Keep me updated, Drake replied.

Erik dropped the legs of his chair to the floor. "So now what, oh, wise one?"

Drake ignored his sarcasm. "We focus on protection while I try to get a hold of Malone and see if she knows more. We'll do what we normally would with a two-man protection detail. I'll remain here with the protectee, and you take the end of the driveway so we have advance warning of any danger."

"Figured you would say that," he grumbled. "Talk about boring."

"Well, don't fall asleep, whatever you do."

"I know how to do my job."

"Yeah, but this is your second shift of the day."

"Same for you, but we do this all the time." He blew out a breath. "You're just questioning me because I'm the youngest."

Was he? Maybe. "I expect things to be quiet, so you can spend your time in the truck doing research on Kirk Gentry."

"Fine." He pushed to his feet and closed his laptop then tucked it under his arm. "Go do your thing. I got this."

"It won't be more interesting in here, you know?"

"But it'll be far more comfortable." Erik went to the kitchen and opened the cabinet.

"Help yourself," Drake said letting his sarcasm flow.

"Hey man, you put me on surveillance duty. The least you can do is provide me with a few protein bars." He grabbed a handful and pocketed them, then filled a travel tumbler with water. "You'll call Aiden and Brendan in for relief in the morning, right?"

Drake held up his iPad. "Will do once I have more information."

"Let me know when they're expected. Wouldn't want to shoot one of my brothers." He grinned and stepped out the door.

Drake shook his head. His brother could be a smart aleck, but Drake was thankful for him. Sure, Erik complained at times. Who wouldn't? But now he was off to spend the night in his cold truck watching the road while Drake had a more comfy spot.

Didn't matter. Comfy or not, Drake wouldn't be sitting. He'd be by the door watching. Waiting. His gut said this Gentry guy was bad news, and Drake wasn't going to let him get anywhere near the woman and kids sleeping upstairs.

Natalie woke with a start and sat up. Where in the world was she? She glanced around the room with a hint of cedar in the air. Willow lay next to her and the other Gentry children were snuggled into twin beds.

Right. She was at Drake Byrd's hunting cabin, and Kirk was doing who knows what. How long had she been out?

She checked her watch. One a.m. She'd been sleeping for an hour and Kirk could be using that time to find her. Or trying to evade the police. Just because they'd gotten to his house didn't mean they arrested him. Natalie had to find out what was happening.

She slid out from under a downy warm handcrafted quilt. *A quilt.* She hadn't put that on before falling asleep. And her shoes. She'd been wearing them. Now they were sitting neatly on the floor. Who'd removed them and covered her?

Drake. Had to be Drake.

A rush of heat flooded her face. Something about him touching her while she slept seemed so personal when she was trying her best to ignore the attraction to him. She got out of bed and padded over the cold wood floor to the door and peeked out.

Heat from the fireplace rose up to greet her at the landing, and she could see him standing by the front door, gazing out the window.

She stepped out.

He spun, his hand going to his sidearm until he caught sight of her and locked his focus on her.

She suddenly felt self-conscious. Why hadn't she thought to take a look at herself in the mirror? She ran her fingers through her tangled hair. No help. It needed a brush. She gave up and started down the smooth wooden stairs, her feet already getting cold on the hardwood, but she didn't want to put heels on her aching feet. The smoky scent of a burning fireplace rose up to greet her, and the air was toasty warm.

She could imagine Drake here on a hunting weekend. Dressed in camo, looking all tough and masculine. Mr. Outdoors. She might not like the outdoors herself, but she was all for a rugged-looking guy.

He smiled at her, a crooked number that got her heart rate going, but she tried to ignore it.

"Everyone still asleep?" His attention remained riveted to her.

This must be how his prey felt on the other end of his rifle. She nodded and tried to smooth her hair again to no avail. It was naturally curly, and she straightened it most days, but the curls sprang back to life while she slept. "Sorry I dropped off."

He crossed the room, his stride slow and almost stealthy.

Why did she feel like she was being hunted?

He stopped at the fireplace and draped an arm on the mantle, emphasizing the width of his biceps. "Aftereffects of adrenaline can do that to you."

"You should've woken me." She tried her best not to look embarrassed at the personal contact, but heat started at the base of her neck and rushed up. She resisted looking away and held his gaze. "At least I figured it was you who covered me and took my shoes off."

He looked down at her feet, and the heat of her blush deepened. She must be quite a sight. Curly hair in tangles. Maybe mascara under her eyes. Could even have creases from sleeping. Her clothes too. They had to be a rumpled mess. She tugged down her jacket and tucked in her blouse.

"I made some coffee," he said. "Would you like some?"

She nodded. "I can get it."

The nutty scent of coffee drew her across the room to the small kitchen. She could only hope her red face dissipated as she retrieved her coffee. How silly to be embarrassed over the guy taking off her shoes. But she couldn't help it. She didn't have a lot of experience with men, and she'd never had a guy remove her shoes before.

"Mugs are in the cupboard above the pot. Sugar on the counter and almond milk in the fridge."

"I like it black." She grabbed one of the many hand-made mugs lined up on crisp white shelf paper. Had he taken the time to line his shelves? Didn't seem like something he might do, but then she'd known him less than a day and virtually knew nothing about him. Except that the desire to hurl herself into his arms for comfort remained strong.

She filled a vivid blue mug with steaming coffee. "Do you want some?"

"Had plenty already."

She turned to find him squatting by the fireplace, poking the logs with a wrought iron poker.

She nodded at the fire. "Looks like you know what you're doing there."

He held up three fingers. "You're looking at an Eagle Scout here, ma'am. Be prepared. That's my motto. All the time."

He chuckled, and she laughed with him, enjoying this lighter side to his personality. Not that he'd been super serious so far. But when it came to Kirk? Yeah, Drake's intensity had been through the roof.

The wood in the hearth caught hold and blazed brightly, and she moved closer to chase out the cold she was feeling. She didn't know if it was a real chill from the cold or a feeling from finding the nail polish. From learning Kirk was a serial killer. An image of the bottles all lined up with so many more colors waiting to be used played out in her head, and she shivered.

"You okay?" Drake asked.

She didn't know how to answer. Not when she didn't know if she would ever be fine again.

6

_____

"Now that you have your coffee"—Drake pointed at a worn plaid couch—"have a seat and tell me what this is all about." He tried not to sound demanding, but it came out as an order, and she cringed.

Great. Nice way to start.

She glanced up at the loft, likely checking on the kids, making sure they couldn't hear. Admirable. But he wished she would just come out with whatever had happened.

He also wished he wasn't distracted by her disheveled state even more than the put-together woman he'd first laid eyes on. Her hair was messed up with curls that had somehow come to life. Her suit was rumpled, her makeup streaked. She looked so different. More approachable. More attractive.

Just what he needed. "Let's get started."

She headed to the couch that had been in his parents' basement rec room for years. The stories it could tell.

She sat near a pile of colorful blankets knitted by his mother and wrapped her fingers around the mug. She took a sip of the coffee and didn't gag. Most people did with as strong as he made it. More brownie points in her favor.

She rested the mug on the arm of the couch. "Before we start can you tell me if you've heard anything about Kirk?"

"All I know is that he didn't answer the door and nothing from Malone yet. So go ahead and tell me what happened at the house."

She gave a sharp nod. "While I was babysitting, I discovered some very disturbing things in Kirk's basement. I'm certain now that he's The Clipper."

"The serial killer?" Drake's words shot out and up an octave.

"Shh." She spun to look up the steps. "The children will hear you."

Shh? Seriously. How could he pipe down when she'd just told him Kirk Gentry was The Clipper? The Clipper, for Pete's sake! Made him one seriously bad dude.

"Erik did a preliminary search on the guy, and he seems like an upstanding citizen, but appearances can be deceiving." He'd seen it often enough as a deputy. People who seemed on the up-and-up aided and abetted fugitives all the time, often lying right to his face. He'd lived it though, that trusting people came hard to him.

He took a beat to internalize her news. "Why do you think that?"

She started to reach for her purse, then dropped her hand. "I forgot I trashed my phone. I took pictures at Kirk's house that'll explain everything. They're in my iCloud account. Do you have a way to access the internet without giving away our location?"

He gaped at her. "You took pictures?"

"Yeah. Why?"

"There you were thinking Gentry was The Clipper, and you calmly took pictures. Seriously? Takes a lot of courage to stay cool enough to snap photos in a situation like that."

"Trust me, I was far from calm, but I knew without

concrete information the police wouldn't take action. But I needed proof, so they didn't laugh at me again."

"Again?"

"Long story." She tried to wave off her concern, but a hue of unease darkened eyes that, in the glow of the flames, he could see were ringed in black. "About that internet access."

Okay, subject change. Not so subtle either. What was she withholding from him? Or was it really nothing and she was just still shaken from the whole night? What person wouldn't be? Shoot. This discovery was unsettling him. Would unsettle his brothers, too, when they heard.

If she was right. Big if. Huge if.

He grabbed his iPad from the table. "Use this. We have an encrypted VPN, so the connection is secure."

"VPN?" She took the iPad and blinked up at him.

"Virtual Private Network," he said. "Our internet connections are routed through a virtually untraceable connection. We'll use emails via the VPN to communicate with the outside world."

"Why can't you make an internet call on that same VPN thing? I mean, I know you can use the internet to make calls," she added. "And you have the VPN, so I figured a call from here wouldn't be tracked."

"What you're talking about is Voice over Internet Protocol or VoIP, and you're right. These calls are hard to trace, but companies who own the app used to make the calls are allowing law enforcement access to call data. If that's true, then an officer like Gentry could potentially access the data too."

"I thought burner phones were safe?"

He shook his head. "No call is completely untraceable especially since we're dealing with a cop. I have a fresh phone, and it would take Gentry a long time and a lot of luck to trace the calls. But since there is even a chance, I won't risk making a call from here unless it's a life or death situation."

"Thanks for explaining." She flipped open the iPad case and held it so tightly her fingertips turned white.

He wanted to do something to help her let go of her fear, but that was going to be up to her. She'd have to trust him and his brothers to keep her safe, and that would take time as she got to know them.

She tapped the screen with her free hand, her tongue peeking out the corner of her mouth as she concentrated. She looked like an adorable kitten, and the cute sight belied the rigid set to her shoulders.

She took a sharp breath and looked up. "Kirk's wife went missing about a month ago. He said she took off, didn't want to be a mother and wife anymore. But I always got the feeling that something bad happened to her, and he was involved."

She paused and took a long sip of the coffee. "So tonight, when I was putting Willow to bed, I had a creepy conversation with her about her father polishing her nails. From there she revealed the fact that he hid their basement by installing a bookcase where the door was once located."

Okay, weird. "So you went into this basement?"

She nodded, her eyes tortured. "And I found the belongings that he reported his wife as having with her when she disappeared. Here's a picture of her things." She handed him the tablet.

The picture on the screen was of a large wooden shelf. It held a pink tote bag with the name Tracey embroidered in the canvas, a small purse in some designer fabric he couldn't name, and a blue rain jacket.

Drake met Natalie's gaze. "So it looks like she might not have taken off. Could even mean Gentry killed her, but that's not as extreme as being a serial killer."

Natalie set down her mug, and a hint of coconut rose up to greet him.

"I also found this." She swiped to the right on the iPad and looked up at him.

The next photo she revealed displayed a multi-compartment storage case similar to the one where he stored screws and other small fasteners out in his workshop. It was sitting on a crowded workbench. The drawers were pulled out, and each drawer held a bottle of nail polish, all different shades.

"They're in order of the colors used on the women The Clipper murdered," she said, her tone flat and emotionless as she dropped back down to the couch.

What in the world? Could she be right? Was this guy The Clipper?

Drake could hardly wrap his head around the idea, but he called up what he knew of the investigation. The nail polish details hadn't been in the news. Of that, he was certain. He and his brothers had been following the case closely. Very closely, as it was the biggest investigation to ever hit Portland, and each of them wanted to be in on it.

How could a social worker possess this information?

He watched her, waiting for any sign of duplicity, but didn't see any deceit in her eyes. "How do you know the order?"

"I overheard it. I didn't mean to listen but..." She shrugged. "I was in a PPB detective's office to talk about one of my children they'd arrested. He's one of the detectives on The Clipper task force. He got a phone call and stepped into the hallway to take it. But he didn't close the door all the way as he discussed the list of colors." She rubbed her forehead. "He doesn't know I heard him, and I haven't told anyone other than you and Malone."

That detective should've been more careful, and Natalie

shouldn't have listened, but Drake would've likely done the same thing.

"And you're sure this is the correct order?" *Or are you wanting it to be? Want to be one of those people who attach themselves to a famous investigation?*

"Positive." The single word rang out in the room, and she glanced up at the stairs.

Her adamant tone spoke to something deeper. Maybe as a female, she was empathizing more with the victims than he could. Or it could just be because she knew Gentry and now suspected him of heinous crimes.

Either way, Drake believed her and believed that he was now looking at protecting her from a man who'd killed four women and maybe his wife too. A serial killer who a major joint agency task force that included highly respected FBI agents had been working hard to find and had struck out. A seriously bad dude.

This news changed things. *Everything.*

Drake needed time to plan, but one thing was clear. Crystal clear. There might be a task force investigating The Clipper, but they wouldn't have the resources to protect Natalie and the kids, and Drake and Erik alone couldn't keep them safe from a cunning killer. They needed their brothers on the job.

He started pacing. Thinking. On one of his trips past the couch, he stopped to look at Natalie. She peered up at him, those unusual eyes boring into him. Into every emotion he was feeling right now and intensifying them.

His phone signaled an email, and he grabbed it from his pocket to see a message from Malone. "Excellent. Malone is working with Detective Londyn Steele. She's one of the members of the inter-agency task force hunting down The Clipper."

"I've worked with her before. Seems like you think it's a good thing Malone called her."

"She's an excellent detective. Tough but fair. My parents have been friends with her family for years. They own Steele Guardians and provide security guards for businesses in the area."

"Does she say if Kirk is in custody?"

"No, but she wants to interview you ASAP."

"Perfect."

Was it so perfect? "One thing you should think about. There's a chance you could be arrested for kidnapping."

"I don't care." Ferocity blazed in her eyes. "If Kirk's The Clipper or he killed his wife, he has to be stopped no matter what happens to me. Let me get my shoes so I'm ready to go."

She jumped to her feet. "Wait. The children. We can't take them with us."

"Erik can't babysit and protect them at the same time," Drake said.

She glanced up the stairs. "Maybe Londyn should come here."

"Too risky. We'll get my family out here. My parents can watch the kids."

"Now?" Natalie asked. "It's the middle of the night."

"Detectives don't sleep when they are hunting a serial killer." He riveted in on her gaze and widened his stance. "From this moment forward until Gentry is behind bars, no matter the time—day or night—we'll be here to protect you and the kids. That goes not only for me, but for my brothers too. Once I share your situation, they'll hightail it out here."

"I understand calling your brothers. You all do this for a living. But your parents? I can't impose on them too."

"Trust me." He almost laughed at the thought of the conversation with his mother. "My mom will be glad to be needed. And my dad is former law enforcement, so he understands. He'll want to get in on the action if he can."

"If you're sure."

"I am." He tapped the email account for his oldest brother Aiden and offered a prayer. For the kids' safety. For Natalie's safety. For the ability to protect them, and for the skills to outsmart a very cunning killer.

~

Overwhelmed. That was the only word Natalie could use to describe her emotions several hours later as she stared across the loft at the sleeping children. She'd been close to losing it since her discoveries in the basement, and she was barely clinging to sanity now.

Instead of melting down while they waited for the Byrd family to arrive, Natalie had come up here to check on the children. She was pleased to see all three were fast asleep, and the loft was nice and warm from the fireplace.

She reached for her shoes and sat down on the empty bed to slip her aching feet into them. And then she did what she should've done from the moment Willow had told her about polishing her nails.

Prayed. Enthusiastically. Almost desperately.

"Why, Father?" she whispered but didn't expect an answer. She'd learned over the years that God didn't often explain, and she really didn't need to know the whys. She just needed to know it was. To see what was happening. Find out His purpose. Find out what His plans were and carry them out.

In this case, she wanted to understand His purpose in bringing her together with the children, and with Drake and his family.

This situation was so different for her. She was a loner.

She only needed God in her life, and things were just the way she wanted them. A cute townhouse, small and efficient so it didn't take much time to clean. It left her more time for her huge caseload. Her clients needed other people. They needed her, but it was a one-way street. Her mother had almost obliterated the need for love or companionship in Natalie's life. Then Gina's murder erased that need, and Natalie vowed never to love again. No point. It always ended up in agonizing pain.

She glanced at Willow's little freckled face. At Sadie's button nose. At Logan's plump cheeks. God's creations, all of them. They needed each other. They needed parents. She knew that. Felt it even. And if their father was a killer, it was her job to find someone to love these children, give them companionship and care. They needed to know someone cared if they lived or died.

Natalie would find it for them, and in the meantime, she would protect them. With every fiber of her being, she would be their staunchest advocate.

Feeling more resolved, motivated, and dedicated, she tiptoed to the door and closed it firmly behind her.

Deep male voices carried up the steps. Drake shushed the guys, and they lowered their voices. She looked over the railing to see a golden lab sitting at attention at Drake's feet and two broad-shouldered guys shedding windbreakers, both with dark hair and features resembling Drake.

Buff. Handsome. Drake's older brothers. Seeing them all together, the confidence they exuded, she had to swallow. If these strapping guys couldn't keep her and the children safe, no one could.

She took a breath and started down the stairs. All gazes pinned to her, and the conversation stopped.

Her stomach tightened. Were they talking about something they didn't want her to hear? Was it about her? About the children? Did they discover something on the internet? Like maybe that The Clipper had killed her sister, and Natalie had withheld that info from them.

Gina was married and had taken her husband's last name. Not that Natalie ever saw him. He didn't like how Natalie wouldn't let Gina's death go. He'd moved on. Too quickly for Natalie's liking. Still, connections between Natalie and Gina could be found. Natalie knew that for certain as she'd found them while searching for information on Gina's killer.

And these looks directed her way. *Wow.* The intensity was almost frightening, and her steps faltered.

No. She wouldn't let them intimidate her. She'd just sworn to take care of these children and find them the life they deserved. Plus, she'd vowed years ago to find her sister's killer. She wouldn't let a few intense guys stand in her way, no matter what they'd found. No matter what they thought of her.

She ran her gaze over the men, making sure they knew that she wasn't daunted. They all wore what must be their work uniform of a black polo shirt with the team's logo on their chest and the cargo kind of pants that she'd seen police officers wear.

Drake knelt by the dog and patted his head. "Erik's dog, Pong. He's an electronics sniffer dog."

"A what?" she asked.

"He sniffs out hidden electronics like flash drives and memory cards that can otherwise be missed in a search."

"Interesting."

"Plus, he's just a fun guy to have around. The kids might like him." Drake smiled lovingly at the dog and ruffled his fur, leaving it sticking up at odd angles. "And he's great at alerting us to unwanted visitors." Drake looked up at her. "These are my other brothers, in case you haven't figured that out. Erik's standing watch out at the road."

She stepped to the closest guy and shoved out her hand. "Natalie Dunn."

"Brendan Byrd." He smiled, looking very much like an older version of Drake. He clasped her hand tightly and gave it a vigorous shake.

She tried not to wince and looked at the other guy, Aiden, and mentally put the brothers in alphabetical order.

"C is missing," she said.

"That would be Clay," Aiden said. "He's keeping tabs on Gentry."

"So she knows, huh?" Drake looked at her. "Erik tell you?"

"About your order? Yeah. It's cute." She smiled at them.

They groaned.

"From a naming point of view," she added. "It would make my job so much easier to keep children's names straight if all parents did that."

"But not from a living with it point of view." Drake focused on Aiden. "Are Mom and Dad on the way?"

"Should be pulling up any minute."

"Mom has agreed to keep an eye on the kids, so we can head to an interview with Malone and Londyn Steele."

"You worried about legal blowback?" Brendan asked. "I mean, inviting Malone to the meeting and all."

"I was just going to ask the same thing," Natalie said, as this was the first she was hearing of it.

Drake returned his focus to her. "You may not care what happens to you right now, but you could later on. So I thought it would be good to have Malone sit in on the meeting."

"Thank you," she said, touched that he was thinking of her. She interacted with a lot of people in her job, and it was rare to find selfless people. Several of her fellow social workers and Malone were an exception to that, and now it appeared as if Drake and maybe his family were too.

"And us?" Aiden asked. "What do you want us to do?"

"Protection detail for the kids, of course," Drake said. "And get started brainstorming a plan of action so when we get back, we can hit the ground running. Not only do we need to protect Natalie and the kids, but it appears as if Gentry somehow escaped the police, and we're going to need to find him."

"He what?" Natalie swallowed to control her fear.

"Didn't Clay have eyes on the guy?" Aiden asked.

Drake nodded. "He says Gentry was moving around in the house until the police arrived, so Clay doesn't know how the guy disappeared, but he did."

Brendan drew in a deep breath. "Out the back, I suppose."

"I'm sure we'll learn more when we meet with Londyn." Drake changed his focus to Natalie. "We'll get going the minute Mom and Dad arrive. I've arranged to meet at the Veritas Center."

"The lab?" Natalie asked. "Why there?"

"We office out of the center, and the building is as secure as a fortress," Drake said. "Top-of-the-line security system and an armed guard at all times."

"Couldn't we just meet Londyn at the police station?" Natalie asked.

"If Gentry thinks you're a witness to the evidence you found in his basement, he might head over there," Drake said.

"Oh, right." She needed to stop questioning these professionals, who obviously knew what they were doing. "I didn't think of that."

"That's why you pay us the big bucks." Brendan grinned.

"Oh, payment." She clamped a hand over her mouth. "I'm so embarrassed. Here I am thinking you'll take care of us, and I didn't even think to ask for your continued help or consider your payment."

Drake waved his hand. "We'll do this pro bono."

"I can't ask you to do that." She ran her gaze over the group.

"We're glad to do it, right guys?" Aiden asked.

The others didn't hesitate but nodded.

"But I—"

"Hey," Brendan said, a smile forming. "Think of it this way. We get to be involved in hunting down an elusive serial killer. None of us got to do that in law enforcement. As much as we hate what the guy's done, it'll be exciting to be involved in bringing the creep to justice."

"Exciting isn't the word I'd use." Drake frowned at his older brother.

"Okay fine. A challenge."

"Better," Drake said.

"Then thank you." Natalie smiled at the men. "Let me know if I can repay you in any other way."

"Honestly, the best way to repay us is to do what we tell you to do." Drake stepped closer to her. "Not question anything we ask, but just act. If indeed we *are* dealing with The Clipper, then we have a very cunning adversary, and everyone needs to be alert at all times."

She nodded and then thought about the meeting he planned to hold when they returned. "I don't mean to be questioning your decisions right off the bat, but if we meet in here, the children might overhear."

"I have a heated workshop," Drake said. "We'll use that space."

"I brought some whiteboards and lights." Brendan tipped his head at the door.

"Great," Drake said. "Someone get them set up."

Aiden arched an eyebrow. "Make me a cup of coffee while I unload, and I'm glad to do it."

"Sure thing." Drake faced Brendan. "And if you'd relieve Erik at the road so he can continue his deep dive on Gentry and his wife, that would be great."

"Offer me the same deal," Brendan said, sounding a bit more laid back. "But none of that spoon-stands-up-in-the-mug kind of coffee you like to drink. Make it palatable."

Drake mocked offense. "You guys just don't know how coffee's supposed to taste."

"We don't need the extra caffeine you crave." Brendan zipped up his jacket and headed for the door. He and Aiden exited like a strong hurricane wind.

She was blessed that Malone knew these men. They seemed capable and willing to protect her and the children. Even so, she would still remain involved in her own and the children's safety and in bringing Kirk to justice. She couldn't leave everything up to them. Especially since her sister was The Clipper's first victim, and Natalie had a personal interest in seeing this man locked behind bars for the rest of his life.

7

Natalie watched Erik step into the cabin from his surveillance detail and set his laptop on the table. He seemed like such an easygoing guy compared to the others, but underneath it, she saw an iron will much like she'd witnessed in Drake. She felt Drake watching her right now and could easily imagine his narrowed eyes. The burning intensity in them. Maybe questions like he seemed to want answered all the time.

She was coming to know him in such a short time. It was like they had an innate connection, or one God was fostering, which made it feel right. But was God behind it or was she just imagining things? Letting her fatigue get to her and make her want something she couldn't have. Maybe she just wanted to hand off all her problems to Drake and let him sort them out instead of her doing the hard work for once. Or maybe she was just plain attracted to the guy.

She turned to face him, stifling her frustration at the uncertainty of everything. She was usually so sure of what she wanted, but now it was all up in the air.

He gave her a tentative smile, seeming out of character.

"My family's a lot to take in at one time. And I'm warning you that our mom is something else."

She didn't know how to respond, so she didn't. "I can make the coffee if you tell me where things are."

"We can do it together." He stepped into the galley-style kitchen open to the living area that consisted of a tiny stove, an apartment-sized refrigerator, a worn enamel sink, and cabinets painted a cheery blue color. His vibrant personality seemed to take up the entire kitchen, and physically he commanded much of the minuscule space, leaving little room for her.

Turns out it didn't matter. Not at all.

The door opened, and a tall woman with silvery-blond spiky hair rushed inside. She took one look around and marched into the kitchen.

"Scoot," she said to Drake, taking the coffee pot out of his hand. "No one needs the kind of coffee you make."

She all but pushed him to the other side of the island and turned to Natalie, a big smile on her face that reminded Natalie of Erik. "I'm Peggy Byrd. Mother to this gaggle of boys and a daughter who's going to birth our very first grandson any day now."

Natalie loved the woman's enthusiasm, so opposite of Natalie's mom, who'd been sullen and noncommunicative. "Nice to meet you, Mrs. Byrd. I'm Natalie."

"Please call me Peggy." She smiled, and her eyes crinkled with the kind of joy Natalie had once imagined seeing reflected in her own mother's eyes. At least imagined it in the days when she still had hopes for a happy childhood like most of her classmates.

Peggy stepped closer. "I don't know the details of why you and the children are here, but you can trust my boys to keep you safe."

Boys. Surely, she didn't mean the herd of testosterone

that had rushed in and out of the front door only moments ago. Natalie loved that this woman still thought of those fierce men as her boys.

Natalie glanced at Drake to see if it bothered him, but he was just giving his mom a tender smile that made Natalie's heart swoon. If she was looking for a relationship, a guy who loved his mother with so much zeal would be a guy worth getting to know.

"My husband, Russ, is unpacking the car," his mother said. "But I knew the boys would want something to eat so I came right in to check on them. They'll want coffee, but what about you? Coffee or tea? I'm a tea drinker myself."

"Coffee for me," Natalie said.

Peggy's firm nod was reminiscent of the certainty her sons possessed. "I'll get it going and if Russ doesn't have things in here by then I'll grab a few snacks from the bins."

"I can help," Natalie offered.

"Thank you, but no. This is my thing, and I've got it." She gathered Natalie up in a hug.

Shock had Natalie standing like a statue, but then she relaxed and enjoyed the warm embrace. When was the last time an adult had hugged her? Probably people at Gina's funeral. Peggy's closeness felt warm and odd at the same time. And it brought tears racing to the surface. Natalie wasn't going to cry in front of these people. She swallowed and pushed back.

Peggy smiled. "Now don't you worry. The boys have you well in hand and so does God. Do you believe in Him?"

"Yes," Natalie answered, liking the woman's straightforward nature.

"Good. Good." She squeezed Natalie's arm. "Then you know everything will work out."

Drake met Natalie's gaze. "You might want to escape the kitchen now, or Mom will be asking for your life story." He gave his mother a fond smile. "We'll need our cups to go, but thanks for making the coffee and for agreeing to watch the kids. They're asleep in the loft. Hopefully we'll be back before they wake up."

"But in case we're not," Natalie said, "Willow's the oldest at eight. Then four-year-old Logan and two-year-old Sadie. I hate to leave them. They're kind of vulnerable. Mostly Willow. She might be difficult."

Peggy waved a hand. "I can handle just about anything after raising five headstrong boys and one super opinionated girl. So don't worry."

"Thank you."

"While the coffee finishes, I'll run out to the car to grab something for you to eat for your trip." She hurried out the door.

Wow. She could move. Especially for her age and for the middle of the night.

Drake looked like he wanted to sigh but held it back. "She just wants to mother everyone and make sure they're happy. She loves everyone with enthusiasm."

"That's special." Natalie inhaled the scent of fresh coffee filling the air.

"Trust me. At my age it can be challenging."

"How so?" Natalie watched as he got two travel mugs from the cupboard.

"Mostly she sees herself as a matchmaker." He opened the mugs and rinsed them out. "She wants all of us to get married and produce grandchildren right now."

"I noticed Aiden and Brendan were wearing wedding rings."

He nodded. "They both got married this spring, and Clay's engaged. Brendan's wife, Jenna, has an almost five-year-old daughter. Mom has Karlie to spoil, and Sierra's due any day, but she wants more grandchildren. Many more."

Natalie looked out the window at Peggy hurrying back to the cabin. Natalie didn't understand the woman's longings. Natalie was a loner—plain and simple—and she had no desire to be a part of such an overwhelmingly large family. She left those yearnings in her childhood with her mother's neglect and her father's abandonment and was well over any angst regarding that.

Peggy rushed in and handed a container to Natalie. "Banana nut and blueberry muffins. Make sure Drake eats. He gets cranky when he's hungry."

"Mom," Drake warned.

Peggy simply smiled up at him and clutched his arm. "Be careful, son, and keep our Natalie safe."

Our Natalie. Already? If Peggy was matchmaking, she worked fast. Something Natalie was going to have to put a stop to as soon as they returned.

The moon hung in the sky, striations of light filtering through the foggy darkness. A fine mist fell, dampening Natalie's body, and a crisp breeze was downright chilly on her bare legs. She moved as fast as her heels allowed to Nighthawk's SUV. Drake remained in sync with her. She got the feeling that he would not only be in charge of protecting her and the children, but be physically by her side whenever she left the cabin.

She climbed into the big SUV and pulled the door closed. Odd. It was heavy under her hand. She hadn't noticed that before. She hadn't noticed many details that she was picking up on now. Like the way Drake's eyes could be darkly intense and just as quickly turn as clear as a summer's blue sky in a flash.

He slid in and cranked the powerful engine. The SUV

rumbled to life under them and cold air blew from the vents as the heat struggled to warm up.

She looked at him and said the first thing that came to mind to keep her thoughts off of him. "Is there something special with your car door? It seems really odd."

"Right. I didn't tell you." He patted the dashboard. "This vehicle is armored, and the doors are bulletproof. The windows are two inches thick. That's why our doors are thicker. They need to support the weight of the windows. We even have electrified door handles."

She looked him full in the eyes. "What?"

"The exterior handles have copper wire embedded in them." A cute grin formed on his face. "With a push of a button the driver can turn on the handles and zap any attacker who grabs them."

Trying to comprehend this James Bond kind of spy stuff, she blinked a few times. "Seriously?"

"Yep." His grin widened. "We have night vision cameras, a loudspeaker, and a siren. Plus bulletproof metal panels for the radiator and battery. The bumper's reinforced steel, and we have run-flat tires. We're virtually a tank." He laughed, the deep rumbling sound bouncing around the space and feeling warm and wonderful after all the tension they'd been going through.

She tried to process this information. "Sounds like you have every option possible."

"Nah." He shifted into gear. "There are tons of additional things you can add. Like a Kevlar blanket for the floors to stop an explosion from harming someone in the vehicle. Too pricey for us."

"This technology is something else. I had no idea." She shook her head. "Nighthawk Security is definitely a first-rate operation. It must've been expensive."

"It was." He shrugged. "Aiden insisted on tricking out

both of Nighthawk's vehicles right up front, and the money came straight out of our pockets. But it'll all be worth it the first time one of the upgrades saves a life."

A vision of Kirk, gun in hand, standing outside the SUV and opening fire on them flooded her brain. She could almost feel the bullets pinging off the vehicle's body. She shuddered, but she knew she'd be safe. Thanks to these guys. A good feeling. Especially if Drake was in the vehicle with her, as she wouldn't want him to be hurt. His brothers either. Or, of course, the children.

She nodded. "Sorry to question you."

"I don't mind questions when your life isn't in immediate danger. After all, I'm the one in my family who's always asking them." He smiled, a slow, lazy one that flip-flopped her heart. The smile disappeared in a flash. "But I need you to listen if we come under attack. No questions."

"And I will. Promise." She crossed her heart and smiled at him, trying to lighten the mood, but his eyes followed her finger's movement, and when he looked up, his eyes were darkly dangerous.

A heated current flowed between them, feeling almost physical. Powerful. Amazing and new.

She'd dated. Not a lot but she'd dated and had never felt anything like this. It was...it was electric. A cliché, but that was the best description for the sizzling warmth.

Her heart stumbled. Paused. Then pounded. Racing.

He jerked his gaze away and sucked in a sharp breath as he released the brakes. His strong fingers gripped the wheel tightly, relaxed, and gripped it again. Over and over, he followed the same pattern as if letting out pent-up emotions. She understood the need. She could use the same release, but she was still too shocked to act.

He got the vehicle heading down the driveway toward the main road, the tires crunching over the gravel. She waited for him to speak, as she couldn't say a word, but he turned onto the road. The pavement rolled under them for miles, yet he remained quiet.

Was he going to ignore the little interlude? Probably a good choice. At least for the moment, but what about long term? Couldn't it fester and become a big problem?

She wanted to get it out into the open, but she didn't want him to think she was coming on to him. She wasn't. Not at all. At least not on purpose. And with his mom into matchmaking, it was all the more important to talk about this so he knew where she stood.

"What was that?" she asked, her voice still unsteady. "I mean what happened between us back there."

"I'm pretty sure you'd call that attraction." He sounded as if he liked and hated it at the same time.

The exact same way she felt. "You didn't expect that to happen, did you?"

He glanced at her. "You're a beautiful woman. So yeah, I expected to be attracted to you. Actually I was the minute I laid eyes on you. But..." He shook his head. "I figured it would pass. Especially since I'm charged with your safety."

"And it didn't."

"Nope." He clicked on the blinker to merge onto I-5. "And it seems you feel it too."

"I did. Do. But it can't go anywhere. I'm not cut out for a relationship. No time or inclination. I live for my job and helping families. And right now I have the added responsibility of the Gentry children."

"Suits me just fine," he said, his tone unwavering.

His answer certainly bothered her. It shouldn't. His response was exactly what she wanted. So why did it trouble her?

"I've got a whole lot of living to do before I settle down

with anyone," he continued. "And I sure don't want to be responsible for kids."

He glanced at her. "I don't mean making sure they're safe. I'm more than happy to ensure their dad doesn't get to them. I mean be responsible in a fatherly way." He mimicked a shudder. "Father. Can't even hardly say the word much less imagine myself being one at this point in my life."

"Right." She was surprised at how much his stance on not getting involved bothered her. And his take on children? If she were ever to decide to get married, she would want children—would want to raise them the opposite way of how she'd been raised. But clearly that wouldn't be an option with this guy anytime soon. He didn't want children or a relationship.

The same thing she wanted right now. So what was the big deal?

He didn't want her.

No big deal.

Or was it?

His quasi rejection brought back the feelings from her first serious crush. The high school quarterback, of course. But the dirt on the bottom of his shoes held more standing in his eyes than she did. Poor girl. Wrong side of the tracks. Crazy mother. Shy. Awkward.

Yeah, that described her perfectly back then, and at times that girl still showed up. Like today, she supposed.

Go away, Hand-me-Dunn.

She hated the nickname—the play on her last name— that her classmates had called her growing up. At her age it shouldn't still bother her, but it did. She'd learned over the years that if you call someone a name long enough, the person starts to believe it. Sure, she wore secondhand clothes—thrift shop clothes, but she knew the slur wasn't true.

Problem was, her emotions didn't always get the message.

The pain and hurt still crept up when she least expected it. Often when she was tired and emotional. Just like now. Add in taking away her control over what was happening in her life, and she had the perfect trifecta of a storm brewing. A storm she wouldn't let loose while confined in a vehicle with Drake, even this big SUV.

Turning this conversation back to the job at hand was the key. If she didn't, she might regret what she said.

She took a breath to banish *Hand-me-Dunn* from her thoughts and sought a safe subject. "I don't think I've properly thanked you for your help. Not only for being so careful, but for dropping everything in your life and coming to our rescue."

"It's what I—we—do."

"But still. You're not taking payment, and I wanted you to know that your kindness is appreciated. For me and the children. I don't hardly know you, but I know you're a special person."

His face colored a bright red. She'd embarrassed him. Not her intent. She wanted to make things easy not more difficult. She resisted sighing and looked at him out of the corner of her eye.

Were things destined to be awkward between them?

She didn't want that, but with the highly charged atmosphere between them, yeah. Yeah, she was most certain things would never be easy.

8

They traveled far enough away from the cabin that Drake felt safe in using a burner phone to call Malone. He placed the call, and the ringtone sounded over the speaker, but his thoughts remained on Natalie. She'd been quiet. So had he. He had nothing to say. He'd said it all. She was gorgeous. He found her attractive. End of story. No matter if what had just passed between them was new to him. He didn't understand it fully, and he wasn't going to analyze it

Just let it go.

He had to. For her safety. That had to come first.

She was the toughest kind of client to protect. An altruistic person who thought of others first. He applauded her selflessness. Respected it. It was rare these days to find someone so driven to help others. Was probably fueled from her past. He suspected she didn't want any child to experience the same pain she'd gone through and would zealously work toward making sure they didn't. Despite being impressed with her passion, he didn't like it. Not from a protection perspective.

Sure, he wanted to protect these children at all costs. He'd die for them if needed. So would she. But he was different. He knew what he was doing—how to handle the danger and threats. She didn't, and even if she promised to listen to him, he feared that, if it came down to her life or theirs, she'd try to save theirs. No questions asked. And that could be the wrong move. The very wrong move that could get her killed.

"Hello." Malone's deep and sultry sleepy voice came over the speaker.

"It's Drake. I'm in my SUV with Natalie, and you're on speaker."

"Is everyone okay?" Worry carried through her tone.

"Yes, thanks to this amazing guy and his family," Natalie said, and smiled at him.

Drake waved off her compliment and focused on the road. "We haven't really done anything other than escort everyone to a safe location."

"No, it's more than that." Natalie gripped his wrist.

He knew she wanted him to look at her, but he never needed or wanted praise. In fact, he hated it. He didn't do what he did for thanks or praise. He did it because his parents raised him to help others, and his faith commanded him to do it. James nailed it in the Bible when he said faith without works was dead. Drake believed that. Completely.

She gently squeezed his arm, and he could almost feel her gaze imploring him to look her way. He gave in and glanced at her, her soft and tender expression brought the unwelcome heat back to his face. Thank goodness he wasn't on a video call with Malone. The last thing he needed was for her to notice the feelings he was developing for Natalie.

No, the real last thing he needed was for his mother to discover them. She would make life unbearable unless he acted on it. And even then, she'd be right there, encouraging him to get more involved.

"You've already taught me what not to do if I want to stay

safe," Natalie said. "And counseled me on my next steps. So don't discount your help."

He stared at the road sliding under their vehicle to ignore those soft fingers pressing against the sensitive skin right above his pulse. She could probably feel her simple touch firing his heartbeat.

He swallowed. Concentrated. Found his center and his strong determination to succeed. That was what he needed to focus on. "We were hoping you'd join us for the interview with Londyn."

"I'm glad to if you think you need me, but I don't foresee any issues." Malone's usual self-confidence was in her voice.

"What about kidnapping charges?" Drake asked.

"I doubt Gentry will bring charges, and even if he tries to, there are extenuating circumstances that the DA will take into consideration."

At the good news, Natalie's expression brightened, like the parting of stormy clouds and the sun shining through.

Drake shifted before he let that bright expression mesmerize him. "We also need to talk about your safety, Malone."

"Mine?"

"Have you given the number for the phone you're using to anyone else?"

"The at-risk teens I work with have the number, but that's it."

"With Gentry being a cop, it's possible he could get a phone company to reveal the cell tower tracking for your location."

"Wait, what?" Malone asked. "The phone company can track calls by location not just by number? This is the first I'm hearing of this."

"They can do tower dumps, which are reports of every

mobile signal from a specific area at a specific time. So the burner phone number would be linked to your location."

"I had no idea they could do that." Malone tsked. "Does that mean the calls I've made with women and troubled teens aren't secure?"

"It's not like just anyone can get this information. It requires a warrant. Or an unethical friend at the phone company. Or even a hack, which Gentry could know how to do."

"What are the odds of that happening?" Malone asked.

"Very slim," Drake replied. "He'd have to connect you to Natalie to even begin looking. But it could happen, and I wouldn't feel right if we didn't provide you with protection. I'd suggest you join us at our secured location, but that means you'd only be able to communicate via email."

"No. No," Malone said firmly. "I can't do that. Not with Sierra expecting. And I have clients who are counting on me."

"Figured you'd say that and was hoping you listened to Reed and are staying with him and Sierra. On second thought, her moods have been swinging pretty wildly and you might want to avoid that." He laughed. "You can bunk at my place while I'm gone."

"I've convinced my brother that I'm fine for now, but I can stop in and talk to him after the interview."

"No," Drake said firmly. She may have convinced Reed she didn't need special protection, but Drake wouldn't let her go without an escort. "I don't want you out there all alone. Give me your address, and we'll pick you up."

"You don't really think Gentry has connected me to Natalie, do you?"

"We're just running background on him now, so I don't know how much he's capable of." He paused and locked gazes with Natalie. "Other than killing defenseless women and eluding the police for years."

~

Two tall towers of shiny glass with twinkling lights greeted Natalie as Drake drove into the Veritas Center's secured parking garage a few hours before dawn. The towers were linked together with a building on the ground floor and a skybridge on the sixth floor. An impressive structure.

"Tower on the left holds the labs and our office," Drake said as he wound the SUV up the ramp to the top floor. "On the right are our condos."

"You must have some view from that skybridge." Natalie turned to catch a final look.

"It's amazing," Malone said from the back seat.

"We take it for granted." Drake parked outside an entrance on the sixth floor. "We'll start by heading down to the lobby to get security passes and escort Londyn to the office."

Natalie glanced at Drake. "We need passes?"

"Yes." Malone removed her seatbelt. "Be sure to keep it with you and that one of the golden team is with you all the time. They get cranky if you don't obey." She wrinkled her nose.

"Sounds like a story there." Drake killed the engine.

"Let's just say I forgot one night when I was visiting Reed, and the guard filling in for Pete didn't know me and blew a gasket." Malone laughed.

"I'm sure you gave as good as you got." Drake chuckled as if they were old friends.

They all exited the vehicle into a gusty wind, and Natalie straightened her rumpled jacket. Malone might not have had much time to get dressed, but she looked the consummate professional. Her sleek black suit jacket emphasized her tiny waist as she carried her overnight bag to the door. Under her jacket she wore a white blouse, and she'd paired it with equally sleek straight-legged pants and designer black pumps. She was nearly six feet tall in her heels and had fragile and delicate features.

She crossed her arms as she waited for Drake to press his fingers on the keypad, and her nails, with a French manicure, stood out against the black jacket. Natalie felt plain and underdressed, and *Hand-Me-Dunn* tried to make an appearance. Natalie shut her down. She took a quick look out the glass walls at the sparkling Portland skyline, but Malone was on the move, and Natalie hurried to catch up.

"I'm glad Drake was able to rescue you and the kids," Malone said as they walked toward the elevator.

"Thanks for arranging it," Natalie said.

"And thanks to you, Drake, for being a knight in shining armor one more time." Malone glanced back at him as she boarded the elevator, giving him a dazzling smile that likely melted countless hearts over the years.

Looking uncomfortable, Drake mimicked rubbing his chest as he joined them in the elevator. "Your calls are getting more frequent. Gonna have to polish up my armor."

Malone laughed. That was one of the things Natalie liked about this woman, and why they'd become friends. Malone had a great sense of humor. Natalie was more serious and could stand to lighten up. It was looking like that was another thing she didn't have in common with Drake.

When they reached the first floor, Drake led them through a spacious lobby that smelled of vanilla and was decorated in calming neutral tones. He approached an older guy dressed in a security uniform who stood alert at the desk. His buzzed gray hair was laced with silver, and confidence oozed from him. Natalie caught sight of Londyn sitting on a sofa under a wide open staircase. She came to her feet, but Natalie kept her focus on the guard.

"You must be Natalie." He smiled and held out a tablet computer to her. "I'm Pete Vincent. Just fill in the form, and I'll give you your pass."

"Nice to meet you." She tapped the screen to add her details and made short work of completing the form. She handed it back to Pete and took the pass dangling from a lanyard.

By the time she draped it over her head, Londyn was shaking hands with Drake. She was of average height with a muscular build and had a tough, rugged vibe, but her tailored navy blue suit, gauzy blouse, and manicured fingernails with a pale pink color gave her a contrasting feminine side too.

Natalie had always admired Londyn. Not because she was a pushover and did whatever Natalie requested for her clients. Just the opposite. She was a strong woman and a very capable detective, but her greatest strength was her fairness and compassion. She evaluated every case on its merits and didn't jump to conclusions about Natalie's clients due to their prior convictions or living conditions. Natalie might not like it when Londyn asked the DA for strict charges to be imposed, but Natalie had never found fault with Londyn's decisions. Ever.

She released Drake's hand and turned her pointed attention on Natalie.

"Good to see you again." Natalie shook hands and forced a smile despite the sudden uneasiness that was rushing through her. She'd never broken the law before. Well, other than speeding. Her intentions were good when she'd taken the Gentry children, but that didn't change the fact that she'd kidnapped three children, and Londyn might not think too highly of that.

"You too, though it's not the best of circumstances, is it?" Londyn tilted her head, and her almost black hair with nutmeg highlights shifted over her shoulder.

"I'm so sorry to hear about your brother, Detective Steele." Malone slipped her security pass over her head. "Always a sad day when someone as young as Thomas is taken from us."

Londyn seemed to deflate for a moment before lifting her shoulders. "Thank you. And thanks to the Nighthawk team we at least caught the lowlife who killed him."

Natalie had heard Londyn's older brother was murdered in his home, but she didn't know that Drake and his brothers helped bring the killer to justice.

"We were glad to help." Looking embarrassed at the praise again, Drake gestured out the door. "If you'll all follow me."

He took them to the elevator and up to the sixth floor. At the end of the hall, he pressed his fingers against another reader. "Our humble offices."

"Might be humble, but you have the penthouse floor," Natalie said, trying her hand at joking.

"The Veritas partners wanted to save the fifth floor for expansion, so it's not because we're special. Though we are. Very." He grinned and locked gazes with her.

Oh, wow. This guy really knew how to smile.

Natalie's breath stalled in her lungs.

"You're safe here. Breathe," he said, oblivious to what caused her reaction.

She was mooning over him right after telling him she didn't want to get involved. And right before confessing to a crime with a strong police detective. Natalie's focus should be pinned on that. She could still be prosecuted for abducting the Gentry children. Plus, she always strived to be professional, and she was coming across as a smitten teenager.

Enough.

She firmed her shoulders and marched into a tiny reception area that held a small desk and two chairs.

"Let me get a light on." Drake went to an open door. Light soon spilled out, and he made a sweeping gesture with his arm as he bent forward. "After you all."

Natalie entered first and took a moment to look at the space boasting exposed pipes and ducts and giving the large area an industrial flare. Cubicles lined the back wall and a long conference table with live edges and black iron legs sat just inside the door. Overall the place was as masculine as the brothers.

"Go ahead and have a seat." Drake told them and pointed at the chairs.

Natalie took the nearest one, and he sat next to her. Malone settled on her other side and Londyn across the table.

"Have you arrested Kirk?" Natalie knew Londyn would be in charge here, but Natalie had her own questions to ask. To know.

"Not at this time." Londyn laid a pen and small notepad on the table.

Natalie kept her focus pinned to the detective. "What are you waiting for?"

"I'll get into that after you tell me what you discovered at the Gentry residence that makes you think Kirk Gentry is The Clipper."

Okay fine. Londyn *was* in charge, and Natalie would have to go along with that for now. She breathed deep, and she glanced at Malone for confirmation that she should tell her story.

"Go ahead." Malone pressed her hand on Natalie's. "If something becomes problematic for you, I'll step in."

Natalie sat forward and shared about Willow's fingernails, trying her best to keep her emotions out of her voice. "I found that extremely unsettling and suspicious. Then when Willow said her dad had remodeled the house and got rid of their basement, that set off my alarm bells."

"And according to Drake, you went looking for this basement," Londyn said.

"And I found it." Natalie described Tracey's items sitting on the shelf. "I think he killed her."

Londyn leaned back, but her expression remained sharp. "I read up on her investigation before coming here, and there wasn't anything pointing to foul play or to Tracey being hurt. In fact, CCTV footage shows her getting on a bus with the items you say are in the basement."

"Can I see that footage?" Natalie asked.

"It's public information, so I don't see why not." Londyn tapped the screen on her phone a few times then held it out to Natalie.

Drake shifted closer, and the musky scent that she was coming to associate with him enveloped her, but she ignored it to look at the screen. Just as Londyn had said, a woman fitting Tracey's description held a tote bag in her hand and a little Gucci bag hung over her shoulder as she climbed the stairs to the bus. She wore the blue polka dot raincoat that was shoved on the shelf in Kirk's basement.

But, and this was a big but for Natalie, the woman's face wasn't visible. "This could be any woman with Tracey's things."

"Keep watching," Londyn replied.

The woman stopped on the top step and looked back over her shoulder, her face fully visible.

Natalie looked at Londyn. "Matches the photos I've seen of Tracey though her lips are swollen."

"Exactly," Londyn said with a satisfied smile. "And on the lips, I think it was a recent cosmetic procedure gone wrong."

Natalie dug the pictures from her pocket that they'd printed at the cabin. "Then how do you explain these items I found in Kirk's basement?"

Londyn examined the photo then looked up. "You took these pictures tonight?"

"Yes," Natalie said. "Like I said. I think he killed Tracey."

Londyn's eyes narrowed. "I agree that it's suspicious for him to be in possession of these items, but jumping to murder is quite a leap."

Drake lifted his chin. "Why else would he have them?"

A flicker of a shadow deepened Londyn's eyes, but she quickly vanished it. "He hired a private detective to find Tracey. Maybe she dumped these items, the detective located them and returned everything to Gentry."

"This is the first I'm hearing of a PI." Natalie rubbed tight knots in the back of her neck. "I think he would've told me about it. It's something that would go in his favor in our investigation."

"Just how did he come on to social services radar anyway?" Londyn asked.

Natalie explained about the neighbor who reported Tracey missing. "Kirk told the police that Tracey couldn't cope with three children and walked out on them. But the patrol officer thought he was acting odd."

"Uncooperative?" Drake asked.

Natalie shook her head. "No, but he was furtive and hesitant in his answers. Still, he allowed the officers to look around the house, and they found Tracey's bloodstained blouse shoved into the back of his closet. He said she'd cut herself in the kitchen, and he was supposed to drop the blouse off for professional cleaning. He claimed he'd forgotten and hid it so she wouldn't get mad. Then he completely forgot about it."

"Yeah, I read that in the report," Londyn said. "The detective's notes also said he thought Gentry was more eager to find her so he could divorce her and get on with his life than concern for the woman."

"It sure looks like he found her," Natalie insisted. She knew she was right about this. She just knew it.

"So you were called in to evaluate the family?" Londyn asked.

"Kind of," Natalie said. "The neighbor's call prompted a welfare check. Nothing that would develop into a full-fledged investigation unless I found something. But before I could go to the house, Kirk failed to pick up his children from school and daycare. He, Tracey, and the nanny who was unavailable were the only people on their approved pick-up list, so when it got late, the school called us."

"Is that normal?" Drake asked.

"Can be or the school could cut the parent some slack and wait for them. In this case, Willow had told the counselor that her dad thought a bad man had taken her mother. This wasn't what he'd told others, and with the aspect of neglect in failing to pick them up, the counselor grew concerned and made that call. So I brought the children to the office until we could locate Kirk. He'd gone out for drinks with a co-worker and said he'd forgotten his nanny was out of town."

Drake swiveled his chair to face her. "Did you believe him?"

"He's very convincing, but no. I didn't buy his story. Which is why I did a thorough investigation and put him on watch status, though I still don't really know why he didn't pick them up. Maybe he'd just snapped under the single parent responsibilities. Tracey was a stay-at-home mother, and my investigation revealed that she and their nanny pretty much handled the child-rearing duties. He didn't know a whole lot about his children's lives, and he was only marginally involved."

"Is there proof of the private investigator in his file, or might it just be hearsay?" Malone asked.

"No proof. Only mentioned in his statement." Londyn set down the photo and rested her arms on the table. "Our investigation into her disappearance ended when the video was located showing Tracey alive and well, and the detective never looked into Gentry's claim of hiring the PI."

"Sounds premature to close the investigation," Drake said.

"Have you seen our caseloads?" Londyn narrowed her eyes. "We barely keep our heads above water. This woman is seen leaving of her own accord. No foul play. I'm not surprised they closed it."

Natalie knew all about high caseloads on the job. "Are my pictures enough for you to get a search warrant?"

Londyn nodded vigorously. "You're a person with expected access to the house, which means anything you found is most definitely admissible both for a warrant and trial."

"Good. Then you'll want to see this." Natalie took out the nail polish photo they'd printed from her iCloud account. She unfolded it and pressed out the wrinkles, her heartbeat ratcheting up just viewing the bottles. She slid it across the table to Londyn. "I also found these in his basement. Check out the names on the bottles and the order. Matches the order of polish colors used on The Clipper's victims."

Natalie held her breath as she waited for Londyn's reaction. The detective made a detailed scan, then her head popped up. Her eyes were narrowed and dark. Suspicious. And she looked like she might be controlling her anger. "How do you know about this?"

Londyn's frightening detective stare had Natalie's heart racing and brought *Hand-me-Dunn* to the surface. She shook her head to still the urge to revert back to her childhood feelings of inadequacy and glanced at Malone to see if she should answer. Not because Natalie really thought she shouldn't for any legal reasons, but because she would have to admit again to being an eavesdropper.

Malone offered Natalie a sympathetic look followed by a sharp nod.

Natalie swallowed hard. "I overhead someone talking about it at your office."

Londyn aimed her chin at Natalie like a weapon. "Who?"

Natalie worked hard not to let *Hand-Me-Dunn* take over and make her shrink under the stare. "I don't think that's important."

"Not important." Londyn snapped her chair forward. "They should be disciplined for their carelessness."

"I don't want to get anyone in trouble." Natalie twisted her hands together, fighting the urge to run. "And to be fair, I could've told the person I could hear the conversation, and I didn't."

"But—"

Malone rested a hand on Natalie's arm, stilling her. "Natalie doesn't want to reveal this person's identity, so let's move on."

"Fine," Londyn said, not at all sounding like she was caving. "But I can't let this go. Not when it's such a high profile investigation. Know that I will revisit it at some point."

"How do you want to proceed after seeing these photographs?" Malone asked.

Natalie was so thankful Drake had thought to invite Malone to the meeting for support, and thankful she was moving them forward before the conversation became contentious.

Londyn looked at Natalie. "I'd like to bring you to Gentry's place to walk me through your night. I'll make the arrangements with the other task force members then give you a call to join me at the house."

Londyn stood and kept her pointed focus on Natalie. "Be ready for my call, and don't make me waste valuable time looking for you."

9

Exhaustion weighed down on Natalie after a brainstorming session with Malone and Drake, and as they walked Malone down the hall to Reed's condo, Natalie stifled a yawn. She and Drake would wait for Londyn's call at Drake's condo and hopefully grab some sleep while waiting. They all agreed talking to the Gentry's nanny was top priority, so after the walkthrough at Kirk's house, they would interview her before heading back to the cabin.

They approached Reed's door, and Natalie glanced at Drake. "You know Londyn's not going to like us talking to the nanny."

"I don't care." Drake curled his fingers. "You saw those pictures. This guy needs to pay and pay big-time. We can't sit around and wait for Londyn to tell us what she found."

Natalie agreed. Of course she did. Especially after Londyn had flipped through her murder book while questioning Natalie. *Murder book.* Natalie couldn't even believe she was saying those words as she'd never been privy to the police insider information. Or believe the glimpses she got of Londyn's photos—The Clipper's victims lying in pools of blood, their chests pierced with a sharp object over and over, their hearts the main target. He clearly killed like he was in a fit of rage, but then he took the time to paint finger-nails and pose the women. The two acts seemed out of sync with each other.

Natalie had struggled not to throw up. Drake's reaction had been strong too—grimacing and muttering something under his breath, and his body tensed up next to her before he lurched to his feet and started frantically pacing. Maybe the movement allowed him to rid his brain of such horrific violence. After all, he'd seen it for so many years already and had to have found a way to remain sane amidst it all.

Natalie couldn't find any peace. Not after losing the one person who'd meant the world to her. Sure, she wanted justice for all the women, but she desperately wanted to prove Kirk had killed her sister.

"It's not illegal for you to talk to her." Malone knocked on Sierra and Reed's door then looked back at Natalie and Drake. "If you remove anything from her property that might be evidence, that could be construed as impeding an investigation. So keep your visit to questioning, and you should be fine. And first thing in the morning I'll call your supervisor, Natalie, to tell her the children are okay and safe with you."

"Are you sure it shouldn't come from me?" Natalie asked.

"Your supervisor could ask where you've taken the kids." Malone's expressive eyes narrowed. "You would either have to reveal their location or lie. Both situations could poten-tially end your career as a social worker. Where I can honestly say I don't know where the children are."

Drake gave Natalie a pointed look. "She's right. Let her do this for you."

Natalie felt like she was shirking her responsibilities, something she would never do in a normal situation, but in this case, she had to agree.

The door opened, and a very pregnant woman with dishwater blond hair and honey brown eyes ran her gaze over them. Natalie had no trouble identifying this woman as Sierra. Not only because of her pregnancy, but because she looked just like Erik and their mother.

Sierra stepped out and gathered Malone up in a hug. "Reed's not too happy with you. Good thing you decided to listen to him and stay with us, or he would be impossible."

"Actually, I'm taking Drake's advice." Malone backed away and grinned. "I can't wait to tell Reed that, and there's no time like the present."

Natalie gave the kind attorney a smile. "Thanks for coming out so early."

"Are you kidding?" Malone grinned. "I get to mess with my brother, and that doesn't often happen." She turned and strode into the condo.

Natalie could hear Reed's deep voice booming from inside, but she couldn't make out his words.

"I'm Sierra by the way." Drake's sister rested one hand on her belly and held out the other one.

"Natalie."

Sierra shook firmly.

"Do you guys want to come in?" Sierra asked.

"We need to catch a quick nap before meeting Londyn again." Drake gave his sister a tender smile. "Now off to bed with you for a few more hours so little Elvis can finish percolating."

She swatted a hand at him.

He took hold of it and drew her gently to him for a hug. "Dang, girl. You're huge."

She pulled back and mocked offense, but a sweet smile tipped her lips. "Be careful so you're around to meet this little guy." She smiled at Natalie. "Nice to meet you. Has my mom got the two of you walking down the aisle yet?"

Natalie's jaw dropped open.

"She doesn't work quite that fast." Drake chuckled. "And if Natalie's look says anything, Mom's got her work cut out for her."

Natalie couldn't come up with any kind of a response.

"Not just with Natalie." Sierra eyed her brother. "You're the least eligible of the group."

Drake cocked his head. "What's that supposed to mean?"

"You're too busy trying to prove something to make time for a relationship."

He frowned. "I don't want to get into this now."

"Hit a nerve, did I?" She smiled sweetly and stepped back. "Bye now. Take care, Natalie. I hope to see you again."

"Okay," was all Natalie could say.

"C'mon, let's go." Drake started down the hallway, taking long strides.

Natalie nearly had to run to keep up with him, which didn't make her feet feel any better in the hopelessly high heels she'd chosen yesterday morning. She could dress more sensibly, she supposed. But looking good made her feel good, and on some of the dismal days on the job, that was all that kept her spirits up.

"Can you slow down a bit?" she asked.

He reduced his speed and waited for her to catch up at the elevator. "Sorry. I forgot you were wearing stilettos."

"They're not stilettos."

"Close enough." He held the door for her. "Still not very practical."

"Trust me. If I'd known I'd be running from a serial killer when I got dressed, I would've worn running shoes."

He punched the number two button. "You and Sierra are about the same height. We could go back and ask if she has something that might fit you."

"I couldn't impose on her."

He paused, hand on the doorknob. "You don't like to accept help, do you?"

She thought to blow him off, but maybe if she explained, he'd understand. "It's not that I don't want help. I've never really had anyone other than my sister around *to* help. So I learned to do things on my own. Now I'm more comfortable counting only on myself."

He didn't answer for the longest time but leaned against the back of the elevator and watched her. "What about when God puts someone in your life to provide assistance at the right time?"

"You mean like your family?"

"Exactly."

He had a point. One she hadn't really considered in the past. "I'll have to give it some thought. But I still don't want to bother Sierra. She's probably already gone to bed."

Drake's eyebrow rose, and he watched her for the rest of the ride down to his condo. It appeared as if he really wanted to say something else but was holding it back. She didn't want to get into a personal discussion when she was this tired and wasn't about to ask him what he wanted to say.

On the second floor, he led her to his condo, his thumbs tapping on the knob as he held the door open for her. The atmosphere was charged with his hyperactivity, and she found it unsettling.

"You're still pretty hyped up," she said, thinking this was a safe subject to approach.

His thumbs stilled in the air, but he didn't respond right away. "I want to hunt Gentry down. Be in on the action to bring him in and lock the cell door behind him. Not being in on the takedown is one part of my new job I hate."

She could easily imagine him tracking and appre-hending a fugitive and suspected he was really good at it.

"Must have been satisfying to shut the cell door after you captured the person you were hunting."

He scratched his jaw. "I didn't actually get to close doors. We turned fugitives over to the local law enforcement agency. They held them in local jails while they waited for the prisoner's return to the correction facility they escaped from or waited for their day in court."

This was another area that they didn't seem to agree on. "I know your job was necessary, but I've always had more of a rehabilitation than incarceration mindset."

He frowned and stepped back, but didn't comment on her response.

Okay. Maybe he didn't want to go there so she would leave it alone. Excited to see his place, she slipped past him to go down a hallway to a spacious room attached to an open kitchen. Light gray paint covered the walls, and the trim was a crisp white. He had little in the way of decorations other than a bookshelf loaded with books about every kind of extreme sport she could imagine.

He passed her by to go into the kitchen. "And on your mindset, I think we're going to have to agree to disagree on that one. I know you often work with offenders, but most of them are in a far different class than the people I hunted down." He gripped the edge of the counter on a big island until his fingers turned white. "Those very dangerous fugitives needed to be off the streets before they reoffended."

"Agreed," she said, though she still believed incarceration often did more harm than good, there were some people who had to be locked up. Unfortunately, way too many people fit that criteria these days. "Like Kirk Gentry. He shouldn't be out on the streets, and he's not a good candidate for rehabilitation."

"We first have to find him." He grabbed a glass from the cupboard. "Can I get you some water?"

"Please."

He got down a second glass, and as ice dropped and water flowed from the refrigerator dispenser, he tapped his left foot at a rapid speed.

She settled on a barstool. "Are you always this antsy?"

"Not always. Just when I don't have a physical outlet for my frustration." He flashed her a cute smile and handed her a glass, but she could see that he was forcing it. "Probably why I like high adrenaline sports so much."

She took a sip of the icy liquid. "I'm not judging so don't take this the wrong way, but how do you reconcile your need for adrenaline with your faith?"

He stared at her, his expression unreadable. "What do you mean?"

"It's like you have to keep moving because you aren't in control of the situation, when in fact, God is in control all the time. Not us."

"Not sure I agree." His thumbs started tapping on the counter in rhythm with his foot, but he didn't look away. "We have free will. We can control things."

"Only if God allows it." She faced him. "Trust me. I know. Growing up the way I did showed me what little in my life I could actually control. I was kind of like you back then. Not in the pacing or adrenaline thing, but I always had to keep busy. I only felt good when I accomplished something. Probably the reason I was able to get my Ph.D."

"And, what happened?" He pinned his focus on her.

"I burned out. Plain and simple. Finished school and was a wreck." She swallowed away the memories so she could tell her story without getting emotional. "That made me dig deep to find out why."

"And what did you learn?"

"Something surprising. I had low self-esteem from being teased as a kid and having parents who didn't show any real affection. That part I knew. But what I discovered was that I found my worth in accomplishment. The more I accomplished, the better I felt about myself. I believed as a kid that if only I did more or did better my parents would love me. And that my classmates would see *me*. Not a stereotype they wanted to see. So I pushed myself even harder. Got more done."

"And now?" He took a long drink and set down his glass but kept his gaze on her.

"I still struggle with doing too much at work, but I make sure it's not for that reason. I do it now because the people I work with need help, and I can't let them down. But I have to stop on a regular basis and analyze my actions just to be sure. And I also have to make time to chill."

He shoved his fingers into his hair and left it messed up. "I've never thought about why I do what I do. I've always kept busy and on the move. Until now, no one has asked how this might not jive with my faith."

"Sorry," she said sincerely. "I don't mean to sound like your shrink. That was pretty forward of me." *And way too personal if I want to keep you at arms-length.*

"No. No. It was good. I need to give it some thought." He started to tap the counter, but then flattened his palm on the surface. "I mean I'm not trying to overcome a difficult childhood like you. Mine was ideal. Mom homeschooled us all, and she loves us with a passion. Dad's more reserved but he shows his love in different ways. So that's not an issue."

"Could it have to do with your birth order? Were your older siblings super-achievers? Good grades, all of that?" She shook her head. "Listen to me. Going all Ph.D. on you and sounding like I have all the answers. You can ignore me if you want."

He perched on a stool near the island. "I don't mind answering. Sierra is the real brainiac of the family, and being the oldest, she set a high bar. Aiden, Brendan, and Clay are smart enough. I struggled with school, though. I'm not so good at sit-down activities when I wanted to be on the go. So I didn't concentrate like I should have."

"Maybe you wanted to keep moving to compensate. If you weren't there, you couldn't fail."

"Yeah, maybe."

"And maybe that's even why you love the adrenaline rush in sports or your activities. It's accomplishing something difficult."

"Could be." His eyes sharpened with an edgy intensity that matched his body language. "I appreciate your insight but now's not the time for me to think about it. Not when we have a serial killer to find."

10

The three hours of sleep that Drake had gotten at his condo wasn't nearly enough and he was bleary-eyed as he signed in with the officer of record outside Gentry's house. As Natalie scribbled her name on the roster, he blinked a few times and rubbed his dry eyes. Wouldn't do to be groggy now that he had a chance to look for leads.

Natalie shed her heels, and he helped her put on the requisite paper booties, doing his best to ignore her sleek legs.

"You're sure you're okay with going back in there?" he asked as he handed her latex gloves.

"If it helps capture him, I'll do just about anything."

He stepped back to let her enter the two-story foyer. The house was grand and far bigger for what Drake expected on a police officer's salary. But it was the sight of Gentry's elaborate video system set up in the office that took Drake's attention. Malone had mentioned Gentry had inherited some money and maybe he blew it on the house and equipment.

Natalie stopped outside the glass paneled office door. "Unbelievable. Kirk had this planned. He knew he would need to escape someday."

Drake took in the large screen facing the window along with a ceiling-mounted projector that displayed Gentry at his desk and then getting up to move through the room. The window faced the road so Clay would've seen this video through the curtains and think Gentry was in the office. Gentry had synced the timer to a similar system in his bedroom.

Londyn stepped into the hallway and joined them. They'd been apart for only a few hours, but dark circles now hung under her eyes. "Crazy, right? I mean, who does this? This is paranoia at the finest."

"With his IT experience, the technology was well within his grasp." Drake stared at the video still playing. "But the fact that he knew he might be watched and planned ahead like this? No wonder he hasn't been caught."

"Exactly," Londyn said. "He had this set up and the one in the bedroom timed to perfection so it looked like he was in the house. Never seen anything like it."

Shaking her head, Natalie turned to face them. "And the evidence?"

"Gone, just like Gentry." Londyn shoved her hands into her pockets. "That's why I wanted you to come over, to confirm where the evidence was located so forensics can give those areas a more detailed search. Not sure how much it will help, but we aren't going to leave anything to chance here."

Drake texted Clay and told him to head out and get some sleep, then turned back to Londyn. "Forensics not here yet?"

"Not yet." Londyn frowned. Maybe she was having jurisdiction issues. "Follow me."

Londyn led them through a neat family room. Drake moved slowly, making a mental picture of everything in the large space open to the kitchen. The chairs. Blanket.

Pillows. Pictures on the wall. Items on the fireplace mantel.

Londyn stopped by the basement door that stood open. "You coming, Drake?"

"Yeah, sorry." He joined them.

From the visible side, the door looked ordinary, but Natalie had said the other side held a bookcase. He wanted an up-close look at that.

When Londyn and Natalie started down the stairs, he studied the door and spotted the tiniest hole by the locking mechanism. He took a better look and spied a camera. Tiny. But it was a camera for sure, plugged in from the other side of the door.

If he hadn't been looking, he'd have missed it. He glanced around the other side, where the body of the camera was embedded in the base of a metal cat sculpture. He snapped pictures of the setup and items on the bookshelf. Who knew? Something else there might just be a lead. He needed to look at everything he could while he was here, as he was just plain lucky Londyn let him in with Natalie. He wouldn't be given a chance to come back.

He hurried down the stairs looking for additional cameras and listened to Natalie point out where the nail polish and Tracey's items had been stored. He didn't miss the scent of bleach and heard Natalie and Londyn discussing it. If Gentry killed his wife down here and there was any hint of blood, the forensic team would find it.

He took his time scouring the workbench for any tool that could've been used to kill the women, but found nothing. Of course not. A killer who would create such an elaborate scheme to make it look like he was home while he escaped wouldn't leave a thing behind.

"What I don't get," Natalie said, "is why he kept these items at all."

"Souvenirs, maybe," Drake said. "The bottles reminding him of each kill, and Tracey's belongings doing the same."

Londyn frowned. "Seems likely. And seems like he's our guy."

"Sure does." Drake took one last look around, noting the contents of the room as he'd done in the family room. Two coolers. Camping gear. Bins of Christmas and Halloween decorations. And the workbench holding copious tools. Something told Drake to get a picture of the tools.

He motioned in the direction of the stairs. "After you guys."

They went ahead of him, and he took a picture of the wall of tools. Not content with that, he shot a few more of the other items then hurried to catch up. Back on the first floor, he looked at Londyn. "Could we have a look at the bedroom? Natalie might see something that you all don't think is important."

"Follow me." She jogged up the stairs, her paper booties whispering on the wood.

He managed to snap pictures of the family room on the way through and kept his phone out for the bedroom. Another screen faced the window where sheer curtains were still closed, but the thick velvet drapes remained open. The video wasn't playing right now, but Drake assumed Kirk had filmed himself occasionally moving through the bedroom too.

The room smelled strongly of perfume, a peppery scent with a hint of flowers. A very unique scent that likely belonged to Tracey. In the corner sat a huge makeup table and mirror littered with cosmetics.

Londyn got out her phone and tapped the screen. "The perfume's a special release of Caron Poivre for the company's fiftieth anniversary. Costs a grand an ounce."

Drake let out a low whistle and took a better look at the bottle. "This is a three ounce bottle. So three grand for perfume. Where did she get that kind of money?"

"A gift from Kirk?" Natalie suggested. "He could've used some of the money he inherited."

Drake made a mental note to have Erik dig into Gentry's finances and looked at Londyn. "You've been through the dresser and closet?"

She gave a sharp nod. "Nothing but clothing and shoes."

Drake glanced inside the very tidy closet with a color-coordinated arrangement of male and female clothing. "So he never got rid of Tracey's things. Not sure if that says he was expecting her to come back or he was just putting on a show for law enforcement."

Natalie joined him. "The last time he mentioned her to me, he was saying he hoped she would still come home. That even if she made a fool of him by taking off, he'd still take her back. She was the children's mother, and they needed her. I guess keeping her clothes helped support his claims, when all the while her things were in the basement, and it seems like he'd killed her."

"Not usual behavior for a man who murdered his wife," Drake said.

Natalie stared ahead. "Everything's organized by color. Perfectly hung. Neat. Just like his personality. And the color organization of the nail polish means something too."

Drake looked at Natalie. "Tracey wore nail polish, right?"

"She's wearing it in this picture." Londyn pointed at a silver-framed photo on the dresser. "She was also very into fashion."

Drake crossed the room to look at the family photo taken in the summer in a park near a flood of purple flowers. Tracey's blond shoulder-length hair was flawlessly combed, her makeup heavier than normal for a park visit. At least it was heavier than he would expect. It was taken before the botched procedure on her lips. She wore what looked like designer clothing with strappy sandals, and her blue fingernails and toenails matched her blouse. The other family members were dressed far more casually.

"She doesn't fit in with the family."

Natalie joined him. "She's beautiful, in a plastic sort of way."

"All the pictures in the house are like that," Londyn said. "As if she only allowed the camera to capture her if she was perfect looking. And they're all older photos. Nothing in the recent months. Likely due to the plastic surgery fiasco."

"Or maybe Kirk was cheating on her, and she felt the need to look her best all the time," Natalie said.

"If he did, it'll likely come out in the investigation." Londyn looked between them. "Now if there's nothing else, we should get going so forensics can take over."

"I'm sure Sierra would love to do the forensics for you," Drake said. "That is, if you want the best."

"An FBI forensic team's on the way. This being a joint investigation, we have to play nice with them. No way I'm going to fight that."

"Nor should you," Drake said. "The FBI teams are top-notch. Maybe not as cutting-edge as Sierra, but top-notch. Besides, she's due this week, so it might not be a good idea to get her out here. She could go into labor and insist on staying on scene to keep working."

Londyn laughed. "From what I've heard about her dedication to her job, that sounds about right."

"What about the evidence that's already been processed in the missing person's case? I assume that's still under your control and at the Portland police lab? Sierra could review it. Maybe find something your local lab missed."

Londyn planted her feet in a no-nonsense stance. "You saying the PPB lab is incompetent?"

"Not at all. Sierra has better toys to work with, is all."

Londyn pushed back her jacket and rested her hands on her hips. "We only have the blouse in evidence, and it'll most likely become part of the task force's purview."

"Can't you get the detective in charge of that investigation to transfer the evidence to Veritas before that happens?"

"I don't like making snap decisions." Londyn shifted her stance. "Especially on something so important. Not to mention something that could potentially lead to career suicide."

Drake understood that, but he wouldn't give up. "Sierra is the absolute best at trace evidence, and she could give you the lead you need right now."

Londyn tilted her head, and he waited, hoping she'd agree.

"Fine," she said. "I'll call him and get the ball rolling."

She got out her phone, and Drake resisted the all-powerful urge to pump his fist. Wouldn't do to gloat. Besides, he needed to use every second she spent on the phone searching for a lead. He took a stroll around the room. The space was still decorated in very feminine fabrics, and a ton of throw pillows were piled on the neatly made bed. You wouldn't catch Drake with a mound of pillows on his bed, even if he was married. Not like that was going to be an issue for him in the near future.

He took a long look at the ceiling. There. In the smoke detector. A hidden camera. Could either be a faux detector or a real one Gentry modified. Either way, it was a perfect place to hide a camera. No way Tracey would suspect it or even find it when cleaning. Gentry probably had them strategically placed to record the activity in the entire house. He could even be watching them now.

Londyn's voice deepened, and she almost demanded the detective comply. She didn't mention the FBI or the connection to the serial murders, but the detective had to know she was working this investigation. Everyone in the office would know. It was such a high profile investigation, even the patrol cops would know her role on the team and would either be dreaming of being her or be very, very glad they weren't involved. Nobody would have a middle-of-the-road stance.

He took a few more pictures of the room.

"Done." Londyn shoved the phone into her pocket. "Evidence is on the way to Sierra."

Drake pointed at the camera and jerked his head at the hallway. Londyn frowned and marched out of the room. Looking confused, Natalie followed, but he didn't want to tell her about the cameras right now and freak her out. Better to do it when they were alone.

On the front stoop, he looked at Londyn. "How did Gentry get away without being seen?"

"Loose fence boards in the backyard lead to a large conservation area."

"So he's on foot?"

"He was." She gritted her teeth. "Based on his plan to dupe us, he likely had another vehicle stowed somewhere close by. We're researching DMV and car rental records now."

"Would you let me know if you find anything?" Drake asked. "If I'm going to keep Natalie safe, it would be good to know what he's driving."

"Sure thing." She looked up at the portico above, and Drake knew she was searching for additional cameras.

Drake scanned the street, the morning sun beating

down on them. He didn't think Gentry was dumb enough to be nearby, but then, killers often returned to the scene of the crime to see the commotion they caused. In this case, though, the hidden cameras might be fulfilling that need. Seeing law enforcement cover every inch of his house and strike out. He'd love that.

So, where could he have hidden other items? If he even did.

"Do you have anyone processing Gentry's car?" Drake asked.

"I wish." Londyn turned her intense focus on him. "Crash happened on a backroad in the boonies. Gentry called his own tow truck before the medics transported him to the hospital. The deputy didn't stay around to write down the company name. Means we don't know where the car was taken. Makes me think that Gentry was trying to hide something."

"Could be a long list of tow companies to go through."

"We'll get started on it right away."

Drake's attention went to three plain black SUVs rolling to the curb near the perimeter marked by fluttering yellow tape. The contingency had *fed* written all over it, and made quite a sight. Neighbors on the sidewalk stared at the vehicles and their many questions floated on the breeze. He couldn't imagine living in the quiet and respectable neighborhood, only to wake up one morning and learn the man living next door was the infamous Clipper.

How did a person go to bed at night and feel safe again after that? And their property value would nosedive. In the short run anyway. Maybe in the long run. It was tough to be these people right now.

Drake offered a prayer for them as men and women in khaki pants and blue polo shirts with a gold FBI emblem on their chests poured out of the vehicles. They paused to size up the situation and wait for their orders. Drake wanted to be long gone before they spread out like ants to take command of the house and grounds.

"Don't envy you," he said to Londyn, who was eyeing the agents warily. "Even if I was once a fed myself."

Londyn turned to Drake, ripped off her gloves, and shook hands. "Keep in touch."

"Will do." He faced Natalie, whose attention was on the agents now storming their way. "Ready to go?"

"More than ready." She took off for the SUV.

Drake kept pace with her and kept his head on a swivel, looking for Gentry or any danger. He opened her door and waited for her to slide in. She smiled her thanks, but her eyes were narrowed and worried.

He closed her door, knowing at least she was safe in the vehicle. For now. But this guy, who'd set up an elaborate scheme and cameras all around his house, knew she'd been in the basement. Knew she'd seen his evidence and would testify against him if he were caught.

He would soon be hunting her down. If he wasn't already tracking her.

And if he found her?

That wasn't something Drake wanted to think about. Not at all. But to keep her safe, it had to be in the forefront of his mind at all times.

Drake quickly pulled away from the curb in front of Kirk's house for the short drive to interview Kirk's nanny. The group of onlookers had grown larger by the minute, but he ignored their stares as he drove off. He was used to this sort of circus, but Natalie wouldn't be.

"Quite a sight." She stared out the window, her fingers

clawing together. "Not that I blame the neighbors. If I lived nearby, I'd be gawking, too."

"Especially at the FBI forensic van pulling up." Drake turned a corner leaving them behind. "Ulani's place is just down the road."

Natalie looked at him. "I sure hope she can give us something to help us find Kirk."

Drake nodded but then kept his focus on the area. Not that Gentry was likely present, but Drake couldn't be too careful. He made a few turns and reached the fourplex where Ulani lived, the building drab and uninviting.

"Wait here until I have a look around." He parked in front then slid out.

The complex was located in an older residential area mixed with retail and restaurants. The building was neatly painted a bright blue and the landscaping was well manicured. A dog barked a few blocks away, but otherwise silence reigned.

He opened her door. "When Ulani answers the door, tell her your name and that we need to see her. Since she knows you, she's more likely to let us in."

"Will do."

"And stay close to me." He stepped back and pushed aside his windbreaker to rest a hand on his sidearm.

Natalie slid out. For once he kept his focus off those incredible legs and took her elbow to bring her close. He felt her gaze on him but ignored it. Keeping an eye on the surroundings was foremost right now. Not talking.

He led her toward apartment 1B, drawing her even closer to place her under his arm, the safest position, before pounding hard on the door painted a cheerful green. No one answered, so he knocked again and also rang the doorbell. He knocked a third time and finally a light came on in the window next to the door.

"She's home." He stepped to the side so she would only see Natalie through her peephole.

"Ulani, it's Natalie Dunn." She spoke in a lighthearted tone, but the nervous clasping of her hands gave away her unease. "The Gentry children's social worker."

"What do you want?" The woman had a high-pitched voice, almost childlike.

"I need to ask you some questions."

"This early?"

"It's important. Please. Can I come in?"

No answer. Not a yes or a no.

Drake started counting in his head and had reached twenty when the deadbolt slid free. The door opened a fraction, and Ulani peeked out.

"This is Drake," Natalie said. "He's helping me with the Gentry children."

"Helping?"

"It's a long story. Can we come in?" Natalie stepped forward and pressed on the door preventing Ulani from closing it in their faces.

Good. Natalie gained access. She'd likely done this a time or two at homes where the occupants weren't so eager to see her.

Ulani frowned but stood back, her turquoise satin pajamas a silky flash in the light. Natalie entered first, and Drake followed. The nanny was petite with gleaming black hair flowing down her back. Her skin was the color of wet desert sand.

Natalie marched into the small living room and sat in a leather easy chair. The savory scent of bacon clung to the air but was mixed with a disinfecting smell. He stood behind her, positioning himself in place where he could act if needed. Not that the five-foot-tall woman looked like a threat, but he'd learned over the years that he could never discount anyone. That was how people were killed and injured, and he wasn't going to let Natalie come to any harm.

Ulani perched on the edge of her beige couch in an equally beige room. She fixed her focus on Natalie. "What do you need to know?"

"Tell us about Kirk Gentry," Drake said, taking her attention. "What's he like?"

Ulani clasped her hands together in her lap. "Natalie knows him. She can tell you that."

"I'm interested in your take."

She opened her mouth then closed it and looked down at her hands.

"It's okay, Ulani," Natalie said softly. "You can tell us. This is an unofficial visit, and it won't go into his file or impact his custody of the children."

She raised her head. "It's not that he's a bad person. He's not. He just can get super focused, and when he does, he doesn't like to be disturbed. Not by me. The children. The phone. Nothing."

"What does he do when someone disturbs him?" Natalie asked.

"Yells. His face goes red, and the veins stick out on his neck." She twisted her hands. "But it's okay because otherwise he's very nice. Especially for a guy who came from a really rich family."

"How often does he get upset?" Drake asked.

"A lot. But he always apologizes."

Drake believed her, but thought she was holding something back. "Has he ever hit you or threatened you?"

"At times, I thought he might, but no."

"How long have you worked for him?" Natalie asked.

"A year or so. Tracey hired me."

Ah, she knew Tracey. Great. That expanded his line of questioning. "What do you think happened to her?"

Ulani looked away.

"Ulani," Natalie said. "Please just tell us what you think."

She swung her focus back to them. "Mr. Gentry said she left, but I think she might've gotten involved in something bad and was killed."

"Bad like what?"

"I don't know." Her eyelashes fluttered. "She hired me because she said she needed time away from the children each day. So I came in at noon, and she left. She always came home at three like she planned, but sometimes she was wearing heavy makeup that she hadn't had on when she left. And different clothes. She would run up to her bedroom to change and wash it off then get Willow from school and retreat to her room."

"She had cosmetic surgeries," Drake stated.

"Yes, and the last one was botched." Ulani shook her head. "Poor woman. Her lips looked oversized. She was so embarrassed. I felt bad for her. She wanted to have it fixed. But apparently it costs more to fix bad plastic surgery than to do it in the first place, and Mr. Gentry wouldn't pay for it. Not that he didn't have the money. But he refused for some reason that they never mentioned."

"Did she continue to go away every afternoon even after the botched surgery?"

"Yes, but she was very depressed and also started taking mini-vacations away from the family. Just a few days here or there."

"Where did she go?" Drake asked.

Ulani shrugged. "I don't know, and it seemed like he didn't either. He would come home from work, and I'd tell him she'd gone on a trip. He seemed surprised every time. And a bit angry."

"Angry enough to do something about it?" he asked. "That's the reason she's missing?"

"I don't know. Maybe. But really, I thought she'd taken one of her trips and ran into some trouble."

Something seemed fishy about all of this, but it was becoming clear that the Gentrys were an odd couple, and it might be normal for her. "Did you tell the police about this?"

She shook her head, quickly. "Mr. Gentry asked me not to. And when he asks you not to do something, you don't do it."

"I don't get it, Ulani," Natalie said. "He sounds like a hard man to be around. Why do you still work for him?"

"Money. Insurance." She blurted out the words then took a long breath. "He pays for it and pays me way above the going rate for a nanny, and there's nowhere else I could go to make that kind of money."

Drake wouldn't stick around for those reasons, but some people didn't have a choice. And if the pictures of a boy at various ages on her bookshelf and the baseball cap on the couch meant she had a child to consider, her choices would be more limited.

Time to change direction. "What can you tell us about nail polish and the Gentry family?"

"What do you mean?"

"Did anyone use it?" he asked, making sure to keep a neutral tone and expression to keep from leading her.

A confused look lingered on her face. "Tracey always had perfectly manicured nails."

"Did she do her own or go to a salon?" Natalie asked.

"Her own, I think. She never mentioned it." Ulani tipped her head. "Why? Is that important?"

Drake ignored her question. "How about Willow? Did she polish her nails?"

"She started after her mom left. She used her mother's polish. Honestly, I think she did it as a way to be close to her mother."

Or not. Willow had kept the method her nails had been done from Ulani. Drake wasn't surprised. "Do you have any reason to think Kirk would've hurt his wife?"

Ulani's gaze snapped to him, but she didn't speak.

"It's okay," he said, trying to sound encouraging. "Be honest."

"I don't know." She brushed her hands against her legs. "He didn't know she took off every afternoon until a week or so before she disappeared. She didn't have any friends so she wasn't going to visit them. Maybe she was having an affair, and he found out."

Drake worked hard to keep his skepticism to himself as he didn't think that she would meet a lover that often. "How could he not know about the afternoons away?"

"She made me swear not to tell him. So I didn't. And she was always home before he got home." Ulani's face screwed up and tears glistened in her eyes.

"But he had to be paying you for that time."

She shook her head. "Tracey paid me. Cash. Please don't report me. Please. I need the money. My son. He's soon going to college. He deserves to go. I can't end up in trouble for unreported wages."

"We're not going to report you," Drake assured her. "I assume you never told the police about this either. Because of the cash payments."

She nodded.

"And you really have no idea where Tracey went?"

She shook her head.

He believed her, but he couldn't let it go as it might be the lead they were looking for. "Not even a guess?"

"I mean maybe she went somewhere to get the plastic

surgery done for less. Like Mexico maybe, and she didn't survive the surgery."

"Do you think that's more likely than Kirk hurting her?" Drake asked.

She scratched her neck. "I don't know. Either way, I don't think she left for the reasons Mr. Gentry said. I think something bad happened to her."

11

___

Natalie buckled her seatbelt and waited for Drake to get into the SUV. The neighborhood was teaming with life. These neighbors would be shocked to hear that Natalie and Drake were visiting their neighborhood because of a serial killer. Unless Ulani became integral to the investigation, they would never know.

Drake settled behind the wheel and plugged his phone into the vehicle's information system. "Call Sierra."

The call connected.

"Before you ask"—Sierra's voice sounded loud over the speaker—"I haven't gone into labor since you were here. Please tell everyone I'll call the minute it starts."

"That's not why I'm calling, but thanks for the update." Drake chuckled, but it seemed forced.

"Okay. I've just heard the question too many times this week, and I'm about to go crazy."

"Sorry, sis. We just love you and little Elvis."

Sierra's groan reverberated through the speaker. "You really should stop calling him that. You're going to forget after he's born, and before we know it, the nickname will stick."

"I wouldn't have to call him Elvis if you'd have settled on a name by now."

"No can do." She sounded resolute. "We have to see him first. Make sure the name fits."

Natalie could see that point, but Drake narrowed his eyes as if it was a foreign concept for him.

"So why the phone call?" Sierra asked.

"Evidence is being messengered from PPB for you to review. A bloody blouse. It's for a missing person case. Woman appears to have left the family, but now we have a reason to suspect the husband killed her. The local lab confirmed the blood is hers, and I want to know if, in your experience, it's enough blood to be from a serious wound. Then find any kind of touch DNA you can on the fabric."

"I take it this has to do with your current client," she said.

"It does."

Natalie waited for him to explain, but he didn't say a word.

"And I'm assuming that's Natalie," Sierra said.

"That's not important. What *is* important is that you have to work fast. There's a good chance the FBI will insist on having the blouse returned to PPB today."

"FBI? But I figured missing persons would be a PPB investigation."

Drake glanced at Natalie, but she couldn't read his expression. "Our client connected the missing persons investigation to a much bigger one being worked by a joint FBI/PPB task force."

"It's The Clipper investigation, isn't it?" Sierra's excited tone bounced off the vehicle's interior. "Ohmygoodness. Are you serious right now?"

"I didn't say that." Drake's tone remained calm, but just

hearing Sierra's excitement got Natalie's heart rate going again.

"But we all know the big joint task force is working on that investigation," Sierra said.

"There are multiple task forces with the FBI and PPB going on all the time," Drake stated calmly.

"Yeah, but I know it's The Clipper. Especially by your evasion. Shoot. This is going to be something else to work on." She let out a long breath. "Let's hope I don't go into labor before I finish it."

"You've changed your tune."

"Hey. It's a once-in-a-lifetime opportunity. I'll call the front desk and tell them to let me know the minute the blouse arrives, and I'll personally log and process it. I didn't schedule anything for myself this week in case I go into labor, so I can do it right away."

"Let me know the second you find anything."

"Might not be possible," Sierra said. "If the evidence comes with the usual disclaimer we work under, you know I can only provide details of my findings to the officer who submits it."

Drake let out a frustrated breath. "You can at least tell me if you find anything they missed. Like locating another DNA sample or other evidence, right?"

"We'll see. Gotta go now so I can get ready." Sierra ended the call.

Drake stabbed the screen harder than necessary and clenched his steering wheel.

"Your sister sounds very dedicated," Natalie said, deciding to focus on the positive.

Drake nodded. "It's going to be interesting to see how she handles work and motherhood."

"She's taking maternity leave, right?"

"Sure, but our condos are a few steps away from work,

and she has a large family of potential babysitters. I can see her sneaking down to the lab for an hour or two during her leave. Not that any of us will let her stay for long." He chuckled.

She loved how he could go from such an intensely focused person to one who could laugh. If needed, she knew he would return to the protector who watched every inch of his surroundings and made sure people in his sphere of influence were safe. Even if a stranger came under attack, he would be right there to help. Just like he was helping her and the children.

He cranked the engine, but didn't shift into gear. His thumb was tapping against the wheel, exuding that same nervous energy, but his focus was sharp and pinned out the front window. "You believe Ulani?"

"I do," Natalie said. "And I really want to know where Tracey was going all those afternoons. And where she got enough cash to pay Ulani when she didn't work. She couldn't have taken it from their joint bank account or Kirk would've found out."

"So she had some sort of income source. Income that she probably wasn't reporting on her taxes."

"Illegal, then," Natalie suggested.

"Or just under the table like the way she was paying Ulani."

"Maybe the makeup and changed clothes is a lead. She could've been having an affair or even been into prostitution. That would give her cash to pay Ulani."

"I was thinking the same thing. But an affair seems unlikely to me. Would she see her lover every day between the same hours? I guess it's possible."

"I know she worked as a model before they got married, but if that was what she was up to, she could be risking Kirk seeing her photo somewhere, and she clearly didn't want him to know about it. And if she continued to go out every day even after she was disfigured, then she wasn't likely modeling. Or her face wasn't in the photos. Could be a hand model for example."

"If she was modeling, Erik will likely find photos when he does her background check." Drake went quiet, and his thumbs stilled. "What about pornographic movies or videos?"

"Again, he could see them." Natalie couldn't reconcile this in her brain at all. "Whatever it was, she had to be coming home with a lot of cash. Good nannies are expensive."

"Like how expensive?"

"Thirty dollars an hour for the best, and Ulani said she was making more than that."

He let out a low whistle. "So Tracey had to be making even better money doing whatever she was doing to afford to pay Ulani. Which rules out entry-level jobs."

"And she didn't have a college education, so I just can't see that she was doing legitimate work to earn this large of a salary. Plus, she would have taxes withheld in a legit job, and she'd have to report it on their tax returns."

"Since they live in the city, there's bound to be CCTV cameras in the area. Once we get back to the cabin, I'll have Erik look, and maybe we can catch her on video near their house and trail her to wherever she was going. Or he can track the bus she took, and we can go from there."

Natalie was looking forward to getting back to the cabin to spend time with the children, but what was she going to tell them about their dad? She could probably evade their questions. For now anyway. Once he was found and arrested, she would be the one to tell them.

Drake glanced at her. "Why so serious all of a sudden?"

"It's looking like Kirk's children will have to be told

about their dad. Willow will be the only one to really understand, but the others have to at least be told he won't be coming home, and they'll be going into foster care." She thought of her sister, and a lump formed in her throat.

He searched her gaze, digging deep. "Are you thinking about when you were growing up?"

She nodded and swallowed the lump like she'd done so many times. "I remember when social workers threatened to take my sister and me away. Not to our faces, of course, but we listened in and heard things we shouldn't have. I always wondered if we would stay together. And there were times I thought about running away, just the two of us so we could be together. But we were too young, and I knew we couldn't survive on our own. I was so afraid."

He took her hand and cupped it between his palm and long fingers. "That must've been rough."

She should probably jerk her hand free, but it felt so good to have someone care about her enough to touch her. That disappeared with Gina's death. Sure, Natalie had work friends, but that was different. They weren't the kinds of friends who hugged or squeezed your hand. She sometimes received hugs from children, but it wasn't the same.

Drake was showing compassion for her alone. Tears flooded her eyes. She took a deep breath and let it out, then freed her hand.

He glanced at her, but she looked out the window, hoping he would get the hint that she needed to think. He pulled from their spot and got them on the road. She felt some sort of vibe still emanating from him, but she didn't know what.

Maybe it had to do with their personal connection. Something she shouldn't be encouraging for so many reasons, but especially since she wasn't being completely truthful with him by keeping quiet about her sister. Natalie had to focus on finding Kirk and making sure he paid for killing her sister and the other women. Then restore the lives of his children to ensure they flourished.

Flourish. But how?

He glanced her way again. "You're lost in thought."

"Thinking about the Gentry children and their future. Few people want to take in three children so they'll likely be separated."

"Will they have a good chance at adoption?"

"Typically younger children do but, in this case, once the potential parents learn about their father, they might think twice—wondering if the sins of the father will revisit the children."

"Does that happen?"

"I've seen it happen often enough when parents are serious offenders. It's unfortunate, but human nature. Thankfully, most people aren't like that, but Adopted Child Syndrome does exist."

He cocked an eyebrow. "What's that?'

"A term used to explain problems adopted children have in coping." She faced him. "Here's a fact that might shock you. According to the FBI, most serial killers in the United States were adopted."

"Seriously, most?"

She nodded. "Not that it's a huge number of people. The syndrome mostly affects adoptees where their adoptive families treat the adoption as a secret and don't openly talk about it. The Gentry children will require very special parents."

"Sounds like you have your work cut out for you to ensure they all find the right match."

"Yes." She let her mind wander. If only she could take them in. She would provide the kind of life and stability they needed. But these children deserved two parents as she suspected it would take two people working together to care for them properly. Still, would it be better if she took them in and kept them together than if they were all separated? She just didn't know, but she had to decide by the time they incarcerated Kirk so if she did take the children, they wouldn't have to be separated in foster care.

She closed her eyes and prayed then repeated positive thoughts to improve her mood. She must have dozed off, as the next thing she knew Drake was exiting the highway near his cabin.

He tapped the media screen on his dash. "Call Brendan."

The call connected, and Brendan answered. "Yo."

"We're just about there," Drake said. "Turning onto the road now. Everything quiet?"

"It's a regular snooze fest."

Drake huffed a laugh. "You okay, or do you need a break?"

"Aiden spelled me, and I caught a few winks while you were gone, so I'm good."

"Roger that." Drake ended the call and glanced at her. "He's watching the road. We want a heads-up in plenty of time if Gentry decides to come out and play."

She smiled at him. "You all really know what you're doing, don't you?"

"Yeah," he said. "It's almost as if we've done this before." He flashed her a quick grin, that playful smile she was coming to love, then turned his attention back to the road. They soon reached an SUV matching the one they were riding in.

Drake flashed his lights, and the other vehicle responded. When they passed it, Drake saluted his brother.

"You all are giving up so much time for this. I need to figure out a way to repay you."

"No need. Honest. We couldn't walk away. We have to be sure you and the kids are safe. It's just who we are."

"Yeah, I can see that now." She also saw a group of men who were selfless and willing to give of their lives for others. Just like that. No questions asked. They were the guys who ran into danger to save others. And that made them a very special breed indeed.

And he was a special man, one she thanked God for putting in her life at the right time. Maybe what he'd said about accepting help was the truth, that she should just accept it as provided by God. Not feel obliged but embrace their assistance.

He glanced in his rearview mirror, and she thought about what it would be like if Kirk were following them. Coming to end her life and take his children. Might she have prevented that? "I keep wondering if I'd done something different if Kirk would be behind bars."

"I've learned over the years that it does no good when looking for a fugitive to think about what could've been. There's only what is and what could be. And that's what we have to do here. Take what is and turn it into the result we need. Review what we know and plan. Hopefully the guys will have a good start on creating a solid background report on Gentry, and we can go from there." He pulled up to the cabin and shifted into park. "But first we get something for lunch and rest."

"Rest? But Kirk might be out there, maybe another woman in his sights. Maybe me. Maybe someone else."

He met her gaze. "We won't be any good to the investigation if we don't sleep and eat regularly."

"Sorry. I shouldn't have said that. You need to rest. I was out of line questioning you."

"No worries." He opened his door then glanced back

with another one of his grins. "And speaking of eating, I can smell my mom's cooking all the way out here."

This boyish smile revealed a dimple in the side of his left cheek. Fun loving and magnetizing. Drawing her to him in a way she hadn't experienced before. She felt almost as if she had to have him in her life. Had to get to know him, and there was no other option for her.

Strange yet captivating.

Tired. Like he said. She was tired. That was it. She was getting loopy and needed more sleep. Sure, that was it. She would take a long nap when he and the children did, and when she woke up, this crazy need to know Drake Byrd would be gone.

Half of her wanted that to be true, but as she slid out of the SUV and joined him, the other half wanted to slip her hand in his and claim him as hers.

At the door he paused to look at her. "I've been dreading telling you this, but you need to know."

"What?"

"Gentry has cameras all over the house. I saw them in several smoke detectors and one in the bookshelf door."

Her heart sank. "So he knows I went into the basement then."

Drake gave one sharp nod, like a guillotine coming down. "And we both know he can't let you live to tell about it in court."

After Drake's last statement, he was worried Natalie would be terrified, but oddly, she appeared calm as she hung her suit coat in the entryway. Maybe she seemed relaxed with Brendan monitoring the driveway so they would be forewarned if Gentry showed up. Or maybe it was because of the warm feeling his mom created in the cabin. The smell of her hearty beef stew and crusty bread filled the air, and a roaring fire warmed the space.

She was humming from an easy chair in the family room, two-year-old Sadie on her lap. Willow sat on the couch with Drake's father. She chewed on her lower lip and stared at a large bin of Legos sitting between them, but she wasn't even touching them. Logan played with Duplos on the floor, building tall towers. Pong stretched out in front of the fireplace, his paws under his head as he cast a wary eye at Logan.

Drake figured his mom had brought the toys. She'd kept many of their childhood things in the attic and cleaned them up when Brendan brought Jenna's daughter, Karlie, over for a visit. His dad slid down on the floor and started building with Logan and talking to him about structures. His dad had always been able to handle kids so well.

Natalie looked at his mom. "The bread smells amazing. I didn't know you could bake it so fast."

His mom got up and settled Sadie on her hip. "I make the dough in advance and always have a bucket of it in the refrigerator. All I have to do is take it out, let it rise for a bit, and then pop it into a cast iron Dutch oven and bake. I learned to do that in self-defense once I had five growing boys to feed." She laughed.

"You make it seem simple, but to someone who doesn't cook or bake, it seems like a big deal."

"I can teach you in a few minutes. Only four ingredients. No kneading. No fuss. Anyone can make it."

Natalie smiled at his mother. "If it tastes as good as it smells, I'll take you up on it."

"Trust me," Drake said. "You'll love everything Mom puts on the table."

"And speaking of the table." His mom held Sadie out to him. "Lunch is ready, so take this little one."

"But I—"

"Have free hands." She nearly pushed Sadie into his arms. "Sadie, this is my son Drake. You'll like him."

The baby's lip quivered but, despite her sad little chubby face, she tugged at his emotions. Or maybe the sadness made her even more adorable. But then she started whimpering, and panic took hold of him.

He started to give Natalie a plea for help. *No. No.* He couldn't let a two-year-old best him. Time to conquer that fear. Her fussing increased. Now what? He shot a quick look around the room for something to help him out. A fish mounted on the wall near the fireplace grabbed his attention. That might work. He bounced her in his arms and hurried over there.

"Fishy. Pet." She reached up to touch it.

Drake lifted her closer, proud of himself for stilling her complaints. But how long would the fish work, and what did he do next? His mom had just been sitting with Sadie on her lap, and the child seemed contented. Had something changed other than a different person holding her? Maybe she was tired. Or hungry. *That* he understood.

He glanced back at his mom, who was placing the pot of stew on a hot pad on the table and looking at his dad. "Will you get Erik for lunch? Clay dropped into bed the minute he got back, so we'll let him sleep. And we'll take a bowl out to Brendan."

His dad patted Logan on the head. "Be right back, sport."

Logan cast a disappointed look at Drake's dad but went back to building. Drake imagined his dad back when he was in his thirties. Did his dad have experience with kids, or did he learn it after he got married? A lot of law enforcement officers knew how to deal with kids. They had to. The job required it. Drake chased fugitives. Not many kids to interact with there.

"Time to wash up for lunch," his mom announced as she carried a crusty loaf of bread on a cutting board to the table.

"Willow. Logan. Come with me." Natalie held her hand out to the kids. They quickly got up and followed her to the bathroom.

Okay. Fine. Now what? He had the little kid. Did she need her hands washed? Did she eat bread and stew?

"In here, son," his mother said.

He crossed the room.

"Time for lunch, sweetie." His mom tweaked Sadie's nose, and she giggled.

The sweetness of the sound felt like a party to Drake, and he smiled with her. But what did he do with her?

His mother moved past him, a pitcher of water in her hands. "Set her on the counter and help her wash."

Sadie patted her hands together. "Wash."

He started water running. Once the temperature was warm, he put some soap on her hands and lifted her over the faucet. She clapped her hands under the water, spraying herself, him, and the counter.

She giggled and did it again. And again. And he laughed with her.

"Might want to curtail the splashing a bit and finish up," his mother said.

"Got it." He hated to ruin Sadie's fun, but he cupped her little hands between his and scrubbed hers and his clean then set her on the counter to dry them.

She giggled, her freckled cheeks lifting. She had a spot of water on one of them so he wiped it dry. She grabbed his hand. "Like you."

"I...um...like you too." He was surprised to find that he meant it.

"Sit wherever you want," his mom said.

He scooped a damp Sadie up and went to the table.

"No booster seats." His mom looked up from the water she was pouring. "She'll have to sit on your lap for lunch."

"But I don't know—"

"She's just a little person." His mom set down the pitcher. "Help her if she needs it. Otherwise let her do her thing."

Natalie looked at him. "I can take—"

"He's got it." His mom issued him a dare with her look, clearly deciding he needed an education in two-year-olds today.

Fine. Challenge accepted. He dropped into the chair where two plates had been set. Sadie immediately grabbed the spoon and started banging it on the plate. Did he stop her or let her have fun?

"Stop, Sadie," Willow said. "You know Dad wouldn't let you do that."

Sadie immediately stopped banging, but she stuck out a trembling lower lip.

Drake grabbed a piece of bread and broke it into a few pieces and handed one to her. She shoved it into her mouth and chewed.

Crisis averted. For now. But what would she be upset about next? Was that what it was like to have a little kid? Go from one crisis to the next. If so, why did people want them?

She leaned back and smiled up at him. Ah, the smiles. That made the crisis worth it. Didn't it?

The door opened, and Drake automatically reached for his gun, but his dad and Erik stepped inside. A deep frown erased Erik's usual cheerful expression. Either he didn't want to be interrupted to eat, which was a common thing with him when he was into a project, or he didn't like what he'd discovered about Gentry.

"Everything okay?" Drake asked.

He glanced at the kids. "We'll talk after lunch."

Drake's gut clenched. Tight. How could he go from the warm feeling this mini-person on his lap was giving him to thinking about a creep like Gentry? How did law enforcement officers with children do this every day? Face the horror of the world, then go home and try to live a normal life for their children?

As a single man, Drake never had an issue with it, but he was gaining a new respect for married officers with children. A new respect for his dad.

His mother came to the head of the table, a big metal ladle in her hand. "If you'll pass your plates, I'll dish up the stew."

"Take Sadie's first. I think she's hungry." Drake handed her plate down the line.

Natalie smiled at him, a warm approving smile, that lit something inside him far different from Sadie's smiles. What would it be like to have children with her? Would it be like today? Working together? Splitting up the duties?

Of course they'd start with one child. Learn the ropes as they went. Not have three children right off the bat.

Wait. What if she decided to adopt these kids? No. Starting with a baby—he could perhaps see that. Think it might even be okay. But three adopted children? Um, no. That he could never do.

12

___

While waiting for his brothers to gather, Drake shoved a log
into the woodstove in the corner of his shop, letting go of all
the warm fuzzies from lunch. He stabbed the log with a
sharp poker and stifled a yawn. He needed a nap. How he
needed it.

He'd tried to rest, but he couldn't sleep. Not when
Gentry would be coming for Natalie. For his kids. Natalie
should probably sleep more, too. Nap while the kids did.
But she refused. Said she'd gotten enough rest. And he
understood that. It was her life they were talking about here.
She clearly had more to lose than he did. But the thought of
losing her? Or these kids he got to know better over lunch
being harmed? Man, that put a pain in his heart. A
sharp one.

He adjusted the logs until the flames licked around them
and closed the metal door with a smoky glass pane. When
he'd bought this cabin, the workshop was more of a lean-to.
He'd roped his dad and brothers into helping him turn it
into a place where he could store and maintain his many
outdoor toys. Fishing rods and reels, nets, lures, and skis
hung on the walls. A kayak rested in the wood rafters above.

He hunted from here too, but he stored his rifles in a climate controlled space at home and where no one could easily break in and steal expensive guns and scopes.

Sure, he was an adrenaline junkie, but a guy couldn't be a thrill seeker twenty-four/seven. So his downtime was spent keeping his toys in mint shape, and he used this space for that too. Although he'd never used it as a meeting room before, there was a first time for everything.

He called Brendan on the iPad and set it on an old door propped on sawhorses so he could join in from his post at the road. "Everything still quiet out there."

"Yes." Brendan yawned.

"Hang tight until everyone gets here." Drake turned to his brothers, Erik and Aiden, who entered the room and dropped into folding chairs. They grabbed a few of their mom's chocolate chip cookies, which he and his brothers called crack cookies as they were highly addictive, and filled mugs with coffee from carafes. Leave it to his mom to bring insulated carafes so the coffee wouldn't get cold. It was like her mom radar always had the right things ready to make their lives better.

Sadie and her siblings didn't have the benefit of a caring mother right now. He thought back to holding her warm little body and the kiss she'd given him when he put her down for her nap. The Gentry kids didn't have anything nearly as special as what he'd grown up with. He was fairly certain their mother was no longer alive. Now that he knew the kids a little better, it bothered him even more. Maybe it was also because they were under his roof, and he felt responsible for them.

Like he felt for Natalie.

Okay, fine, that was a totally different feeling, one he wasn't going to think about too hard. No point. They were as incompatible as a cat and a mouse.

She took a seat nearest to him, sipping from one of his favorite mugs, the one with a fish-shaped handle. She'd freshened up but still wore the same suit and those heels that made her legs look a mile long. He and his brothers had all changed, and his dad had gone to the nearest clothing store to get something for Natalie to change into. Thinking about his father picking out unmentionables for her brought a smile to his lips.

"What's so funny, bro?" Erik scratched Pong's head.

"Nothing." Drake grabbed a cookie.

"We gonna get started soon?" Erik leaned his chair back on the rear legs.

A risky move as far as Drake was concerned, as he'd gotten the ancient folding chairs at a church rummage sale and some of them were a bit rickety.

Clay drifted into the room, yawning and stretching. The moment he reached the table he filled a mug.

"Now that we're all here let me bring you up to speed on Gentry's house." Drake stepped to the whiteboard and used a red marker to write *Kirk Gentry* and told them about the videos.

"Would've loved to see that," Erik said. "I mean, I hate seeing IT being used to foil us, but gotta give the guy props for being creative and prepared."

"The preparedness isn't a surprise." Clay scratched his cheek and sat. "He's former military."

"What branch?" Aiden asked, likely because he once served as a SEAL.

"Marines." Clay took a long draw on his mug. "MARSOC Raider."

Aiden let out a low whistle. "These guys are swift, silent, and deadly."

"You ever run an op with them?" Drake asked.

Aiden shook his head. "But before I trained as a SEAL,

my company worked a night op with them. We set up an ambush, and the Raiders moved down the heavily forested road. Finally our CO comes up the road and tells us to stand down. The Raiders had gone past us fifteen minutes before that, and we never heard them. Not a sound. Impressive."

"Yeah, they're top-notch," Brendan said. He was a former Delta Force operator and would know too. "If he was a Raider, he'll be hard to stop, and I don't feel so bad about his eluding us at the house."

Natalie clutched her hands on the table.

"Not impossible to stop, though." Drake firmed his stance. He didn't like even the hint that they might think this guy could best them and get to Natalie. Or even his kids. Though Drake doubted Gentry would kill them, they wouldn't have any kind of a life on the run with a serial killer. "There are five of us and one of him."

"Six," Natalie said. "Though my role will obviously be limited. But I know people and can read them well. That's a valuable skill in finding someone like Kirk."

Drake gave her a tight smile. "Tell us more about the guy before we get started on what we've learned."

"Sure." She sat up straighter, and her hands relaxed. "He's conceited, but very charming when he wants to be. He has a feeling of self-importance. He has a lot of friends at his workplace and is well respected. He's smart and creative. And he *always* has to be right. Always. That could be his downfall."

"Do you get the sense that he loves his kids?" Aiden asked.

She tilted her head. "Yeah. Yeah. As much as he can. But if he's a serial killer, and let me say I'm no expert on serial killers—he most likely suffers from antisocial personality disorder. In that sense, he probably doesn't care for others the same way we do. I don't know if he indeed suffers from this disorder. I'm just throwing this theory out."

"Do you think he'll even make an effort to find his kids?" Drake asked.

"Yes, but again not for the same reasons we might have. I doubt he has the kind of emotional connection we all might have with a child. He likely sees them as his possession. He won't let anyone take what he believes to be his. So that means, in addition to wanting to stop me from testifying, he wants to get his children back. He surely can't let me best him."

Erik leaned forward. "Antisocial personality disorder. Is that the same as being a psychopath or sociopath?"

"Sort of. At least, to me they're the same thing, but some people in my field distinguish between the two using severity of symptoms. Generally, a sociopath is someone who doesn't cause serious harm or distress. A psychopath on the other hand puts others in danger or is violent. But we evaluate all people with ASPD—antisocial personality disorder—using DSM-5 diagnostic criteria, and all of these symptoms can be found in the ASPD category. Sociopath is just one of the terms to describe someone with ASPD that most people recognize."

Drake was so impressed with her knowledge that he knew he was beaming like a proud parent. Or more like a boyfriend or significant other. "I should've probably mentioned that Natalie has a Ph.D. specializing in children and youth."

"Uh-oh, maybe we should've been calling you doc." Erik grinned.

She laughed. "Natalie is fine."

"So our takeaway is that he doesn't think the same way we do," Drake said to keep them on track. "Doesn't care about others."

Natalie's smile evaporated, and she nodded. "If I have him pegged right, he's into sensation seeking and has a lack of remorse or guilt. He's impulsive, but he needs to control, and if he is indeed The Clipper, we know he engages in predatory behavior."

Aiden grimaced. "And what does that mean for his actions now?"

"He has no remorse for killing or committing other crimes, and he'll risk everything to find me and his kids." Natalie stated the danger in a matter-of-fact tone, but her trembling hands gave away her real emotions.

"Which means he could use the IT skills he learned on the job to try to track you down," Erik said. "Being an officer would give him access to a great deal of personal information."

Drake focused on his brother. "Can you get us a—"

"List of the women and their details?" He got up and carried his laptop with him to the end of the table where Drake was standing. "Still working up detailed profiles, but I'll write their names down for you."

He listed four names with a date beside each of them. "The day they were murdered."

"I've been thinking about the nail polish," Clay said. "Specifically the names. *Angelic. Chameleon. Bewitching. Vixen.* Do they mean anything? Tell us something about the women?"

"I haven't found anything to suggest that," Erik said.

"Did they all live in Portland?" Aiden asked.

"No. Cities around Oregon." He tapped the first and fourth name. "Gina Green and Laura Zimmer were the only women killed in Portland. They died four years apart. Because he murdered the women in different cities, it took a while for the link to be discovered. But his big mistake was killing in Portland again."

"How's that?" Brendan asked. He'd been quiet for so long Drake had almost forgotten his brother was on the video call.

"Londyn Steele linked the current murder to the one four years ago, and then she searched for others," Natalie answered before Drake could.

Erik sat back down. "I'll try to track him to see if he traveled to the other towns when the women were murdered."

"Do that," Drake said. "And get us a full report on the victims as soon as you can."

"You think the victims are the key to finding him?" Natalie asked.

"Not necessarily," Drake said. "But Erik will already be looking at things like car rental, video surveillance, banking records, etcetera and this will just be part of the big picture and give us an idea if he has a connection to these locations or a reason to return to them."

Erik eyed Natalie. "And I need to look into you, Natalie."

"Me?" She gaped at him. "Why me? I'm just the person who found the polish in the basement. I haven't done anything."

"We need to determine if any of your connections could lead to this location and leave us vulnerable," Drake said. "Starting with Malone."

"But they don't," Natalie's voice rose, her panic raising Drake's concern. "Malone said her burner phone was secure."

"It's not likely traceable, but all phones can be traced with the right information," Erik said. "And Gentry is proving he has the right skills and resources to gain that information. If he connects you to Malone, it's not unreasonable to believe that that connection could lead to us and this location."

Natalie should be fearing for her life, but, at the moment, she only cared about the list Erik wrote on the board of the women's names. Women. Four of them. But Natalie could hardly focus on anyone but Gina. Her sister. The girl Natalie had protected all those years from her mother's depression, had mothered, had practically raised. Gina, her only true friend.

And now, here she was on a list on the whiteboard. A statistic to these men. Not a real person. None of the women were. Sure, the guys were upset over their murders, but they didn't know them. Didn't know that Gina liked honey not jelly on her toast. That she only ate eggs if they were scrambled. That she had a nervous habit of picking at her cuticles until they bled when she was uneasy. Or that she was terrified of the dentist but had no fear of going to a doctor or getting a shot.

Natalie looked around the table at the men staring at her. Could she trust these guys? Tell them the truth?

They were going to do a background check on her, and they would find out about Gina anyway. Wouldn't it be better for her to tell them before they discovered it and didn't know her reason for keeping it from them? Especially from Drake.

Help me, Father. Please help me do this.

She stood and cleared her throat. "There's something I need to tell you."

As one, their eyes narrowed, and the force of four pairs of eyes locking on her almost had her bolting from the room. But she swallowed instead and moved to the whiteboard where she tapped Gina's name.

"Gina Green was my sister." She let her statement hang out there and watched the men.

Mouths fell open, but she only cared about Drake's reaction. He was watching her with a quiet intensity that speared her with guilt and insecurity.

Hand-Me-Dunn tried to make an appearance. Tried hard. But Natalie wouldn't let her. She raised her shoulders and mentally prepared for the first comment.

"Way to bury the lead," Erik said, but she couldn't pull her focus from Drake.

He stared at her, his lips pressed tight, putting an ache in her heart. She had to explain. "I'm sorry I didn't tell you. I was worried you would ignore me or think my lead was made up."

"Why?" He continued to eye her.

"Because the police did before." She forced herself to look at the others too. "When Gina's investigation went cold, I couldn't let it go. So I did some digging and went to the police with my findings. Many times. Each time Detective Archibald discounted me because I was Gina's sister. I mean, he was polite, but like I said, I'm good at reading body language, and I could tell he was just patronizing me. I doubt he took anything I said seriously."

"And what does that have to do with not telling me...us?" Drake asked.

"I thought as former law enforcement that you all might think the same thing. That maybe I fabricated the evidence to make Kirk look guilty."

"You have to admit it's quite a coincidence that you were in the home of the man you searched years for but didn't know it," Drake said.

"See. That's just what I expected you to say and why I didn't tell you everything." And her first sign of Drake playing the devil's advocate, as he'd said he was so good at doing.

A knock sounded on the door before it opened.

Good. Whoever it was, Natalie was thankful for the interruption.

Russ stepped in carrying a pot of coffee. He took one look at the guys and frowned. "Seems like I interrupted at the wrong time, but you know your mother. She says bring you guys more coffee, and I jump." He chuckled, but nobody laughed with him.

"It's okay," Natalie said. "I need to check on the children anyway."

She finally gave in to her instincts to protect herself and fled out the door. She stood outside gulping in the cooler air and wondering if admitting to lying to the Byrd guys might be the end of the investigation. She knew they would still keep her and the children safe. They were fine men and wouldn't bail on her or the children. Of that she was certain, but might they leave finding Kirk to the task force?

No matter what they did, she wouldn't stop looking for Kirk. He killed Gina, and he needed to pay. But it would be sheer foolishness to go after him on her own. From what the guys said, Kirk's military training and IT skills made him a very worthy foe, and she was no match for him.

So what should she do? Just what?

She looked up at the downy white clouds in the sky, pleading for an answer. Hearing nothing. Finding no answers.

Carrying an empty coffee pot, Russ stepped outside and paused next to her. "I found some clothing that the woman at the store assured me would fit you. Put them in the bedroom."

"Thank you." Despite her efforts to sound normal, her voice trembled.

"Everything okay?"

"Not really." She told him about her sister. "I lied to

them. I know it's hard for them to understand why, and I don't know if they'll forgive me."

"They'll come around."

"How can you be so sure?"

"'Cause I've walked in their shoes before, and I know how they think. Right now, they don't want to believe one of their fellow officers didn't do his job as fully as would be expected. Then they figure out with the high caseloads that sometimes a detective might not handle things as well as he should and could've been dismissive."

"High caseloads? You're defending the detective who blew me off?"

"No. No." He held up his free hand. "Just saying I can see how it happened. But that doesn't mean I wouldn't listen to you now and understand why you withheld the info. They'll figure that out too. But it might take Drake a minute or two to come around."

"Why's that?"

"He was the first person to assist you. Means this protection detail and investigation is more personal to him, and he's more emotionally invested than the other guys."

"I didn't realize that."

"Happens all the time. You catch a case, and you take it personally, even if you don't want to. In this situation..." He grinned. "I also think my son has found a woman who has him thinking about letting go of his wandering ways to consider a relationship. But you didn't hear that from me. If Peg thinks I've even got a hint of matchmaking in my skillset, I'll never live it down."

13

Dumbfounded, Drake didn't move. What should he do? Should he go after Natalie? Tell her it was okay that she'd kept the truth from him and his brothers?

It wasn't okay. He was putting his life on the line for her and the kids. So were his brothers. The very least they deserved was the truth.

"I know Detective Archibald," Erik said. "He's an OG and know it all. I can see him being dismissive."

"Just because he's an old guy doesn't mean anything," Drake said. "Dad was an OG before he retired and was still a heck of a detective."

"That was Dad." Erik crossed his arms. "But this guy's disillusioned by the job and let it get to him. He retires this year. I hear he's been phoning it in for a while."

Drake gritted his teeth. "Still no excuse for her lying to us."

"She didn't lie," Aiden said. "She just held something back. I don't blame her. She didn't know us. Didn't know how we would react. Now she does and trusted us with the information. So think about it from that point of view before you go all righteous on her because you got your feelings hurt."

Drake clamped his hands on his waist. "My feelings—"

"Save it," Clay said. "This is personal and you know it. You've got a thing for her. We get it. Understand even. Just don't expect us to jump on board your bandwagon when she didn't do anything wrong."

Drake stared at his brothers. How could they accept what Natalie had done just like that? Were they right? Was he being a baby because he got his feelings hurt?

"How does it feel to have one of us calling you out instead of the other way around?" Brendan's voice came loud and clear from the iPad speaker.

"I'm not liking it much," he said. "But I'm gonna let it go. I need to talk to her."

After he started for the door, one of his brothers made a kissing noise. He spun to see who, but they all stared blankly at him.

Right. He was getting payback for all the times he'd called them out on so many things. But he couldn't help it. That was who he was. Who God made him to be, and he was glad of it. At least most of the time. Having discernment was hard at times. It often made him the odd guy out.

"Seriously, man," Clay said. "Glad to see you found someone who stopped you in your tracks long enough to see what's out there besides putting your neck on the line in some crazy sport."

"Never thought I'd see the day," Aiden said. "But like Clay said, it's a good thing."

Drake held the doorknob, feeling the coolness against his palm. "I don't know if it's such a good thing or if it's even true. Sure, I'm attracted to her. Not hard to be. She's very easy on the eyes. But I don't think it goes further than that."

"Aw, man, you're blind." Clay laughed. "What she did wouldn't bother you if you didn't care."

"But it bothers you guys, right?"

"We're over it," Clay said.

His other brothers nodded their agreement.

Okay, fine. He might be developing feelings for Natalie, but what difference did it make? None. He wasn't going to get involved. Not with her. Not with anyone. Period.

"You guys get to work on reviewing the victim's backgrounds. And someone look for other properties Gentry or his wife or extended family might own. Maybe he's holed up at one of them. And let's see if we can hack into the account for his in-home surveillance cameras. Maybe we'll find a lead there. I'll be right back." Planning to march into the cabin to let Natalie know what he thought, he jerked the door open and stepped out.

He spotted her leaning against the wall near the cabin door, her eyes closed. His feet stuttered to a stop. A ray of sun landed on her face, and her skin had a healthy glow. She looked so vibrant and peaceful—like a woman who had indeed pierced that armor he'd kept up. All fight and disappointment went out of him. Just like that. Gone.

She'd lost a sister. Her only sister. Not just of natural causes but in the most horrific way. In a senseless violent crime. That was what he needed to focus on. Not his needs. Not his hurt. Not the fact that Natalie didn't tell him about her sister but the fact that she had to be suffering.

He wanted nothing more than to scoop her into his arms and hold her. Tell her everything was going to be okay. That he would make sure of it. But would it?

She opened her eyes, and her gaze lazily drifted to him. When she saw him, he clearly felt the force of his attraction to her, and he felt her pain so deeply it almost seemed like his own.

Eyes locked with hers, he took the last few steps to her. "I'm sorry."

"For?"

"For your loss. I can't even imagine losing one of my siblings much less my only one."

"Thank you." Her voice broke. "It's been four years, but I don't think I've processed her death. I've filled my life up with work and finding her killer. Then to discover that it could be someone I knew, someone I saw on a regular basis. That was something else."

She shuddered and wrapped her arms around her slender waist. "But I put the pain away. I had to. To get your help. I'm sorry about that. It must look like I used you. Maybe I did. I'm so, so sorry."

She needed comforting. Desperately. He didn't care if he shouldn't encourage whatever was developing between them. His mom had always taught them that human touch could do wonders in balancing out a person's pain, and he would provide it.

He gently took her hands. Held them, felt her trembling, and his anger rose again. Not at her but at the lunatic who hurt this amazing woman. "We'll make sure Gentry's apprehended and put on trial for what he did."

Her eyes widened. "Then you still believe the pictures are real? That I didn't fabricate them?"

"Of course. I don't know you that well, but I know you have integrity and live by your faith."

"Thank you. I try to."

"What else can I do to help with your loss?" he asked, feeling bold and terrified at the same time.

"Nothing really."

"I'd like to give you a hug," he said, shocked at how timid he sounded. He hadn't acted this way with a woman since he was an awkward teen. "Would that be okay?"

She sighed, her breath seeming to go on and on. Was she horrified by his question? Fine. He got it. She didn't want a relationship. Just because he was starting to think in that direction didn't mean she was.

The last thing she needed was for him to hug her. He got that. Prepared for it.

"Yes, please." Her words came out on a whispered plea.

He didn't waste a single moment, not even the time to breathe, and scooped her into his arms. Her slender body melted against him, and he tightened his hold. He reveled in the touch. Felt each point where they connected. Inhaled her simple coconut fragrance.

He almost sighed but kept his feelings to himself. This hug was for her. Not him. She felt fragile and strong at the same time. More importantly, she felt right, as if holding her like this was meant to be.

Is it? Did You bring us together for more than the business of hauling Gentry in and keeping her and the kids safe? If so, I don't know if I'm ready for it. I have so much more to do. See. Experience.

Natalie's words came back to him. Was he just keeping busy—seeking the thrill to prove his worth by accomplishing something?

I love you for who you are–My priceless child—not for what you do.

Whoa. He leaned back. He'd really have to give that some thought. But not now. Now he *did* need to be doing something. Finding a killer and keeping the kids and Natalie safe.

"I should go in and check on the children," Natalie said. "Your mom has been watching them a long time, and I can't take advantage of her like that."

"I'll walk you in." He couldn't resist tucking a stray strand of hair that landed on her cheek behind her ear before clasping her hand and leading her toward the door. He might be enjoying holding her hand, but he squeezed it and let go before opening the door. No way he would encourage his mother's matchmaking.

She was in the kitchen, and a new savory smell filled the cabin. Willow sat on the couch with Drake's father, that same large bin of Legos resting between them. Willow's lip was between her teeth again, and Drake didn't know how she could stand the chapped skin there. But obviously it brought her comfort. Logan and Sadie must still be napping as they were nowhere to be seen.

His mother looked up from a bowl of dough she was forming into a ball.

"Dinner smells great. I know we only ate a little while ago but..." He grinned and patted his stomach.

"You always were the son who appreciated my cooking the most. Maybe because you burn it off so fast and come back for more." She chuckled and turned her attention back to the dough.

His dad got up and joined them, lowering his voice. "Willow's in a funk. Not sure what's going on, but something is."

Drake looked at his dad. "I see you tried your usual trick to get a kid to open up."

His dad glanced back at Willow. "You mean the Legos?"

"Yeah."

His dad arched an eyebrow. "You knew about that, huh?"

"Was pretty obvious." Drake grinned. "We were down or troubled by something, and out came the Legos. It took a lot of time to build whatever item you came up with and gave you plenty of time to ask us pointed questions."

"He's right, dear." Drake's mom smiled. "You thought you were being the stealthy detective, but we all knew. I

often wondered why you didn't build Legos with the crimi-
nals you arrested."

They all laughed, and Willow stared at them as if she
took their good humor as a personal assault. Drake could
see that. He'd have been sulking as a kid, and he could
remember times he wanted to stay mad and his family went
on enjoying life without him.

His father's smile faded. "Might've worked on you kids,
but Willow didn't bite."

"Let me try." Shocked at the fact that he was offering to
help a kid, Drake started across the room. He stopped in
front of Willow. "Since you're not using the Legos, mind if I
build something?"

She looked up at him. "Whatcha gonna build?"

Yeah, what? Something an eight-year-old girl would like.
"I think I'll make a castle like in *Frozen*."

"You know about *Frozen*?"

"Sure, who doesn't?" he said, thankful that one of his
fellow deputies had a daughter who was obsessed with the
movie.

Willow frowned, her adorable freckled face screwed up
tight. "You don't have the right colors. It needs to be pink
and purple."

"True. But I can pretend." He smiled. "Say. You know
what? I might get it all wrong. Can you help me?"

"I s'pose, but you haveta listen to me or it won't work."

"I can listen." Feeling thankful for the breakthrough, he
offered a prayer for guidance and picked up the bin. "How
about we go to the table so when the little kids get up, they
don't get into them?"

"The pieces are too small for them," she said as she slid
off the couch. "My mom always told me to make sure to put
them away so they wouldn't eat them."

"Sounds like your mom's pretty smart." He opened the

bin then dumped some of the Legos onto the scarred oak table that had lived in his parents' walk-out basement for years.

He sat and felt eyes on him, so he looked up to find Natalie quietly assessing him from the kitchen where she remained. He nodded, and she jerked her gaze away as if she didn't want him to catch her looking at him. She was struggling too. Maybe fighting feelings that were developing between them. Having her return his feelings should make Drake feel good, but it didn't. Not really. Not when he knew it added to her struggles right now. She didn't need to have another hardship in her life.

"We can pretend the blue is purple," Willow said, drawing him back. "And the red can be pink."

"Okay." He turned his attention back to the plastic bricks. "I like to sort mine by color first. What about you?"

"Doesn't matter."

"What do you usually do?"

She turned a red brick over and over in her fingers. He noticed the pink nail polish, reminding him of the creepy conversation about Gentry polishing the child's nails that Natalie shared. Was Willow's nail color one of the ones used on one of the victims? Was the guy playing out some sick fantasy with his child? Or maybe it was a future color. Or maybe his actions were tied to his wife.

Anger burned in Drake's gut. How could any adult hurt a child? Especially a child of their own. Drake could never do that. And finally he understood that fierce Mama Bear instinct his mother possessed in droves, and he appreciated her and his dad all the more.

Please. Please, Father, let these kids know the love I did. Do. Know Your love too.

Willow kept turning the Lego, her eyes fixed on her hands.

"What's wrong, kiddo?" he asked softly.

She looked him in the eye and let go of her lip. "Is my dad dead?"

"Dead? No. Why do you think that?"

"He was in an accident, and nobody will tell me where he is."

"Oh, right." He'd gotten the child to open up, but he was stepping in treacherous waters now. Waters he had no experience swimming in, and he feared he would drown.

Willow dropped the brick. "If he's alive, where is he, and why doesn't he come get us?"

"We're not sure where he is," Drake answered truthfully.

She pushed all the bricks away from her and propped her elbows on the table. "Does he even know where we are?"

Drake searched for the right answer. "He knows you're with Natalie, and that means you're safe and taken care of. So he doesn't have to worry about you and is free to do whatever it is he's doing." *Like tracking Natalie down. Or even killing another woman.*

"He's never gone somewhere without telling me where he was going. Not since Mom left."

"Who babysits you when he's gone?"

"Our nanny. Ulani. She's nice, but I like Natalie better. I wish she could be our nanny."

"She *is* pretty nice." Drake looked at Natalie, who was leaning against the counter talking to his parents, about what, he had no idea. He hoped the tightness in her eyes and her slumped shoulders didn't mean his mom was trying to matchmake.

"You like her," Willow stated.

"I do," he admitted, surprising himself.

Willow's little red eyebrows arched. "Do you *like her* like her?"

When was the last time he heard anyone ask him that? He held back a laugh to keep from hurting Willow's feelings. He was trying to gain her trust, so he went with the truth. "A lot, I think."

Willow crossed her arms and slouched in her chair. "I don't want her to get married."

"Why not?"

"Because then she'll have to quit working and become a mom."

Interesting take on things. "Some moms work."

"Yeah, but it's wrong. Daddy told me that. Moms have to stay home and raise their kids. That's why Mom had to quit her job before I was born. She didn't want to. She liked working with clothes and makeup. She loves that stuff. Not me. Yuk." She made a sour face, but then tears wet her eyes. "If she comes home, I'll pretend to like that stuff this time."

She picked up two red bricks and pushed them together. Then added a few more. Drake wanted to ask additional questions, but she seemed talked-out, so he started sorting the Legos into colors.

She suddenly looked up. "Is a bad man going to come here?"

"Why do you think that?"

"You and your brothers have guns."

They'd tried to hide them under their shirts, but they were often revealed when they moved around. "We always carry guns."

"Always?"

He nodded.

"Does it make you feel safe?"

"Safer, yes."

"I wish I could have a gun." Her words came with such emphasis that it tore at Drake's heart.

"Are you afraid of something?" he asked, trying to keep those emotions out of his voice.

She nibbled on her lip. "Dad once said he thought a bad man took Mom. Now he says she went away on her own. But I think he was lying so I wouldn't be afraid. But I am. I'm afraid the bad man is going to come back to get us."

"No man is going to come get you here," Drake said with vehemence. "I'll make sure of that."

"But sometimes you're gone."

"Then my brothers or father and mother and Natalie will make sure you're safe."

"I like Nana and Papa." She glanced at his parents. "They said we should call them that because they love being grandparents, and they already consider us their grand-children."

He knew his mom meant well, but this child didn't need to have hopes for grandparents when those hopes would never be fulfilled by his parents.

"But when Dad comes back, they can't be our grandpar-ents." Willow's mouth turned down.

"No, they can't," Drake said.

She curled her arms around her body and looked down. Drake had never known such insecurity in his childhood. If only he could give Willow the same security.

What could he do to make her feel safe all the time? Like when she was lying in bed at night, hugging George tight and worrying that the boogeyman was going to climb through her window.

A thought sparked.

"Hold on, kiddo." He jumped to his feet. "I've got an idea. Be right back."

14

Natalie watched Drake bolt out the door. She was about to follow when she glanced at the time. She had to go get Sadie and Logan up from their naps. She'd been talking with his parents about her family, giving them the barest of information, but mostly she tried to listen to Drake's conversation with Willow. He did great. He handled Willow's questions and concerns beautifully. He didn't lie to her, and yet he managed not to tell her the truth about her father. Okay, supposed truth. They had no proof that Kirk was The Clipper, but Natalie hoped they soon would.

Peggy said Drake hadn't had any interaction with children before now, but he appeared to be a natural at it, at least with kids Willow's age. But Sadie? He'd struggled with her at lunch but had managed. Natalie hadn't yet seen how he would do with Logan. Maybe she would find out now.

She changed into the clothes Russ had bought, glad to see that they did indeed fit, even though the jeans were men's and hung low on her hips. The relaxed clothing was far more comfortable than the suit and heels.

After she put on the basic white sneakers, she woke the children and took them to the bathroom before heading downstairs. Sadie toddled over to the stack of books and grabbed a Dr. Suess book. Willow watched it all from the table filled with Legos.

"Story," Sadie demanded.

"Sure." Natalie sat on the stone hearth in front of a crackling fire chasing away the chilly May weather. "You want to listen too, Logan?"

"Uh-huh." He charged past the blocks he'd been building with earlier to sit beside her.

She started the story.

A few moments later, Drake entered the room holding something concealed in his hand. He knelt down next to Willow.

"This will help you feel safer." He flipped open his hand and revealed what almost looked like the remote for a car resting on his palm.

"Read," Sadie demanded.

Natalie turned back to the book but couldn't concentrate. She had to hear what Drake was saying.

"It's called a personal alarm," he said. "You pull this out and push this button, and it will send a text to me and my brothers telling us where you are and that you need help."

She looked wide-eyed at him but didn't speak.

He held out a bright blue lanyard. "You can wear it on this cord like a necklace so it'll always be with you."

Willow tipped her head and studied the device. "Even in the bathtub?"

He nodded. "It's waterproof, but you might just want to set it on the tub next to you so you don't have to dry it off."

"Okay." She stared at the alarm but didn't pick it up.

"Want me to put it on the cord?" Drake asked.

She nodded.

He attached the lanyard and lifted it over her head. She cupped the alarm in her hand and held it close to her chest.

The unease that had been lodged in her big brown eyes since they'd left her house cleared.

She tucked the device inside her T-shirt then threw her arms around Drake. "I like you. You're the best one."

"Best one?" he asked, sounding truly baffled.

"Of the big men. I'm kind of scared of all of you."

Logan tugged on Natalie's arm to continue the story, but she had to see how Drake handled Willow's announcement.

He leaned back. "You have nothing to be afraid of with me or my brothers. I can tell you silly stories about all of us, and you'd know that we're just a bunch of big goofballs. So you, my friend, have nothing to be afraid of." He tapped her on the nose. "How about we get back to those Legos?"

"Promise you'll tell me the stories." She held out her pinkie.

He locked pinkies with her. "Promise."

Willow cast him a shy smile. Oh, wow. That was so sweet. The child was smitten.

Natalie's heart split wide open, letting more of Drake inside. Any guy who so sweetly cared for a little girl was a guy she should never let go. Even if he didn't want to get involved. Even if he didn't want kids of his own right now. And even if she vowed never to get involved again. Drake was a guy a woman just had to give a chance to, and from this moment forward, she would keep an open mind on that front.

Drake went to the whiteboard in his workshop as Natalie took a seat. He approved of her change of clothing. She looked like she was more comfortable than before and like she fit into the surroundings better. Or did he just wish she fit in his life more? That she might someday be able to embrace the more rugged way of living. Maybe.

Oddly enough he also wished he was back in the cabin with the kids. How crazy was that? He'd actually enjoyed the break with them. Now that he was back to work, he had to stow the warm feelings for all of them and do his job.

He looked at his brothers remaining in the room. Aiden had relieved Brendan, and Brendan was napping. Until this killer was found, none of them would get a full night's sleep. And even then, Erik needed to stay glued to his computer as he was the one who could locate much needed information. And as lead, Drake would go until he dropped and had to take a few hours. He was running on adrenaline and wasn't even close to crashing.

He looked at Erik and Clay. "Who wants to go first?"

"I will," Erik said, his tone sharp and concerned. "I hoped the backgrounds on all of Gentry's victims might give us a hint as to where he might hole up. No such luck. I finished the search including for images, which didn't return any leads, but I've included them in the report anyway." He slid a report down the table to Drake. "You can read it, but the CliffsNotes version is that the women have nothing in common. And I mean nothing. And no connection to one another either. And there's nothing in the case notes to suggest a motive for the murders. There was nothing sexual in the attacks. Ages ranged from mid-twenties to sixty-one. There's no evidence that they knew each other or that they frequented the same places."

"Nothing?" Drake shoved his hand into his hair and considered pulling it out. "Not even Gina and the other woman killed in Portland?"

He shook his head. "Rebecca Vann was sixty-one. Had a well-to-do husband, never worked except as a mom and housewife. Husband died a few years ago. She stayed in the

162

same house and lived a quiet life. Was a master gardener, which was how she spent her time when she wasn't with her two grown daughters."

"Maybe the daughters knew my sister," Natalie said. "Though Gina sure wasn't a gardener. She was like me. We don't like the outdoors much."

Erik shook his head. "There's no evidence of that connection either."

"There has to be a connection," Drake said. "Maybe not a physical link, but in Gentry's motive."

"What about money?" Clay asked. "Were they robbed?"

Erik shrugged. "I don't have access to the banking records. And before you ask me to get it, the only way to do it is to hack the bank, and that's not something we want to do."

"Agreed." Drake stared at the report Erik created as if a link would pop up.

"On another note," Erik said. "I found out Gentry was in both of the towns when victims two and three were killed."

"That can't be a coincidence." Drake gritted his teeth.

"No," Erik said. "All the evidence points to him being The Clipper."

Natalie clenched her hands on the table but didn't speak. It was looking like she was right, but this was likely one of those times when no one would want to be right.

"So let's quit spending time on trying to prove he's The Clipper and shift our efforts to finding him," Drake said. "One thing we haven't considered is his car. If he has a navigation system, we could trace his movements via GPS. Maybe one of the addresses in the file will lead to him."

"Car's likely at a body shop," Erik said. "I can get a copy of the accident report to see who towed it."

Drake explained how the deputy failed to note the tow company.

Clay scrubbed a hand over his face. "Talk about incompetent."

"Londyn is looking into this, but I don't want to leave it up to her alone when we could work it too."

"I'll print out a list of body shops in the area and sort by the most likely places," Erik offered. "And we can start calling them and the tow companies."

"We could have Stella make the calls." Drake would email their receptionist and have her make this her top priority.

Erik leaned back but his fingers continued to rest on his keyboard. "I've also been looking into rental car companies and banking information along with property records for Gentry and his wife. So far, I found Tracey's distant cousin owns a cabin in central Oregon. A remote place. Kind of like this one. Check out the monitor, and I'll put a map of the place up."

The screen came alive with a map, and Drake studied the address located in a wilderness area. "Do we know anyone in law enforcement up there who could do a drive-by to see if the place is occupied?"

"Already ahead of you." A cocky grin lit Clay's face. "Got a college buddy in that area, and he's en route to the cabin right now. Should know something within an hour. And I've also contacted Gage Blackwell. He'll get a helo in the air for us the moment we need one."

"Gage Blackwell?" Natalie asked.

"A friend who owns a tactical company in Cold Harbor," Drake explained.

"If he's looking for Natalie and the kids, why would he go so far away?" Clay asked.

Drake gave it some thought. "Natalie mentioned that he might not care about his kids like we would if we were him.

That he wouldn't let her best him. So he could be lying low, trying to find us."

Natalie nodded. "But remember, in his eyes, he's the most important thing. Means his number one priority is self-preservation."

"What if he thinks the police are involved in protecting the kids and has given up on getting them back and seeking revenge?" Clay asked.

"Then he could be at this cabin figuring out his next move," Drake said.

"Why don't we wait to see if he's even there," Clay suggested.

Drake wasn't one for waiting on anything, but it sure seemed like the right plan at this point. He was just going to have to learn a bit of patience, and learn it quickly.

15

"Is that guy ever going to call?" Drake jumped up from hours of research and paced the length of the workshop and back.

"He always keeps his word." Clay crossed his arms and glared at Drake.

Fine. Clay was mad at Drake for questioning his friend. He'd get over it.

"His word said he'd have eyes on the cabin in an hour, and it's going on three." Drake took long strides, pausing to give his brother a frustrated look.

"Something must've come up, but he'll call. Just be patient."

"Not his strong suit." Erik cocked his head. "In fact, not his suit at all."

His brothers laughed. Okay. Fine. But Drake couldn't find the humor right now. He was getting tired of trying to be patient. Gentry could be hightailing it out of there, and they wouldn't know where to look next. Drake wanted to be able to give Natalie positive news when he went to the cabin, where she was spending time with the kids.

Clay's phone finally sounded in a police car woop-woop siren ringtone.

"See." Eyeing Drake, Clay picked it up and tapped the screen. "Putting you on speaker so my brothers can hear what you found."

"Place was dark when I arrived." The guy's deep voice rumbled over the speaker. "Watched it for an hour then slipped inside."

"You what?" Drake shouted.

"No one told me not to."

Clay shrugged. "I asked for a drive-by. Didn't think I needed to warn him to hang back."

"You want my report or not," Clay's friend said.

"Of course," Drake snapped.

"Ignore his attitude." Clay fired Drake a chill-out look.

Drake ignored it and stared at the phone.

"There wasn't a sign of anyone staying in the place," the friend said. "Nothing in the fridge. Trash was empty. Beds made. Fireplace cleaned out. And the place smelled stale. No one's been there in some time."

"Thanks for checking it out," Clay said.

Drake slashed a hand across his throat to tell Clay to end the call before the guy started asking questions.

Clay rolled his eyes. "We'll let you know if we need you to drive by again." He punched the disconnect button and looked at Drake. "Hey, man, relax. For all of our sakes."

"So that was a bust." Drake looked at his brothers. "Anyone else find an actionable lead?"

Erik shook his head. "He doesn't have any other family or friends that I could find."

"He and his wife are both kind of odd," Clay said. "Nothing on the wife either. No social media accounts at all."

Drake stopped at the end of the table littered with plates from the lasagna dinner their mom had delivered so they could keep working. "Not everyone embraces social media. But not counting law enforcement professionals most do."

Drake ran through in his head everything he knew about this couple. "Willow told me her dad didn't believe in women working. I wonder if he controlled Tracey's social media too."

"Maybe he controlled everything." Clay rested his elbows on the table. "Like her clothes, etcetera. So she goes out in the afternoon in search of some freedom. Maybe does all the things he forbids."

"Controlling her would fit with his personality." Erik leaned back and yawned. He looked totally exhausted and despite the work he still had to do, the guy needed a nap.

"We need to take a break. It's been a long day." Drake locked gazes with Erik. "And you, little brother, need to hit the sack. I need your techie brain ready and raring to go."

"You could be right." He stood and stretched, Pong coming to his feet next to him. "I'll grab a couple of hours and get back to it."

"Go ahead," Drake said. "I'll clean up."

Clay gaped at him. "You gone loco, man? Volunteering to clean up?"

"Just accept it before I ask you for help." Drake chuckled and stacked up the plates and silverware and carried them into the cabin.

His mother was in the kitchen mixing bread dough in a tall bucket. Keeping enough bread to feed this hungry hoard was almost a full-time job. He searched for Natalie, but she was nowhere to be seen. His dad sat in a chair reading a book, and Willow was still at the table, the castle starting to take shape. Erik and Pong were on the floor by the fireplace with Logan, who was hugging Pong and giggling. Erik obviously didn't make it to the bedroom yet, and Drake didn't have the heart to tell his brother to head to bed or Pong would follow, leaving Logan alone.

His cabin didn't have a dishwasher, so he set the dishes in a sink of soapy water and started to wash them.

"I'll do that," his mom said.

"I can help."

"I'd rather you go talk to Willow again. She's still been sulking, and I hate seeing her so down. She seemed to warm to you, so could you give it a go?"

He rinsed his hands and dried them. "I can't even imagine what she's going through. At her age, my biggest trauma was getting picked last for the baseball team."

His mother chuckled, but quickly sobered. "Our family is so blessed, and it's up to us to share those blessings with these kids."

"Agreed." He hugged his mother's shoulders. "Thanks for being the best mother a guy could ask for."

"It's my pleasure." She smiled up at him. "Raising you all is my greatest accomplishment, and I'm so proud of each of you. At least most of the time." She laughed again.

He gave her another squeeze and set off toward Willow before his mom moved on to her matchmaking with Natalie, which she was prone to do whether the female subject was in the room or not. In this case, with Natalie missing, his mom might really go to it.

He assumed Natalie was putting Sadie to bed as his favorite two-year-old wasn't in the room either.

Drake had hoped to spend a bit of time with Logan today, but Erik and Pong were engaged with Logan right now. Drake sat at the table with Willow, who was chewing on that lip again and clutching the alarm that hung around her neck. Drake wanted to give her a chance to start talking if she wanted to, so he watched his brother to see how he handled the little boy.

"He's really your dog?" Logan asked.

"Yes."

"I like him." Logan petted Pong's head. "He's pretty."

Erik looked horrified at his rugged dog being called pretty but said nothing.

"Can he do tricks?" Logan asked.

"Hmm. Well. He sits, stays, and rolls over on command. And he'll give you his paw if I tell him to."

Logan's eyes widened. "Tell him. Oh, please tell him."

Erik smiled at the boy. "Hold out your hand near his front feet."

Logan poked out his hand and gave Erik an intense look. "Like this?"

"Perfect." Erik turned his attention to Pong. "Pong. Paw."

Pong placed his paw in Logan's hand. Logan giggled, and then hugged Pong, who started to move away.

"Stay," Erik said, and Pong froze in place and accepted the hug.

"I like him," Logan said, releasing the dog.

"I like him too." Erik smiled.

"And I like you!" Logan threw himself at Erik.

Pong whimpered his unease.

"It's okay, boy," Erik said to Pong. "Logan's our friend."

Drake expected Erik to extricate himself, but he held the boy, who didn't seem to want to let go. Maybe Logan missed his parents more than he'd been letting on. Drake was proud of his brother for spending time with Logan and for holding him when he needed it. Drake had always known Erik was a good guy who lived his faith, but this just proved it.

"Logan likes dogs." Willow picked up a blue brick and

clipped it onto a tower. "He wants us to get one, but Dad said no 'cause we already have a cat."

"And what about you?" he asked. "Would you like a dog?"

"Sure. It would be fun."

"Do you want to pet Pong too?"

"Nah. I'll let Logan have fun."

Drake respected how kind she was to her brother. Drake didn't know what it felt like to have the kind of responsibility that Willow was carrying. Erik was Drake's only younger sibling, and only by a couple of years. Plus Drake had three older brothers and a sister who fulfilled that role.

After a few minutes of Willow's silence, he turned his attention to the Legos. "Looks like you're making good progress."

"Could do better if you didn't keep running out to your workshop." She tilted her head, her curls shifting as if they had a life of their own, and focused on him. "What are you guys doing out there anyway?"

Drake took a moment to make sure his answer was appropriate. "Just working on one of our jobs."

"What kind of job?"

"We investigate things and help people who are in trouble."

She clutched the alarm. "Is that why we're here? Are we in trouble?"

He should've been even more vague. "Not at all."

"My dad would get really mad if we were." She sighed. "But not Mom."

"Sounds like you miss your mom." Drake connected two bricks together to give her a chance to answer.

Willow gave a sad nod, those Little Orphan Annie curls bouncing. "I love her."

"Of course you do. She's your mom. I love my mom too. She's the best."

Willow frowned, but Drake had no idea what he'd said to upset her, so he sat back and waited for the child to continue.

She pushed a few bricks around on the table. "My mom isn't like yours. Not at all."

"No?"

"Nuh-uh." She stared at the kitchen where his mom still had her hands in the dough, a flour kissed swatch on her face. "Nana makes all kinds of good things to eat. And she sits with you and acts like she wants to be with you instead of doing something else."

He wasn't surprised about the cooking and baking as a lot of mothers these days were too busy to spend much time in the kitchen. Didn't make them bad moms, just different ones. But it sounded like Tracey Gentry didn't much like being a mom at all. "Your mom didn't do those things?"

"She stayed in her room a lot, trying to make herself look prettier." Willow's chin trembled. "She had a video camera. I snuck in once and saw her using it. She was showing off her outfit and talking about her makeup like someone was listening to her. It was weird 'cause she was all alone. I don't think Dad knows about it."

"Sounds different," Drake said.

What was Tracey doing? Creating videos for social media? Was that where she was making her money? But if so, why go away from home in the afternoons when she could record them there, and did that have anything to do with Gentry murdering women?

"She got mad if any of us went up there." Willow chewed on her lower lip. "I didn't like it when she got mad. I had to keep Sadie and Logan busy so they wouldn't bother her."

Drake got mad all over again for this poor kid. Eight

years old and forced to be the adult in the family. Still, it was probably better than getting split up from her siblings and being placed in foster care. And once Gentry was behind bars, with their mother missing and the father a serial killer, social services would likely petition for parental rights and make the children available for adoption. Likely individual adoptions as Natalie had said, and as an older kid, Willow would have an even harder time of finding a forever family than her siblings.

His gut cramped at the thought of the kids' future and especially of them being split up. They would have a tough road ahead, and he wanted to hug this little munchkin. But the investigator in him took hold. Were the videos a lead they needed to follow? He would have Erik look into it.

Natalie came down the stairs and went to Logan, smiling at Erik, who flashed her one of his cute grins that had girls falling all over him. He had such an easygoing personality and could talk to anyone, anywhere. With that smile and his outgoing personality and Drake's more introverted tendencies in high school, Erik often won over girls who Drake wanted to date. Until Kennedy Walker moved to town when they were seniors. The love of Erik's life, he'd said, but then they'd broken up in college. To this day, he'd never said why, but he came out with a broken heart, and Erik hadn't had a serious relationship since then.

Holding Logan's hand, Natalie walked toward him.

"Okay, Willow," Natalie said. "Time for you and Logan to join Sadie for bed."

"I wanna go home," Willow said, her right eyebrow arched just like in a photo Drake had seen of her father.

"I'm sorry, you can't." Natalie's sympathetic tone didn't have any impact on Willow's expression. "Your dad's not there."

Willow jutted out her chin. "But you could stay with us at our house, right?"

Natalie looked like she didn't know how to respond.

"You don't like my cabin?" Drake asked, exaggerating an offended look.

Willow crossed her arms. "There's nothing fun to do around here."

"Sure there is. I do plenty of fun things. Like hunting and fishing."

Willow wrinkled her cute button nose. "Yuk."

Drake knew she would like fishing if she gave it a chance. At least most kids did. "Have you ever been fishing?"

"You havta use worms." She shuddered. "Gross."

"I rarely use worms." Drake stood. "Tell you what. When my brothers and I get done with our current job, I'll take you fishing, and I promise you'll love it so much you'll want to go again."

"Really?" Her eyes brightened. "You'll take me?"

"Sure thing." He held out his hand. "But now it's time for bed."

She slid her small hand into his. For a moment he just stared at the two of them together. Was there anything more important than helping a young child become a fully functioning and successful adult? To make sure they knew Jesus? To teach them to be God's ambassadors on earth?

Drake tugged Willow to her feet and she held on tightly to his hand. "Can you tuck me in tonight?"

He tried not to look shocked at her request. "Sure. Run up and get your pjs on, and I'll be right up."

"But be quiet," Natalie said. "You don't want to wake Sadie. Can you go with her too, Logan?"

"I'll help him." Willow took his hand and raced up the stairs, his pudgy little legs working hard to keep up.

Drake turned to look at Natalie. She gave him a broad

smile. He had no idea why, but he would bask in it for as long as he could.

"You've made a friend in Willow," she said.

"The kid has wormed her way into my heart," he replied.

And so have you.

But that was something he wasn't going to say. Ever. Right?

16

Natalie didn't know what Drake was thinking, but his jaw was clenched and his eyes pensive. Confused maybe. Surely, he understood what was happening with Willow.

But maybe not, and Natalie needed to tell him. "Willow's really searching for love and attention that her parents didn't give her. And it seems as if Ulani didn't either."

"Breaks my heart to see kids suffering because of screwed-up adults. And these kids have some seriously screwed-up adults in their lives."

"They do."

"But you see stuff like this all the time."

"Yeah," Natalie said and resisted sighing. "I mean not serial killers, but unfit parents. I also see parents who would be good role models if they only got some help. I can do the most good with those parents, but I have to give the others more of my time because the children are at greater risk."

He didn't speak for the longest time. "I'm amazed at how strong you are. You help these families and haven't become jaded. And you're doing such a good job of coping with this situation."

"It's really all thanks to you and your family. You're giving me the strength."

"You'd do fine on your own. You need us to provide protection, but caring for the kids in a tough situation? You don't need us for that."

Natalie wasn't quite as confident. Sure, her determination didn't allow her to fail often, but caring for three children was a huge responsibility that she wasn't sure she was cut out to handle for much longer. She never thought she'd have children at all, but in the rare times when she did think about it, she always imagined having a baby and learning the parenting ropes along the way. She might hold a Ph.D. that included child development, but it was one thing to know how a child grew and developed and give advice to other parents. It was another thing altogether to put it into practice for three young children who were thrust into her care when emotions were running high.

"I'm ready," Willow called from the landing.

Natalie spun. She'd forgotten that Willow could hear their conversation. Natalie had to be more careful.

She stepped back to let Drake take the lead, but she would join him in saying good-night as rules prohibited leaving a man alone with these children. Even a fine responsible man like Drake. It was great that he was bonding with Willow, but he wouldn't be around after Kirk was found and jailed. So Natalie needed to keep a close relationship with Willow. No matter how much Willow had come to like Drake, Natalie would be the one to break the hard news of her father's extracurricular activities.

In the loft that was toasty warm, Logan was tucked in and Willow was snuggled in bed, covers up to her neck.

Drake sat on the edge of the bed. "Can I tell you something?"

"Sure."

"I've never tucked a kid in, so I don't know what to do."

"Really?" She blinked up at him, her feathery lashes a pale red. "Someone as old as you?"

"Yeah, I'm, like, ancient." He grinned, and the cute dimple showed up again.

Willow gave Drake an odd look. "How come you're not married?"

He didn't even bat an eyelash at the question. "I've never found someone I want to marry."

Willow's expression turned very serious. "Natalie's kind of nice. And she's old too. I didn't want her to before, but maybe she should get married."

Natalie's mouth dropped open, but she quickly snapped it shut.

"She is pretty nice, isn't she?" Drake grinned back at her. "And you're right, she *is* old. She should be married too."

Willow nodded. "If you married her, then you could get some kids too."

"We could," Drake agreed.

"I think you'd be a good dad."

"Thanks, Willow."

She turned onto her side and hugged George close. "'Night, Drake."

"Good night, kiddo." Drake tucked the covers close then got up and stepped back.

Willow gave Natalie a longing look, and Natalie wanted to hug the child and kiss her good-night, but physical connection of any kind was discouraged on the job, and she'd already crossed that line once.

Natalie's job wasn't to make these children dependent on her. It was to be kind and caring but keep a wall up so that, when they moved on to their foster families, they didn't want to cling to her.

"Good night, Willow. Sleep tight." Natalie turned on the

nightlight and swallowed her desire to hug the child while following Drake out of the room.

On the landing, she closed the door firmly so Willow couldn't listen in and she jogged down the steps, Drake's footfalls sounding solidly behind her. At the bottom, she took a few deep breaths before they went out to join the others in the workshop again.

Drake stopped to look at her. "You okay?"

"The rules of my job prohibit me from giving children the hugs I think they need."

"Willow does seem like she could use one. I even thought about it, but figured it would be odd for her." Drake looked at the living area. "Tell you what. I've really come to appreciate my parents more. No more taking them for granted."

"You hit the parent lottery with them. They're great." She shook her head. "I just can't believe I spent so much time with Kirk and had no idea what a terrible person he is."

Drake ground his teeth. "Did he ever do anything to make you uncomfortable?"

"No. But as you can imagine from what I told you, his personality makes a person uncomfortable—that whole self-centered behavior thing. And as I said, I suspected him of killing his wife. He professed his love and need to find her, but the way he talked about her was creepy. He always changed the subject. Very evasive. I'm surprised the detective didn't pick up on it. Or maybe he did but ignored it because Kirk is a police officer too."

Drake nodded. "Let's get back to work finding Gentry."

On the way out to the workshop, he stopped near his parents, who sat on the couch. Peggy was nestled up to Russ, and he had his arm circled around her. "Could I ask you to keep an ear out for the kids so we can go back to the workshop?"

"No need to even ask." His mother smiled. "Of course we will. I've already become quite fond of them."

"Thanks, Mom," Drake said. "I can always count on you. You too, Dad. I'm lucky to have you guys as my parents."

"What's wrong?" Peggy jumped to her feet and put a hand on Drake's cheek. "This is the second time tonight you've said something about our parenting."

"Nothing's wrong." He smiled. "Seeing the Gentry kids, I've realized I've taken you guys for granted all these years."

His mother waved her hand. "No need to even think about that. We do what we do because we love you and the Lord. And trust me, I'm praying like crazy that things will work out for these kids., and God will give us the answer we need."

Drake hugged his mom. "Love you, Mom."

"Love you too, son." She squeezed his arm. "Now go find that terrible man and make him pay. Not only for what he's doing to these women, but to these precious children too."

"Will do." He gestured for Natalie to head for the door and shared a fist bump with his dad on the way past.

A bolt of jealousy pierced Natalie. She knew she shouldn't be jealous—that it was a sin. That God had given her the life she was living for a reason. But for the first time in many, many years, she didn't want to be alone anymore. She wanted people she could count on in her corner. Honest, caring, loving, God-fearing people like the Byrds.

She grabbed the sweatshirt Russ had bought for her and slipped into it as they strode to the workshop. In the daylight, she'd seen the beauty of Drake's property. Soaring spruce trees mixed with maples. Ferns, hostas, and other plants she couldn't identify scattered beneath the trees along with pine cones and a thick bed of needles. Now they were cloaked in darkness, and the area seemed threatening. Seemed like a bear could be hiding in the shadows. Worse yet—Kirk.

She moved closer to Drake, and their hands brushed. She went to jerk hers away, but he latched onto it with his warm fingers until they reached the door.

The guys were seated at the table, and they looked up when Drake opened the door.

"I think we start at the beginning," Aiden said, having just come back from watching the road. "Until Erik completes his background search on Tracey and we find an actionable item, I say we look into his victims to see if there's any leads missed there. And I suggest we start with Gina. See if we can find any motive for someone to kill her."

"I disagree," Drake said as he stepped past Natalie to enter the room. "I think it's a good idea to look into the victims, but we'd have better luck talking with the family and friends of Laura Zimmer. She was murdered a few months ago, so the trail isn't nearly as cold."

"I have to agree with Drake." Erik rubbed his eyes, and the dark circles under them attested to his shortened nap due to playing with Logan.

Clay, looking far more alert at the end of the table, nodded. "We go with Laura."

Aiden tapped a thick stack of papers in front of him. "According to Erik's report, she lived with a roommate."

"Roommate is Faye Babcock, and she still rents the same apartment where Laura was killed." Erik mimicked a shudder. "Wouldn't catch me living in a place where someone was murdered."

"Me, either." Natalie took a seat. "Especially if it was a rental and not a place I owned."

Drake grabbed one of the reports on the table and

flipped a page. "Babcock's a nurse. Works the night shift and gets off at nine. I'll go talk to her then."

Natalie looked him in the eye. "If your mom will watch the kids, I'm coming with you."

He widened his stance and worked his jaw muscles as if he were restraining himself from saying something. "I'd rather you stay here where it's safe."

"Your SUV is armored." She raised her chin. "So I'm fine, right?"

"Yes, but—"

"She's got you, bro," Erik said.

"Plus I've talked to Faye before, and I know she's uncomfortable around men after what happened to Laura. She's more likely to open up with me."

"No good excuse to leave her behind," Erik said.

Drake glared at his brother.

"You're the one in charge for once, vacating your devil's advocate role. I need to take over." Erik grinned, a boyish smile that seemed to fit the youngest member of the family. Natalie hadn't noticed any other behaviors of a younger child, like acting spoiled. In fact, he seemed well-rounded and an all-out good guy. So why was he still single?

Drake scowled at his brother. "Not necessary."

"That's odd." Erik tilted his head. "It's always necessary when *you* weigh in."

Drake's fingers curled into fists, but he unfurled them and shook his head. "I guess you're right."

"Say what?" Erik gaped at his brother. "You actually said I'm right. Mind repeating it so I can get it on video."

The brothers laughed, including Drake, who gave Erik a friendly sock in the arm. "Just know when this is over, I'll be returning to my role as the family bad guy."

"Fine," Erik said with an easy acquiesce. "You can have it. Too much responsibility."

"Footloose and fancy-free," Aiden said. "Both of you."

"Not a bad thing to be," Drake said, grinning at his brothers.

Despite his desire to be free when her opinion was swinging in the opposite direction, her heart twanged. He was so devilishly handsome, and his bad boy vibe was almost impossible to resist. She didn't see Drake fully in that role, but he fulfilled enough of it—a rebel, walked on the wild side, and volatile at times. All the opposite of her staid existence. She really fit the stereotype of a librarian, not a social worker. Prim and proper. Socially, on the shy side.

They complimented each other well, but Drake wasn't looking for a woman to compliment his personality. He wasn't looking for a woman at all.

"I just talked to Willow," he said to the group. "She told me her mom filmed videos of her makeup and clothes. I got to thinking she might've been making them for the internet, somehow making money on it. Maybe if we find those videos, we can find a lead in the background or in something she says."

"I'll get going on looking for them," Erik said. "Starting with YouTube, which is the most likely place she'd post videos. But you should know, if it's a private channel, finding the information will be next to impossible."

"Thanks for doing it, man," Drake said. "I'm gonna owe you a lot when this is over."

"You know it." Erik grinned.

Drake was sure Erik would hold him to it. "If everyone's good with us taking off for the interview, I'd like to spend the night in Portland so we don't have to fight rush-hour traffic in the morning."

"We've got things here," Erik said. "As long as you make sure Mom and Dad look after the kids. I'm glad to do whatever you need on this investigation, but I draw the line at babysitting."

Drake smiled, but the unease that had been in his gut since he learned Gentry was a serial killer remained. He knew the kids were safe with his brothers, and he was needed where he would be. Right by Natalie's side at all times.

~

Natalie crashed on the plush sofa in Drake's condo, but he paced at supersonic speed on the far side of the room. He was acting like a caged animal. She wished they could've stayed at the cabin, where he'd seemed more relaxed. This fiercely intense guy striding across the floor, pent-up energy oozing from his pores, felt like a stranger.

"You okay?" she asked.

He spun. "Too much sitting and not enough doing. I need to burn some energy off."

"You're making me nervous."

"Sorry. I didn't think about that." He ran a hand through his hair, leaving a few strands sticking up.

She could almost see the thoughts of how he was going to find this serial killer racing through his brain. She would suggest going for a walk, but he would veto that.

"You mentioned a gym in the building. Why don't we go there?" she suggested. "Some physical exertion could help us both get a good night's sleep."

He studied her. "That would be great for me, but are you sure you want to do that?"

She stood. "Just show me where to get changed, and I'm good to go."

"You can sleep in my bedroom tonight and can change in there." He grabbed the bag holding her limited clothing, carried it down the hallway, and set it on the king-size bed. "Let me grab some clothes, and I'll change in the bathroom."

He went to a long dresser and took out shorts and a T-shirt then picked up sneakers from the closet. At the door he glanced back at her as if he wanted to say something else but gave his head a quick shake and left the room.

She didn't even look around the room but quickly slipped into a pair of sleep shorts his dad had gotten for her and left on her T-shirt. By the time she joined Drake, he was dressed in athletic clothes and filling water bottles in the kitchen. She admired the muscles in his legs. She would be no match for him in the gym. And she was taken aback by the fact that he was wearing his gun holstered at his hip and it looked totally odd with the athletic attire.

He turned. "Ready?"

"As I can be in this outfit. Good thing it's a private gym." She chuckled.

She shouldn't have said anything as it drew his attention, and he ran his gaze from her head to her toes, and the heat of a blush rose over her cheeks. His eyes flared with interest, a place neither of them needed to go, so she bolted for the door like a startled deer.

He caught up and led her through the halls and down to the large room with a wall of glass overlooking the hallway. The room was spotless and smelled of lemon cleaner. She wasn't a gym enthusiast but thought the equipment was top-of-the-line. She went straight to a treadmill and got it moving. He stepped to the one next to her and was soon jogging along. They settled into a comfortable routine, but still, she was acutely aware of him. Of his confident stride. The fluidity of his body. Of his masculine form.

She nearly groaned at her wayward mind and forced it back to thoughts of finding Kirk.

"Would it be okay if I read the reports Erik compiled?" she asked between breaths.

He arched an eyebrow and didn't miss a beat on the treadmill. "You think he missed something?"

"No, but sometimes something stands out to another person."

"I don't think reading them is such a good idea."

"Why not?"

"Gina's report will have graphic details of her murder. Things you won't want to see."

"Doesn't matter." Natalie firmed her shoulders. "If it might help to have fresh eyes on it, I can handle it."

He slowed to a walk and looked her deep in the eyes, mining for something she couldn't fathom, and she needed to know the answer to. "What?"

"I...it's just..." He shook his head. "I hate that you're suffering in all of this, and I don't want to add to that. I want you to have a wonderful life not filled with such strife and turmoil."

The challenges of her life flashed before her eyes, and she came to a stop. "We don't often get what we want."

He jumped down from the treadmill and took her hands between his long warm fingers. "You've gone through so much already. And here I am, pretty much skating through life with very few issues. I actually feel guilty."

"Hey, don't." She had to work hard not to focus on the touch of his hands. "God has a plan for each of us. His plan for me is different than His plan for you."

"I don't know how you stay so positive, but I respect it. And you."

"Thank you," she said as she didn't know how else to respond.

She expected him to back away, but his gaze seemed to search even deeper, and his expression changed. Gone was the pity. Replaced by blatant interest in her. She warmed under the fire in his gaze. Loved it, in fact. Loved having someone show they cared for her.

He inched closer. Cupped the side of her cheek. His touch mesmerizing. "I want to kiss you."

She wanted that too. So much. But it wasn't a good idea. Not at all. It could go nowhere for either of them.

She opened her mouth to say no. Stopped. Let her emotions run free.

What was one kiss? Just one, and then she'd go back to her everyday existence.

That was what she wanted, right?

17

Natalie was going to say that she didn't want a kiss from him, and Drake didn't know how he was going to handle it. Sure, he didn't want to get involved in anything long-term, but he sure wanted to kiss her.

She stepped off the treadmill and inched closer. "Please. I want to kiss you too."

His mouth almost dropped open, but he caught himself and swooped in before she changed her mind. Her lips were warm and insistent, as if she'd been wanting this kiss for some time. He didn't know when he first thought about kissing her, but it didn't matter. It was all he wanted right now.

He circled his arms around her back and drew her closer. He couldn't get carried away, but he did deepen the kiss. She matched his passion, clinging to his neck and sliding her fingers into his hair. Holding his head fast.

He was vaguely aware of his phone buzzing in his pocket but ignored it. Nothing was more important than her right now. The buzzing stopped. Then started again.

Okay, it had to be critical.

He broke off the kiss and took a long breath. "My phone. It's ringing."

She backed away with such speed it was as if she was embarrassed at her response. At the kiss. He sure wasn't, not in the least. He liked her. A lot. She was everything he could want in a woman. So what if she wasn't the outdoorsy type? But man, she brought up emotions in him that he hadn't known existed.

She brushed a hand over her hair that he now knew was as soft as it looked as he grabbed his phone.

An alarm squealed from the back door just feet away from him. *Gentry.* Was Gentry trying to break in? To get to Natalie.

They were sitting ducks with a glass wall facing the hallway. The closet. He had to get her in the closet behind closed doors.

Now!

"What is it? What's happening?" she cried out.

"A breach at the back door. Come on." Drake grabbed her hand and tugged her into the storage closet. He joined her to call Pete to see if he'd seen an intruder on the security cameras and noted the missed calls were from him.

"We've had an attempted break-in," Pete said, sounding out of breath. "But he didn't breach the door. The building is still secure."

"Where is he now?" he asked Pete.

"Gone. I saw him on the monitor messing with the fingerprint reader. I asked for him to identify himself over the intercom and scared him off. I couldn't leave the front door unprotected so I couldn't pursue him, but caught him on another camera taking off in his car."

"Describe him."

"He wore a Spider-Man mask, so all I can give you is his

build. I'd say five-eleven about one-ninety. Caught a glimpse of his hands. Caucasian."

"Fits Gentry's build. Maybe he knew Natalie was here, and he was trying to get to her." Drake didn't like to think that was possible, but it was the most logical explanation. "Did you call it in?"

"Yeah. Got his plates. Vehicle's a white Toyota Camry."

"Can you get Nick to check out the print reader?" Nick was the Veritas Center's computer expert.

"Already on his way down. So are Piper, Reed, and Hunter. Figured we could do with some extra eyes down here."

Drake had never been more thankful for all the law enforcement officers living in the building. Piper, an FBI agent, was married to Nick, and Hunter, also an agent, was married to Maya, the toxicology and substances expert.

"I'm in the gym with Natalie. Will stay put until they clear the building, but I want security camera footage to review ASAP."

"I'll email it to you."

"Thanks, Pete. And thanks for acting before this guy made his way inside." Drake ended the call and shoved his phone into his pocket.

He turned to find Natalie with her arms wrapped around her stomach. He brought her up to speed on the situation, wishing he didn't have to tell her and could just whisk her upstairs to safety.

Her face paled. "Do you think it was Kirk?"

"He'd have to have connected you to us. Only way is through Malone, and if he discovered the connection to her, he could've been coming for her. In any event, if he knows about me, he could know about the cabin." Drake dug out his phone. "We need to find an alternate safe site with zero ties to any of us. Then move the kids."

"You really think moving them is necessary?"

"Better to be cautious and wrong than blow this off and someone gets hurt." He worked hard not to grimace. "I hate to split our focus right now, but I also need to protect my extended family. Everyone, including my brothers' significant others could be in danger."

She grabbed his hands. "Your whole family?"

"You know Gentry. Do you think he's the sort of guy who'd take one of them hostage if he thought he could get them to talk?"

"Yes. You're right. I'm sorry to bring this mess to your family."

"We can handle it," Drake said, trying to sound like he believed it.

But honestly, if Gentry made the connection to them, Drake wasn't sure they could protect everyone from a man who'd successfully escaped arrest after committing several heinous murders.

He dialed Aiden and instructed him to move everyone as soon as possible.

"Okay, we're out of here." Aiden remained calm.

"Make sure Mom rides with the kids. She'll keep them calm and know what to do if one of them freaks out at the quick departure."

"Got it."

"And don't call me back on this phone. I'll contact you via email."

"Roger that."

Drake hung up and looked at Natalie.

Her eyes were dark with worry. "Can Aiden get them out of there on time?"

He wanted to say yes. Of course. His brothers could do anything, but they weren't invincible. No one was. "We'll just have to pray that he does."

In the morning, Drake let the water from the shower beat down on his back, the sharp hot beads pinging against knots formed in solid ridges. He'd gotten very little sleep again, what with spending time emailing with his brothers as they found a new safe house. Natalie slept in his bedroom, and he'd taken the couch, a comfy piece of furniture and one he'd fallen asleep on dozens of times. Not last night. But then he hadn't had a woman in the other room who he couldn't get out of his brain. A woman he'd kissed. And a woman who was in danger. Serious danger.

He slammed a fist against the gray tiles. Thankfully, Hunter guarded the hallway. Probably not necessary, but Drake would rather be safe than sorry, and he didn't want to pull anyone off the kids' detail. They were compromised until they were moved. His brothers had found a place and were getting everyone ready to go now.

He shut off the shower and dried off to get ready for the day. By the time he got into the kitchen, Natalie was there, and the nutty scent of coffee filled the air. She'd put on her suit and heels again for the interviews. It really wasn't necessary, but she'd told him she felt more in charge when she was dressed right. He guessed it was a lingering feeling from her childhood, but he couldn't be sure.

She looked up from pouring the rich brown liquid into a mug. "Want some? I tried to make it strong."

"Please." He grabbed a mug and held it out. "You sleep okay?"

She tipped the pot over his cup. "I was surprised that I did, and I'm pumped about interviewing Faye. Maybe she'll turn out to be a good lead for us."

Drake nodded then blew on his coffee and took a sip. "Good."

She nodded. "Guess we're coffee compatible."

"Well, then. What else is there?" He laughed, loving how it felt to have her in his home first thing in the morning, no matter the circumstances. He glanced at his watch. "We have time for breakfast. I could rustle up some eggs and toast."

"That would be great." She slid onto a counter stool.

He scrambled the eggs, and they talked about the Gentry kids, the weather, his interest in sports, and anything other than Gentry. He liked it. Liked it a lot. Usually, he grabbed a large cup of coffee and a protein bar and ate it on the way to the office. Or to an op. But preparing a real breakfast settled his hyper ways. He actually felt calm even with the threat of danger lingering outside his door.

They finished breakfast and took off for the morning interview with Faye. The drive was made with companionable silence and bursts of small talk like a long-dating couple might experience. He was stoked over their compatibility even if it could lead nowhere.

They turned onto Faye's street, and Natalie faced him. "I've been thinking about what might stand in our way of finding Kirk."

"And did you come to a conclusion?" he asked though he'd much rather go back to small talk.

"I think the hardest thing is that he'll blend in with others, and it takes time before you know something's off about him. Even then, you can't name anything specific. It's just a gut feeling."

"Which is why he could get close enough to these women to kill and then interact in society where no one suspected him."

She crossed her legs. "Of course, once you know he's a serial killer, it all makes more sense."

"I really wish you'd never met him. That you didn't have

to meet the people you do on a regular basis." He took her hand. "I've never felt this way before, but I want to protect you from everything bad in this world and make up for the rough things you faced in your childhood."

She blinked a few times, opened her mouth then closed it.

"That's okay. You don't have to say anything," he said. "I know you don't want a relationship. And honestly, I don't either. But if I did..." He shrugged.

"Yeah, me too," she said. "And don't worry about making up for the way I grew up. I know God has a plan, and I am who I am today as a result of it."

"Then His plan was flawless because you're an amazing woman." Drake kept his focus pinned to her and was likely transmitting all the crazy unexplained feelings he was having for her in one look.

She blushed, the red starting at her neck rushing over her face, and she gently eased her hand free. "We should stick to finding Kirk."

"Yeah," he said. "I know his kids are better off without him, but I hate the thought of them being split up." That was as close to work as he wanted to go with all these emotions swimming in his gut.

"Unfortunately, that's probably what's going to happen."

Her matter-of-fact response made him mad. "No. I won't let them be split up. I'll find a way to stop it."

"How on earth are you going to do that?"

"I don't know, but I promise I will." He clamped his mouth closed before he promised something else he couldn't deliver. But something about this woman made him want to promise her the moon and sun and stars and everything in between.

∼

Outside Faye's place, Natalie unbuckled her seat belt and looked at Drake who was drawing his weapon to pop out the thing that held the bullets and looked at it for a long moment.

"You like guns?" she asked, trying not to let him know how uneasy she was around weapons.

"My passion, you might say."

"Do you always carry a gun?"

"I do." He locked gazes. "Does that bother you?"

"I don't know anything about them, but I wonder how I might feel if I were married and had children." There she went talking children again. Maybe he wouldn't notice. Of course he'd notice. It wasn't like he was particularly skilled at observation or anything.

"You've been mentioning children a lot lately," he said.

Yep. He didn't miss a thing.

"I guess having responsibility for the kids is making me more conscious of what it would be like to have them in my life." *And maybe my growing feelings for you is making me wonder what having* your *child might be like.*

"I can see that. I've kind of been thinking the same thing."

She had to work hard not to gape at his response, and she didn't know how to reply so she quickly returned to the safe topic of guns. "So, what would you do with your guns if you had children?"

"Hmm." He stowed the gun in his holster. "I'd have to really think about that. I not only carry, but I keep one in the pipe at all times, and living alone, I don't use a gun safe for my every day carry."

"What does that mean exactly?" She listened to the birds chirping in nearby trees as she waited for him to answer.

"A bullet in the chamber. So in the event of an emergency, I'm locked and loaded. I mean, if you're going to carry a weapon, you gotta carry hot. Makes no sense to carry when the gun's not ready to go."

"Sounds like some people don't do that."

"A lot of them don't. They're afraid the gun's going to go off. But it won't, not in the holster."

She believed him but... "No accidental discharge then."

"Oh, that happens but not with the gun resting in its holster." His expression and tone grew animated. "Think about a gun like a TV remote control. A remote does nothing lying on your table. You have to do something to make it work. Same thing with a gun. So if you're uncomfortable with carrying one in the pipe, that means you've just got to train more."

"Makes sense, but then I've never even touched one, so you could tell me anything about guns, and I'd believe it."

"Maybe we need to change that. Get you out to a shooting range."

She didn't even need to think about that while the children remained in danger. She shook her head. "I'd fall under the uncomfortable group."

"Not after I gave you the right training. I promise you'd change your mind." He watched her for a long moment. "I hope never to use my gun, but we need to be sure we can protect our clients. Especially when they're being stalked by a crazy person."

"Like when you protected the skier, Harper Young. She had a stalker."

He flashed her a look, his eyes wide. "You heard about that?"

"You're not the only ones who can do some research."

"Touché." He grinned then opened his door.

Natalie joined him, and they made their way to the high-rise apartment building where Faye Babcock lived on the first floor. The building was sleek with an all glass exterior and the sun glistened from the glass. Still, the place looked cold to Natalie, but she didn't comment as they approached the door and knocked.

When the door opened and the scent of buttery popcorn drifted out, Natalie explained the purpose for their visit.

Faye peered out at them and scratched a thick head of inky black hair. "I told you before. I didn't really know Laura all that well."

"Please." Natalie firmed her stance. "We really need to talk to you."

"I don't know." Faye ran a hand over her face. "I told you everything I know last time I talked to you, and I'm kinda beat. Was a tough shift."

"It'll just take a minute." Natalie tried her hardest not to sound like she was desperate, but if she had to beg to find her sister's killer then she would.

"Okay. But just for a minute." She stepped back, and her purple clogs squeaked on the tiled floor.

Natalie hurried past Faye into the small living room before the woman changed her mind. Drake's footfalls sounded right behind her. The door banged closed, and Faye joined them.

"Go ahead and take a seat." Faye rubbed her shoulder, wrinkling the blue patterned uniform top. Faye was very down to earth. Very Oregonian in her appearance. Hair natural. Clean skin. No makeup. Earthy.

Natalie settled on the soft beige couch, and Drake sat next to her.

Faye kicked off her clogs, dropped to the carpeted floor and drew her legs in to lean on the bright blue uniform pants. The coffee table next to her held a large bowl of popcorn that looked like it was going to serve as her breakfast.

"You were the one who found Laura," Natalie stated, hoping to get the conversation started.

"Yeah." Faye clenched her hands and tipped her head to the left. "Bedroom's over there. She didn't get up for work that day. I wondered what was wrong, so I knocked on her door. She didn't answer. Normally I didn't bug her 'cause we weren't friends or anything, but something told me to check on her. Found her on the bed. Blood everywhere. Multiple stab wounds to the chest."

Natalie cast Faye a sympathetic look. "That must've been hard."

"I work in the ER, so I've seen worse."

"Where did Laura work?" Drake asked.

"She'd just started as a makeup consultant at a department store. Not sure which one." Faye shook her head. "It's weird that she worked at all. Her family's loaded. They're the Zimmer behind the Zimmer Corp. Ever heard of them?"

"Real estate mogul, right?" Drake asked. "The one who bought nearly a ton of coastal properties and rents them out for a fortune."

Faye nodded.

"Maybe they didn't support her," Drake said.

"Yeah, maybe. I don't know. She paid the rent on time, and that was all I cared about."

"How long did you live together?" Natalie asked.

"Only three months."

"Do you have any idea who might've wanted to kill her?" Drake asked.

Faye shook her head. "Like I said, I didn't know much about her. We lived together but didn't socialize at all. Neither of us was looking for a friend. Just shared accommodations. Plus we worked opposite shifts. She'd be heading to work when I got home."

Natalie glanced at the door. "Wasn't it hard to stay here after she was murdered?"

"A little bit. But I have a lease, and the landlord said he wouldn't be able to rent it out so I was on the hook for the money for the rest of the lease. I don't have that kind of extra cash. Plus he offered me half price rent if I would stay. Said it was better than leaving the place empty." She picked at a hangnail on her finger. "So I agreed and just pretend that room doesn't exist."

"And you're not afraid this killer will come back?" Natalie asked.

"The police said they usually didn't return to the same place, and that the crime was so violent it was likely personally motivated."

"Did Laura's family pick up her things?" Drake asked.

Faye shook her head. "They said to get rid of it. But I figured they might change their minds so I boxed it all up and left it in the room."

"Can we take a look at it?" Drake asked.

"I suppose." She jumped up, grabbed up a handful of popcorn, and padded in her stocking feet to the bedroom door, tossing kernels in her mouth as she moved. She paused for a moment and made the sign of a cross over her chest, the first indicator that Laura's death might have impacted her.

She pushed the door open and swallowed her bite before stepping in. "I got rid of the bloody mattress."

A queen-sized box spring sat in the middle of the room on a steel frame without a headboard. A small white nightstand that looked like an inexpensive flatpack piece of furniture sat next to the bed. It held a silver lamp with a gray shade. Faye had put three cardboard boxes on the box spring and stacked the bedding next to it.

"As you can see, she didn't have much." Faye swept her arm out to encompass the room. "Something else I found odd when she came from money."

"Maybe the police took some of it for evidence," Drake suggested.

"They took her phone and computer. The only electronics they left were a webcam and microphone, but I don't remember them taking much else."

"Can we look in the boxes?" Drake asked.

"Sure." Faye opened the top box. "This one is mostly makeup. Cosmetics and clothing were the only things she spent money on."

Natalie looked into the box. "Wow, she really did like makeup."

"She was always perfectly put together. Makeup, hair, and clothes. A fashion icon at all times. I met her family once. They're very pretentious. Figured she got that from them, though she seemed a little bit more down to earth than they did."

Natalie pointed at a lipstick tube. "Dion Holistic. That's a pretty pricey brand."

"You're familiar with it?" Faye asked. "Laura was always getting packages from them so I asked about it. She said it was an invitation only makeup club of some sort and only members could buy their products."

"My sister used Dion too," Natalie said, thinking of all the money her sister threw away on the latest and greatest makeup products when they came out from the many cosmetic companies.

"A waste of time and money as far as I'm concerned," Faye said. "So opposite of me. Never touch the stuff. Give me an all-natural shampoo, conditioner, and deodorant, and

I'm good to go. Either a guy likes me for who I am or he doesn't. Guess since I'm still single at my age, they don't." Faye huffed a laugh and set the makeup box aside to open the next one. "The last few boxes are all clothing. Designer and pricey. I saw a lot of Nordstrom and Macy's bags come in the door."

"How could she afford these items on a sales associate salary?" Drake asked.

"Family money, maybe," Faye said.

Natalie gave that some thought. "If they were supporting her, I wonder if they expected her to work."

"Yeah, I never understood what was going on there, and she never talked about it."

"You discussed makeup but not her job," Drake said, mimicking Natalie's thoughts.

"I handed her a package from Dion on the way out to work one day. She offered the info. I didn't ask."

Natalie still didn't understand their relationship, but Faye acted sincere so Natalie let it go. "When you met the family, did they seem to get along or was the relationship strained?"

"Hmm, well." She tapped her chin. "I didn't pick up on any tension, and she seemed close with her mother."

"Do you have their phone number or address?" Natalie asked. "I'd like to get their take on things."

"Let me get it." Faye rushed from the room as if glad to be leaving.

Natalie looked at Drake. "What do you make of all of this?"

"It's all very odd," he said. "Laura lived in a modest apartment with a roommate. Worked in a department store. Yet, had access to money for designer clothes and pricey makeup. Raises all kinds of red flags for me, but I don't know what they are. Good idea, talking to the parents."

They stepped from the room in time to find Faye leaving her kitchen with a bright pink sticky note. "Here's their info. I hope you or the police find the guy who did this."

"We will," Natalie said at the front door, trying to sound confident. "You can be sure of that."

18

Drake eyed the three-story contemporary house, an oddity in an area of quaint bungalows. The newer contemporary box-like place had a glass wall facing the beach, and the corners consisted of exposed steel girders. There would be magnificent city views from here for sure. It was the kind of house Drake liked, but he suspected the neighbors didn't much appreciate having such a tall structure built in their neighborhood.

He glanced at Natalie. "Ready?"

She gave a reluctant nod and took a fortifying breath. "It's not going to be easy questioning them. Not with the pain of their loss. I know it firsthand and how hard it'll be for them. Especially since she only died a few months ago."

He didn't know the pain, and didn't want to mess up and make it worse for the family. "If I do or say something insensitive, go ahead and call me on it."

"You sure?"

"Yeah. I don't want to add to their pain, and I'll try to be diplomatic." He glanced around. "We weren't followed, and the possibility of Gentry showing up is next to nil, but not impossible. So stick close to me."

She nodded, and he noted the hint of fear his warning had put in her eyes. He'd rather do just about anything, even his brothers' laundry for a month, than scare her, but she had to know that the risks existed here even if they were slim.

They hurried up the huge pavers mixed with gray river rock to the front door of frosted glass. He rang the doorbell and stepped back. He hadn't wanted to give the parents a chance to say no to the interview, so hadn't called ahead for an appointment. Might mean Drake would get a door slammed in his face. Wouldn't be the first time and he doubted it would be the last.

A tall slender man who resembled Laura Zimmer answered the door, his cool blue eyes narrowed. "Can I help you?"

"Stefan Zimmer?" Drake asked, just to be sure.

Those blue eyes iced over. "Yes."

"I'm Drake Byrd of Nighthawk Security, and this is Natalie Dunn, a Multnomah County social worker." Drake handed him a business card, paused to let that information register, and wished he had law enforcement backing to help him persuade this man to cooperate.

A grimace formed on the man's face. Okay. Fail. The news didn't sit well with him.

He tightened his eyes and tapped the card on his other hand. "What's this about?"

"We hoped to ask you a few questions about Laura's death," Natalie said.

A flash of pain sharpened his eyes as he shoved the business card into the pocket of his designer jeans. "I have nothing to say to you."

"Please," Natalie said.

He started to close the door.

Drake shoved his foot in the way, earning a glare that

Drake imagined had been used in many a contentious real estate deal.

"I lost my sister to the same killer." Natalie stepped close and peered up at Zimmer. His expression softened a fraction. "We're following up on leads, and if we could just have a few minutes of your time."

He hesitated, and Drake gently pressed his foot on the door, subconsciously encouraging the man to fully open it.

He did and stepped back. "A few minutes is all."

"Is your wife here?" Drake asked as he followed Natalie into a foyer with polished concrete floors and a floating staircase encased in glass.

"No, and I'm glad she's not. Wouldn't want her to have to rehash things." He gestured toward the back of the house, another wall of glass but with sliding doors that ran the width of the room. "Straight ahead to the family room."

They passed under a second-story landing, the wall also glass, and into a two-story room that held a soaring fireplace covered by huge marble slabs. They'd grouped contemporary leather furniture in the middle of the room. White and pristine, the leather was well cared for, hardly used, or both.

Natalie sat on a sofa, and Drake perched on the arm next to her. Zimmer took a seat in a sleek chair with shiny chrome arms across from them. He locked his focus on Natalie. "I'm sorry to hear about your sister."

"She was his first victim. Four years ago now." Natalie drew in a deep breath and clutched her hands in her lap. "The loss still hurts like it happened yesterday."

"I get that. Believe me." The real estate mogul had to be used to wheeling and dealing with other big players in the business, but right now, his eyes looked haunted. He swallowed and masked the expression. "So what can I tell you that I haven't already told the police?"

"We were hoping you might shed some light on why

Laura worked and shared an apartment when she seemed to have family money at her disposal," Drake said. "Seems like she could easily have had a nicer place to herself and not worked an hourly wage job."

A smile flashed on his face. "She was going through a phase. Consciousness raising, I guess she called it. She wanted to find out how the *real* people lived." He frowned. "And man did she. Especially with that weasel Owen Odell."

He clenched his hands on his knees next to purposely placed holes in his jeans. "He scammed her. A bunch of other women who came forward too, all who trusted him, and he emptied their bank accounts. He was arrested with a large quantity of cash in his apartment. I don't mind telling you I was glad to see that lowlife go to prison."

"Please," Natalie said. "Tell us more. This wasn't in her file."

"Not sure why. With Odell behind bars, he couldn't have killed her, so the detective didn't really seem interested when I mentioned him."

"What can you tell us about him?" Drake asked as every bit of information could be important.

"Young pup. Good-looking. Charismatic. Preyed on naïve young women and got them to hand over their money." Zimmer gritted his teeth.

"Naïve?" Drake asked.

"I get what you're thinking." Zimmer's expression hardened. "You figure since Laura came from money that she was spoiled. Ran free. Did drugs and hung with the wrong crowd. The typical stereotype you see on TV. But you'd be wrong. We raised her right. Gave her a simple life and made sure she didn't hang with those kinds of kids. So yeah. She was naïve to most of the things that go on in the world today. Her only vices were clothes and makeup. She loved to look good. But yeah, she was naïve in so many ways. Out in the world for the first time. And this guy got his hooks into her."

His hands curled into fists. "I could see right through him. Tried to pay him off. It put a rift between us until she saw his true colors. Then she wanted us to help. And we did. Brought in the police. We wanted her to move home. She wouldn't, so we got her to move and not give out her address to anyone. She moved in with another woman for a little safety. You know the old saying, safety in numbers. She was shell-shocked by then and started keeping to herself. I hated seeing her withdraw like that and wanted the guy to pay. So I worked behind the scenes to get the police looking into the creep, and he was brought to justice."

"How long ago was this?"

Zimmer tapped his long index finger on his knee. "Going on four months now. Her pain and struggle with this guy put him behind bars for years."

"That's what I'm trying to do too," Natalie said. "The monster who killed her and my sister should be locked up forever."

"Wouldn't disagree with you."

"Do you know where Odell's incarcerated?" Drake asked.

"Oregon State Correctional Institution. Salem."

"Do you have any idea who might've wanted to kill your daughter?"

"I was thinking it was his buddy. Odell called the guy Ziggy. Don't know his real name. He showed up at her trial, all angry and blowing smoke at Laura to try to get her to recant her story. But the detective said he had an alibi for her time of death, and he had zero connection to the other victims."

"Do you know the name Kirk Gentry?" Drake asked.

Zimmer tilted his head then shook it. "Don't believe I do. Why? He a suspect?"

"A lead we're developing." Drake had to downplay the lead. The last thing they needed was for this guy to go off on his own looking for Gentry or put a PI on it and get them both killed. "Is there anything else you could share that might help us find out who killed Laura?"

He shook his head. "I hired a PI to work the investigation. He followed up on all of this, on Ziggy and the other leads the police ruled out. Didn't find a thing. And nothing about this Gentry guy you mentioned. Maybe I should have my PI dig into him."

"I wouldn't do that, sir," Drake said. "My firm is working on it, and you can be assured we won't miss a thing."

"How can I be sure of that when I've never heard of you?"

"They're top-notch," Natalie said. "Five brothers. All former law enforcement. They office out of the Veritas Center in Portland."

"Now them I've heard of." Zimmer studied Drake. "Any affiliation?"

"My sister is the trace evidence expert."

He gave a sharp nod and stood. "Then if you'll excuse me, I'll let you get back to finding this killer."

He didn't wait for them to accept his pronounced end to the interview but headed for the door at a fast clip. Drake gestured for Natalie to go ahead of him and followed them both to the door.

On the stoop, Drake turned and offered his hand. "Thanks for talking to us, Mr. Zimmer. I know it's difficult."

"You don't know the half of it until you lose someone." He shook Natalie's hand, and a connection passed between them. A horrible connection to have with anyone.

~

Natalie rarely visited prisons. If her adult client was incarcerated in prison, she couldn't help them. They'd already been sentenced and would be serving their time. She saw some in jail where they awaited trial. She did sometimes visit prisons to talk with family members of her clients, something she might have to do when Kirk was incarcerated if she wanted to arrange adoptions for the children.

Sitting across a table from Gentry and holding a civilized conversation. Imagine that? No. she couldn't. He'd be locked up, likely for the rest of his life, but he wouldn't change. Despite being incarcerated, that smug, superior look would still be etched on his face. He would somehow make every conversation all about him.

She shuddered and followed Drake and the deputy down a damp concrete hallway. A combination of body odor and whatever meal they'd eaten that day filled the air. Not pleasant, and she had to resist plugging her nose.

He pulled open a door labeled *Visitors* and stood back. "Have a seat while I get Odell."

She settled on one of the metal stools affixed to the concrete floor.

Drake sat on a stool next to her, his long leg brushing hers. "Place is clean, but man it stinks."

"I'm glad I'm not the only one who can smell it." She wrinkled her nose. "Not that I'm glad you get to suffer too, but glad that I'm not imagining it."

"Let's just hope Odell isn't the inmate who's stinking the place up."

"Agreed."

They fell silent. Not a comfortable silence. Seemed neither one of them knew what to say to each other in the strange surroundings. A prison definitely wasn't the place to have a personal conversation. Besides, as their interest in one another was growing, she was avoiding those talks at all costs. She focused her thoughts on the background report Eric had pulled together on Odell so she was ready for the interview.

Thankfully, footsteps sounded in the hallway, and the deputy led in a tall, lanky guy with a thick head of curly blond hair and a freckled face. He moved awkwardly, but was a good-looking guy. If he had any kind of game with women, Natalie could see how he could get them to fall for him.

He dropped onto a stool and glared. "Didn't ask to see you, whoever the heck you are."

The deputy chained Odell's cuffs to the table and glared at him for a long moment before turning his attention to Natalie and Drake. "I'll be right outside."

The door closed, and Natalie didn't waste any time. "I'm social worker Natalie Dunn." She hoped a title of any kind might gain her some standing with this guy. "And this is Drake Byrd of Nighthawk Security."

Odell tried to cross his arms, but his chain wasn't long enough, and he lowered his arms. "What do you want?"

"To talk to you about the reason you're in here," Natalie said.

"Ain't no good reason I'm here." He jutted out a narrow chin. "Didn't do what those witches accused me of, and I'm gonna go free as soon as soon as my appeal is heard."

"Tell me your side of things, then," Natalie said. "Because what we've been told is that you made a habit of dating young women and suddenly their bank accounts were emptied."

"Didn't do what they say. Sure, I mighta let some chicks pay my way for a while. What guy doesn't these days? I mean it's equal opportunity for women. But it's not a crime."

"Why would Laura Zimmer rat you out, then?" Drake asked. "Not to mention the other women who came forward."

"She was mad I dumped her. They all were." A cocky smile slid across his face, and he locked his focus on Natalie. "I mean, you wouldn't say no to this, right?"

That grin widened, and she scowled at him.

His smile evaporated. "But still. Calling the cops? That's just nutso."

He lied well. Seamlessly even, and Natalie got how women believed him, but she doubted it would take long to see through him.

He leaned forward, and his eyes held an ugliness he'd hidden so far. "Sure, I mighta let them pay the way, but I never told 'em I'd do anything different. They got what I advertised. Me. That's what they really wanted. Me. I'm all they *could* need." He sat back, that satisfied smile on his thin lips again.

"You're delusional," Natalie said, trying hard not to lose her temper. "These women trusted you. And you not only took advantage of their kindness to pay for dates, but then you stole all their money."

He shrugged. "Like I said. I don't know what you're talking about."

Natalie gripped her knees under the table. "Did you work at all?"

"Sometimes."

"Doing what?"

"I'm in IT."

Kirk was a police officer focusing on IT too. Could there be a connection? "You had no legal employment and were found with a large supply of cash in your apartment."

A grin tipped the corner of his mouth, but he clamped down on his lips and erased it.

"If you didn't steal money from these women, where did it come from?" she asked.

"This and that." A snide look found its way to his face.

Natalie's anger flared higher, and she had to swallow before she could speak again.

"Tell us about your buddy, Ziggy," Drake said. She was thankful he'd jumped into the conversation. She was only making a mess of it.

"What about him?" Odell asked, losing a bit of his bravado.

"His real name for starters."

"Why would I tell you that?"

"Because you have the tiniest shred of decency in you," Natalie stated.

"You must be thinking of someone else."

"Was Ziggy involved in your schemes?" Drake asked.

"What scheme is that?"

Drake leaned across the table, his iron-filled gaze threatening, and Odell jerked back.

"Nah." The man's voice had lost some of its confidence. "He really doesn't have the looks or charm to get the ladies. Not that I did anything wrong with them."

Drake sat back, but his jaw was clenched tight. "Do you know a man named Kirk Gentry?"

"Nah. Should I?"

"He's in the same profession as you," Drake said, sounding disgusted.

"Which does he do? This or that?" Odell laughed.

Natalie's anger reached boiling point and she wanted to get away from this jerk, but they hadn't asked questions about Laura. "You dated Laura Zimmer."

"So?" Odell shifted in his chair and held out his fingers to study them. "That's not a crime too, is it?"

"I assume you know she was murdered," Drake said.

"Yeah, so what? You gonna try to do me for that too? 'Cause I was in here when she died."

"We wanted to ask if you have any idea who might've killed her," Natalie said.

"Nah. She was an okay chick. Not spoiled and bratty like a lot of the ones who came from money. Can't imagine anyone was out to get her. Unless it was one of her crazy viewers."

"Viewers?" Natalie and Drake asked at the same time.

"Yeah, man, she had this makeup and fashion channel online. Not like she had many viewers. She was a true wannabe and a has-been before she ever got started." He laughed.

Drake glared at the guy. "Have some respect. We're talking about a murdered woman here."

Odell's smile evaporated, but the cocky expression remained.

"The channel couldn't be under her name or the investigators would have located it," Natalie said. *As would Drake and his brothers.*

"Not in her name. She used a one-word name like Rihanna or Pink. Not that anyone had a clue who she was, and it was kinda funny. She didn't know that everyone was laughing at her. Sad in a way."

Natalie tightened the grip on her knees. "What was the name she went by?"

He angled his head, and his eyes narrowed. "Honestly? I don't remember."

"Well, think." Natalie finally snapped and slammed a fist on the table.

"Okay, okay. Don't make me get the guard to protect me." He sat back, and that snide grin returned.

Natalie had worked with all kinds in her line of work, but never had she been this frustrated. They needed information he might possess to find Kirk, but this guy hadn't cooperated in the least.

"I think it mighta started with an O like my name." He tapped his chin. "Or maybe I just like O. Or I'm thinking of Oprah." He bent down to scratch his jaw. "Anything else I can help you with?"

She shared a look with Drake, who gave a sharp nod. He knew as well as she did that they weren't going to get a straight answer, and they were wasting their time.

Natalie stood and took one long last look at the creep, sitting there in his prison garb, pretending like being locked up didn't bother him. But once she looked past the snide and cocky appearance he'd thrown in their faces, she glimpsed an underlying unease and maybe even fear.

The report Erik created said he'd had a difficult childhood with a drug addicted mother. He'd likely become who he was because of his upbringing. She imagined him as the scared little boy sitting in a low-rent apartment or even a motel room, car, or abandoned building, hungry and watching his mother shoot into her veins the drug she'd spent their money on instead of food. Instead of a decent apartment or clothing. Or any other need he might've had.

Sure, some people overcame difficult childhoods. She'd succeeded, but many didn't. Odell was a prime example of that. If he didn't overturn his conviction on appeal, she hoped he got the help he needed to come out a reformed man. And she especially hoped he didn't emerge from this place as one of the many who became even more depraved while locked up.

19

In the Nighthawk Security office at their long conference table, Erik described the new safe house location to Drake and Natalie. So far Drake approved. From their father's days at PPB, he knew of an old lodge out in the middle of nowhere. The owners rented the former resort to groups, and PPB had used it for getaway weekends. He was more than willing to rent it to the Byrd's for a few days.

"So there's plenty of room for everyone and no connection to us." Erik grabbed a handful of peanut M&Ms from a bowl on the table, and sat back, looking pleased with himself.

"What about the ability to set up an early warning situation?" Drake asked.

"It has a private drive, so we have someone stationed at the road just like at the cabin."

"Good. Good." Drake gave his brother a fist bump.

"How are the children doing with the change?" Natalie asked.

Erik crunched his candy then swallowed to face Natalie. "Sadie and Logan are doing good. Mom's keeping them busy. Willow is still sulking. Keeps asking when Drake will be back."

Natalie looked at Drake. "You made a friend."

"We connected, but honestly, I think it was a fluke." Drake shifted his focus to his brother. "Now tell me why you're here."

"I did everything I could to find internet videos for Tracey and a video channel for Laura. Thought maybe the information about the makeup channel from Odell and Tracey's videos might connect the two of them. Then in turn link her to Gentry."

"I was thinking the same thing," Drake said. "So what did you find?"

"Nada." Erik looked at his hand as he turned the colorful M&M's. "But my gut says there's something there. So I asked Nick to work his magic for us. Do a more detailed search. He's swamped and can't do it right away, but he agreed to show me how to dig deeper. We're meeting in an hour."

"Good work." Drake was about to elaborate on his praise for his little brother taking initiative when the office phone rang. The blinking light indicated an internal call.

"It's Sierra." He stabbed the button to put her on speaker. "Hey, sis. Baby coming?"

"No!" she said emphatically. "It's the FBI. They're in the lobby demanding that I turn over the blouse."

Great. Just great. The last thing Drake needed was more bad news. Was it too much to ask for a break?

He gripped the receiver as tightly as he could to keep from snapping at his sister. The FBI being here wasn't her fault.

And not a surprise to Drake. "We knew this might happen."

"I know, but I'm not finished, and I don't want to hand it

over." Sierra's breath came in a long sigh over the speaker. "What do you want me to do?"

"Hang tight. I'll be right down and we can talk about it." He hung up and focused on Natalie. "You can stay here with Erik or come with me."

"With you," Natalie said.

Erik popped a green candy in his mouth and chewed. "If you decide to grab some dinner, I'd be all over that."

"You got it." Drake opened the door for Natalie.

Drake looked at Natalie. "It's only two floors. Stairs okay?"

She stood. "Moving sounds good after all the time we spent sitting today."

"Then let's move." Drake quickly led her to the other tower then pressed the fingerprint reader outside the stairwell, and they started down to the second floor. He could easily imagine the FBI chomping at the bit in the lobby, trying to bully the sweet receptionist, Lily. She might be sweet, but she knew how to hold her own and how to keep law enforcement officers at bay. They frequently stopped by thinking a visit would get their results faster, and she sent them packing.

As Drake jogged down the steps, his mind ran over possible ways they could keep the blouse here until Sierra finished her work. But when he opened the door to her lab, he hadn't come up with a good answer. He'd barely noticed Natalie behind him so he paused to refocus. Her safety still had to be top priority, even in a secure building.

He opened the door, and they hurried to the lab.

At the door, she looked at him. "What are you going to tell Sierra to do?"

He pressed his fingers on the reader. "No idea. Except not turn it over."

They entered the lab where Sierra's assistant and two

techs were working at tables to the left. Though they had state-of-the-art filtering systems, the usual chemical odor filled the air. Straight ahead, Sierra was leaning over a stainless steel table covered with white paper. Tracey's blouse with a blood stain the size of a small fist lay spread out in front of Sierra.

She glanced up. "Good. I'm glad you came right down. Go ahead and have a seat, Natalie, while we work this out."

"Thanks." Natalie slipped onto a nearby stool. "Let me know if there's anything I can do to help."

"Pray for a miracle." Sierra wrinkled her nose and changed her focus to Drake. "What do you want me to do?"

She wasn't going to like his answer, but it was the best he had. "Tell them it's missing."

"Right." She rolled her eyes. "Like I would ever tell the FBI that we lost evidence. Would do wonders for our reputation. Besides, you know I won't lie."

"Yeah, I know." Drake shoved his hands into his pockets. "Well, then...then...refuse to give it to them."

She sat on a stool and rubbed her back. "You know I can't refuse the FBI."

"Sure you can," he said with as much enthusiasm as he could muster. "They didn't submit the evidence to you, so they have no right to take it. Unless they have a warrant, which I doubt."

"Technically you're right." She shifted on the stool as if getting comfortable at this state of pregnancy wasn't easy. "But we all know they're working a joint investigation with PPB."

He didn't want to argue, but... "The evidence was submitted under an investigation unrelated to the task force. I assume PPB still has it classified as such. So you *do* actually have the right to refuse them."

"Okay." She pushed off the stool. "I'll try that, but you

come stand by the door and keep it cracked open. Give me three minutes and then tell me you need my attention. It's not a lie. You do need me to get back to the blouse."

"Okay. That I can do."

"Chad," she called out to her assistant. "I'm stepping out for a moment but leaving Natalie here. She's all yours."

Sierra marched off. Or more accurately, lumbered off, and Drake trailed after her.

She glanced over her shoulder. "And you better hope this doesn't come back to bite us or Reed."

"He's tough. He can handle it." At least Drake hoped so. Politics ran deep in law enforcement agencies, and the FBI wasn't any different.

She called Lily on the way to the elevator and told her she would talk to the agent outside the door on the first floor.

"So how are things going?" she asked in the elevator.

"Not much progress, but everyone's safe, so that's a big win."

She nodded. "And you and Natalie. How's that progressing?"

"Come on now," he said. "You did not pick up on vibes between us in that short visit to the lab."

"The matchmaking is strong in the Byrd females." She chuckled as she leaned against the back wall.

"Then thank goodness you're having a boy." He smiled.

"I hope anyway." She cupped her belly. "Not that it's not a boy, but that I'm having him soon."

He took a good look at her. "You look uncomfortable. I can't even imagine. I mean you're growing a human. How cool is that?"

"Way cool." She smiled, a dreamy kind that he'd only seen when she looked at Reed.

What would Natalie look like pregnant with his child?

Man, oh, man. Where did that come from? Seriously, he was way out of his element here.

"I knew it!" Sierra pushed off the wall. "You're thinking about Natalie, and you have a thing for her. Your look just told me."

"You cannot possibly know I was thinking about her."

"No, but you just told me." The doors opened, and she gave him a playful grin.

"Showtime." She stepped into the hallway and to the lobby door.

He held it open far enough so he could see her and the agent and hear how she handled him, but not be seen by the agent.

"Sierra Rice," she said. "What can I do for you?"

"Special Agent Ewing." He flashed credentials. "I'm here to collect evidence from the Gentry missing person's investigation."

"Sorry, what investigation?" Sierra had participated in community drama when in high school, and she actually sounded like she hadn't a clue what he was requesting.

"Come on, now, Mrs. Rice." He shoved his creds into a sleek suit pocket. "You know what I'm talking about."

"We process evidence for many law enforcement agencies, so I don't know the details of every investigation we're working." She clamped her hands on her lower back. "But now that I think about it, I don't know of any evidence we're currently handling for the FBI."

Ewing didn't stand a chance with Sierra. Drake had seen her in action as a teenager and already knew she was a master at telling the truth but still being very evasive.

Ewing widened his stance. "The evidence was submitted by Detective Archibald at PPB."

"Detective Archibald. Yeah sure. I know him. We've handled evidence for him in the past. But if what you're looking for was submitted by him, I'll need a transmittal form to return it to him. He has an account and can complete the form online." She turned to leave.

"Come on now, Mrs. Rice." His sharp tone had her looking back. "That's all going to take some time, and this evidence is top priority for our investigation."

"You're working this missing person's investigation now?" she asked.

"We are. Now will you retrieve the evidence, or do I need to go over your head?"

"Sierra," Drake called out. "I need you in the lab. Now."

"Gotta go," Sierra said. "Give me your card. I'll look up the information and get back to you."

"I'm not going anywhere." He glared at her. "I'll wait right here."

"Then I'll get back to you within the hour."

He flashed a card, but as she reached out for it, he held on to the end. "Seems to me you're stalling. You haven't lost the evidence, have you?"

She stood straight, her back up. "Never. Our evidence is secure and tracked. In fact, we recently started using RFID tags to monitor every item."

"Radio frequency identification," the guy said, sounding impressed. "Then you should be able to locate it immediately."

"I'll do my best. Now I really must go." She pulled the card from his fingers.

Drake held the door for her, and she marched through the opening.

In the elevator, she got out a small box of raisins from her lab coat. "You are *so* going to owe me, little brother."

"You handled him really well."

"Yeah, well, we'll see how I handle it when he gets mad in an hour and insists on seeing me again." She stabbed the fourth floor button and leaned back to open the box. "I wouldn't put it past this guy or his supervisor to call Reed to put pressure on me."

"And will Reed do that?"

"He'll have my back, but he's going to ask about it, and I won't lie to him or sidestep."

"I wouldn't expect you to."

"Wouldn't you?" She sighed and popped a few raisins in her mouth "No. That's not fair. You wouldn't. I'm just confusing you with every officer out there who wants something and will go to any lengths to get it."

"Guess that's what I just did," he admitted. "There's just so much at stake here."

"As there is for most every investigation we work on," she said. "We don't work the basic breaking-and-entering cases, but we take on murder and other major crimes."

"Yeah, I know, and I'm pushing you on this. Sorry."

She waved a hand as she swallowed. "I'll do whatever I can within reason to help you." A cute grin crossed her face. "Besides, I'll always have bragging rights that I helped bring The Clipper to justice."

"You are the best sister ever." He scooped her into a hug.

"Don't I know it."

The doors opened, and she waddled down the hall to her lab, tossing raisins in her mouth on the way. The moment she stepped inside, she tossed the raisin box and clapped her hands. "Okay, everyone. Join me at my table. We have less than an hour to finish processing this blouse, and it's at least four hours of work. So let's get moving."

"How is that even possible?" Drake trailed behind her and gave Natalie a smile as he passed her.

Sierra stepped behind her table. "We pull out our lab-on-a-chip and give it the best test it's had yet."

"Lab-on-a-chip?" Natalie asked.

Sierra slipped on gloves with practiced ease. "A microfluidic device we're testing for the manufacturers."

"Oh, right, that explains it." Drake rolled his eyes.

Sierra pulled a box out from under the table. "I don't have time for a detailed explanation, but think pregnancy test. We load a sample into the device and get a yes or no. *No* means move on. *Yes,* means human DNA is present and will be great for profiling."

"And that means, you can finish the blouse before the agent gets too cranky?" Drake asked.

Sierra looked up and smiled. "That's my plan, and we should soon know if there's DNA other than Tracey Gentry's on her blouse. If so, I'll get it down to Emory to process." Sierra looked at Natalie. "She's our DNA expert."

"How long before she'll have results?" Drake asked.

"She could better tell you, but a minimum of twenty-four hours."

"I was hoping you'd say sooner than that," Drake said. "But I know you're doing this as fast as possible."

Drake moved back to Natalie's location to watch Sierra work for a minute.

"This is exciting and boring at the same time," she whispered.

He laughed, the sound bouncing off the high ceiling.

"We're working here," Sierra called out without looking up. "And on a tight deadline. So behave or take off."

"Guess we've been told," Drake whispered, grinning at Natalie.

"Guess so."

They fell silent, and he studied Natalie as she intently watched his sister and her team pour over the fabric.

"Got something here." She leaned closer. "Another speck of blood. Could be Tracey's or belong to someone else. Won't know until Emory processes it."

Drake's phone rang with a call from Erik. Drake answered.

"I've been monitoring Gentry's phone," Erik said.

"How did you do that?"

"Don't ask. Anyway, the body shop that's fixing his car, left a message on his voicemail. His car is finished and ready for pick up."

Drake had no idea how his little brother pulled this off, but he owed him big time. "Give me the name and address of the body shop, and we'll head over there right now."

Natalie walked next to Drake in the parking lot that surrounded the small body shop. The scent of paint clung to the air. Despite it being dinner time, the sun was still high in the sky and wouldn't set until after eight, but the temps had dropped and a cool wind blew over the lot.

Drake took her elbow and drew her close to lead her toward the small building with bright blue paint and striped awning. She had to smile at his protectiveness even though Kirk was smart enough to know that once the police located his car, they would stake the place out and that would be the last place he would want to be.

At the shop door, Drake shifted the hard case he was carrying and peered through the glass. "There's a security camera by the register. Keep your head down and take a seat in the corner right away. It'll be out of the camera's angle."

She followed directions and tried not to look suspicious as she dropped onto a hard plastic chair. She'd developed an honesty gene when she was a kid, thanks to her pastor. Her parents dropped her and Gina off at church and picked them up after service. Not because their parents thought it was necessary for their upbringing, but because they wanted a couple of hours alone. Her stomach churned over their deception, but she knew this could be the best way to find Kirk.

After her dad had walked out on them, her mom stopped taking them to church, but Natalie always found a ride for her and Gina because even as a kid, Natalie knew she needed God in her life. He was her only hope in her dismal world. If only she could share that hope with the children she worked with. Alas, her job prohibited it. The best she could do was to refer them to church-based resources.

She looked around the tidy shop where the odor of paint and rubber grew stronger. A cute blond that Natalie put in her late teens sat behind the tall reception desk looking bored. Her eyes perked up when Drake approached the counter, and she gave him a dazzling smile. "Can I help you?"

Drake casually leaned on the counter, keeping the case that he carried out of view, and returned her smile. "Someone left a message about picking up a car for Kirk Gentry."

"Right. It was me. I left the message."

"Great. If you'll just give us the keys, we'll get going."

"Let me pull up your record to be sure there aren't any charges."

Natalie sure hoped insurance was taking care of the bill, or Drake was going to have to do some fast thinking as he couldn't produce a credit card in Kirk's name. But she didn't doubt for one second that he would figure it out if needed and achieve his goal.

The young woman squinted as she stared at the screen. "Here you are. You're one of the lucky ones. Insurance's covering it all, and you're good to go." She reached for a folder with keys attached and laid it in front of Drake. "Just need you to sign here."

Natalie watched him scribble something on the pad then snatch up the keys. "Thanks for your help. Where's the car?"

"Spot seven."

Drake spun and held out his hand for Natalie. She rushed out the door. "You know we're likely on several cameras, right?"

"Probably. But I'm going to call Londyn as soon as we're done to tell her where to find the car. Hopefully, when we locate Gentry for her, she'll choose not to bring any charges against me."

Natalie stared at him. "You mean us."

"I'll make sure she knows I dragged you along, so you won't be charged with anything." He pointed ahead. "There it is. The red Mazda Miata. Sweet car."

Natalie recognized Kirk's flashy red sports car all repaired and shiny clean.

Drake held the remote in his hand, and the locks opened. "Keyless entry."

He put on gloves, opened his case, and held it out to her. "Hold this for a minute, would you?"

She took it. "You never said what's in here."

He leaned into the car. "It's a toolkit. I have to take a few things apart to access the telematics and infotainment system."

"And you just happen to know where that is on a Miata?"

"Nah. Erik texted the information to me."

She grew more impressed with the Byrd brother's skills all the time. "I get that the infotainment system can give you the GPS and things like phone calls and internet access—stuff like that—but what are telematics?"

He grabbed a tool from the kit and leaned back into the

car. "It's kind of the black box of a car. It stores turn-by-turn navigation, speed, acceleration, and deceleration information. It can even tell us where the lights were switched on, the doors were opened, seat belts put on, or airbags deployed. So we can tell how many people were in the vehicle at any given time."

She'd never heard of that. "Is that just for a Miata?"

"Most newer cars record that information."

"And you know how to access it? I thought Erik was your electronics guy."

Drake lifted out a cable from the toolbox. "This hardware kit provides the cables and interface boards I need."

"So we can print out the information when we get back to your office and figure out where he's been."

"Not quite that easy. Erik will need to use specialized software to review the data and track what was going on with the infotainment unit at the same time. That will give us the most complete picture of Gentry's whereabouts."

She shook her head. "I can't believe all that information is there waiting for you to access."

"It's not always available." He looked over his shoulder. "There are companies out there who provide owners with a service to clear their history. Sort of like you clear your internet history."

"But why do that if you're not up to no good?"

He backed out of the vehicle and took the toolkit. "Because someone could access the info and use it against you. And some people are just freaks about privacy. We use the service to clear our history when we close-out a case so no one can track our clients."

She shook her head. "All this interconnectivity is great, but nothing is private anymore."

"That's the truth." He glanced around the lot. "Keep your eyes open, and give me a heads up for anyone coming."

She did as asked, but kept checking to see what he was doing too. He removed a car panel and unhooked connectors, which he promptly connected to a device from his toolkit. Time ticked slowly by as she nervously watched around them. She felt like a kid waiting to be caught and was thankful when he closed up the panel and snapped the toolkit lid closed.

"Finished. Let's go." He flashed her another smile, and they hurried to the SUV. He set the toolkit in the back seat and slid behind the wheel then called Erik.

"Yo," Erik answered over the speaker. "Get the data?"

"I did, and we're heading straight back there. I wanted to make sure you were ready and had everything you need to process it when we get back."

"I can do it, but I think there might be a faster method. I'm heading down to see Nick, and I'll ask if he's written an algorithm that can process the data faster."

"Great idea," Drake said. "We'll be back in less than thirty."

"If you want me to do this quickly, bring burgers and fries. And a chocolate shake. Maybe two."

"Two?"

"I'm still a growing boy." He laughed and hung up.

Drake turned to smile at Natalie. "Won't be long now, and we could very well know where to find Gentry."

20

————

Drake placed the burgers, fries, and shakes on the table next to Erik, and the savory scent filled the room. Drake and Natalie had smelled the goodness for the last ten minutes in the SUV, and Drake was fairly salivating, but he stood back to let Erik and Natalie go first.

Erik grabbed a burger and unwrapped it. "Now get out of here so I can work alone."

"I thought we'd eat here so we'd be nearby when you find something," Drake said, not wanting to put off scarfing down a burger any longer.

"Not if you want to live, you won't." Erik chuckled and shoved a few fries into his mouth.

"But I—"

"Apparently you have a death wish, since you're still here." Erik cocked his head. "Seriously. I'll work a whole lot faster alone. Take your food to your condo. Have a nice meal with Natalie, and I'll call you the second I have anything."

Natalie laid a hand on Drake's arm. "I'm a pretty good dinner companion. And I don't bite"—she nodded to Erik —"unlike him, apparently." She laughed.

Erik laughed with her and dipped a fry into a mound of

ketchup. Drake couldn't even manage a smile. He wanted the information the moment Erik found it, but his brother had the right to work alone if that's the way he worked best. Drake would expect Erik to flake off if he needed to be alone, and Drake needed to respect that.

He grabbed the food bag then marched to the door and held it open for Natalie.

"It really won't be *that* bad," she said, preceding him into the hallway.

He shook his head to clear away his frustration. "I don't mind having dinner with you. In fact, I'm all for it. I just feel like this is the lead we've been searching for, and I don't want to waste even a second. Gentry could skate before we get to him."

Drake fell into step with her as they started down the hallway to the skybridge. The sun still burned high in the sky, but would soon drop and the whole city spread out before them would be glowing with vibrant oranges and reds.

"Wow." Natalie paused to look around, her eyes wide and luminous. "Some view. Looks like it's clear enough that stars will be out later."

Drake's stomach rumbled, and he was tempted to open a bag and get out a burger but he couldn't pull his focus from the wonder in her eyes. Even for a juicy burger. He was captivated by her. Plain and simple. Under her spell.

How did she have that calming effect on him? Or was it the city view?

He stared out the window. Nah. It was her.

She turned, her lips curving in a beaming smile. "When this is all over, you'll have to bring me up here so I can spend some time watching the day change to night."

He'd love to. Man, how he would love to. But now that they might be getting close to finding Gentry, it was time for

Drake to face facts. Once they captured the guy, he wouldn't likely see Natalie again, would he? Maybe at Gentry's trial, but not in any other capacity unless he did something about that.

"We should eat before everything is cold." He motioned for her to continue across the bridge.

She looked at him for a moment, her gaze assessing, then she turned and strode ahead of him. He'd probably hurt her feelings by not replying to her request, but he didn't want to get into a discussion of the future in the skybridge.

His heart felt heavy as he got the elevator open, and they rode in silence to the second floor. In his condo, he put the bags on the island and reached for plates in the cabinet.

"I don't need a plate." She slid onto a stool and opened the bag.

"My mom would be horrified if I didn't give you one." He set it in front of her. "And you don't want to get me in trouble with her, do you?"

Natalie's pensive expression evaporated, and she laughed. "I like your mom. She's just like the fake mom I conjured up as a kid when mine was so lame."

He dug the burgers and fries from the bag. "I think back to my childhood traumas, like why wasn't I starting in a baseball game, and after hearing about your childhood and seeing what the Gentry kids are going through, it all seems so trivial."

"It was a normal childhood and normal is good." Her expression darkened.

"Hey, what's wrong?"

"If this lead pans out, I'll need to tell the kids about Kirk and find them homes." She unwrapped and set burgers on plates, releasing more of the savory aroma.

He sat on a stool and stared at his burger as he decided

what he might want to say, if anything. He heard her unwrapping a straw and then saw her pick up her soda and take a long drink.

"After spending time with you, I kind of figured you'd end up taking the kids yourself."

"I've thought about it. How I've thought about it." She shoved a fry into her mouth and dipped another into ketchup. "Who knows? I might still be considering it."

He didn't like that answer. Not at all. Because thinking he might never see her again gave him the courage to ask her out. Maybe more than that. Ask for an exclusive relationship. Sure, they hadn't even gone on a date, but they'd been together for days, and through some very tough times. He honestly couldn't imagine life without her now.

Question was, did he tell her how he felt? And what about the kids? How did he feel about her having children? He still wasn't ready to have kids in his life. Too much of a responsibility and a requirement to settle down.

He chomped off a huge bite of his burger but hardly tasted it. He was too concerned about potentially losing her. "What if I asked you out when Gentry was behind bars and the kids were settled?"

She took a long pull on her straw. "What if they're settled with me?"

"I don't know," he answered truthfully.

She twirled the tip of a fry in the ketchup, leaving a swirly pattern on her plate. "You and Willow hit it off, and it looked like you were getting used to Sadie by the time the meal was over."

"Yeah, but what if it's a fluke? What if Logan doesn't like me?"

She looked up. "I'm pretty sure he will."

"And if the kids weren't an issue?" He looked her in the eyes. "Would you go out with me?"

She didn't answer right away, and his gut cramped around his food. Did she not have the same feelings that he thought she had? Was she going to blow him off?

She tilted her head. "Am I really your type?"

"No." He laughed. "Not in the least bit, but it doesn't matter. You're the one who's got me thinking about settling down for the first time in my life. And I hope I've made you rethink not getting involved."

"Yes, but until I sort out what happens with the children, I can't make any plans."

"So it sounds like you're pretty seriously thinking about taking them in."

"Yeah, I guess I am."

He lost his appetite and pushed his plate away.

His phone rang from the counter.

"It's Erik." Drake grabbed it. "Tell me you have something for us?"

"We have months of data, but Nick's algorithm worked like a charm in comparing the data from the telematics system to the infotainment system. You know this isn't his everyday car, so very few trips to the grocery store, or of course, never picking up the kids from daycare."

"Not like he could get car seats or boosters for all three of his children into this vehicle," Natalie said.

"So what *did* you find?" Drake nearly demanded.

"The address where he'd gone right before the accident. It's in Cannon Beach, and GPS shows him arriving at the destination and crashed on the return trip."

Drake's heart started to pound. "You look up the address yet?"

"It's a house in Cannon Beach. Sending a screenshot."

Natalie sat forward, her eyes alive with excitement. "I remember Kirk mentioning that the family used to rent a house every summer in Cannon Beach."

"But it makes no sense that he would need GPS to find it," Erik said. "Or that he would go there at night."

Thoughts pinged through Drake's brain. "He could be having an affair, and it has nothing to do with the beach house they used to rent."

"Give me a second to check property records." Drake heard Erik's fingers clicking on his keyboard. "It's a rental listed on one of the rental sites. Owned by a Melissa Nagy."

"I know that name." Natalie locked gazes with Drake. "She was interviewed by the police. She's a friend of Rebecca Vann, our third victim."

Drake jumped to his feet. "We need to head out there." He looked at his watch. "We can be there in little over an hour."

"Don't you think we should call Londyn?" Natalie asked.

"I say we first get eyes on the place and see if Gentry is present," Drake said already thinking ahead to surveilling this place. "Then we let her know."

21

Wind pummeled in from the ocean on the sparkling clear night, and Natalie shivered in the gusts. She would never in her wildest dreams—or nightmares—have expected that she would be hunkered down behind a sand dune and tall grasses with two former law enforcement officers watching a beach house for signs of a serial killer. Just craziness. Total craziness.

She'd been surprised Drake had agreed to let her come along, but at a distance they weren't in any danger, and she was the only one who'd actually seen Kirk. So if he'd tried to alter his appearance, she would likely be the only one who could confirm his identity.

Not that they'd seen him. So far, they'd only spotted a light on inside the house, but no sign of movement. No cars in the driveway either.

Erik lifted his night vision goggles and looked at Drake. "What do you think?"

Drake kept his focus pinned on the house. "Best guess? He's in there, but asleep."

"No way to ID anyone unless they look out a window." Erik's discouraged tone mimicked Natalie's frustration.

"The Radar-R is in the SUV," Drake said.

"I'll get it and do a sweep." Erik duckwalked away.

"What's that?" Natalie asked.

Drake lifted his goggles and looked at her. "A handheld Doppler radar device that sees through walls. Erik will run it along the exterior walls, and it'll pick up movement as slight as breathing, telling us the number of people in the house, if any."

She shook her head in amazement. "Is there anything you guys can't do?"

"See through the walls to know who's inside the house." He lowered his goggles and focused on the house.

She was getting bored and cold and needed something to occupy her mind. "What does it look like through your goggles?"

He glanced at her, looking like a frog man she'd seen in movies. "Want to try them?"

"Sure."

He lifted off his goggles and scooted behind her to settle them on her head and adjust the headpiece. His touch vanished the cold and set off a fire of emotions burning inside. She gave in to the feelings she'd been fighting since she'd met him and leaned back against the solid wall of his chest.

He dropped his hands from the headpiece, circled his arms around her shoulders, and held her tightly as he rested his head next to hers, enveloping her in his strength. Power.

Security.

That was the main thing that came to mind. She felt physically secure for the first time in her life. As if for once she wasn't alone and not everything was up to her. She had an ally. A partner. Someone who had her back. Literally right now. Someone who would be with her and see her through in life's challenges.

Oh, how wonderful it felt. Joyous.

Tears sprang to her eyes, and she started crying.

"What is it?" he asked, his breath soft against her skin. "What's wrong?"

"You...I...I never knew." She sniffed.

"Knew what?"

"How wonderful it could be to have another human on your side. I've always had God with me, but this is different. Wonderful."

"It's great for me too." He lifted his head and kissed her neck, his lips soft and sending a tingle from her head to her toes. "I've never felt this way before."

"Me either." And just what did she plan to do about it, other than taking some time to figure out what she wanted. She couldn't react in haste and say something that she might want to retract later. She lowered the goggles to her eyes. "Wow. I didn't think the images would be so clear."

He released her and scooted back to her side. "Yeah. Take away the green tint, and it's almost normal."

She took in tiny details she'd missed from only using her naked eye. She caught movement and zoomed in. "Erik's on his way back."

"Then I should probably take my goggles again," Drake said.

She didn't know if she was imagining the disappointment in his tone or if she just wanted him to be disappointed that she didn't continue their interlude. She didn't know what she wanted at all.

He held out his hand. She lifted the strap from her head and placed the goggles on his open palm. Their hands touched. The memory of those powerful arms around her came rushing back, but before she could do or say anything, Erik joined them.

He squatted by Drake. "One heat signature in the front room. Not in motion."

"Asleep maybe."

"Seems like it."

"Then he could be there." Drake sat back on his haunches.

"Oh, it's him all right."

"What?" Drake gaped at his brother.

"Got a look at him through a gap in the curtains."

"Way to bury the lead." Drake shook his head.

"We should move on him, now," Erik said.

"Not happening." Drake got out his phone. "We're talking about a serial killer here. Not just some routine criminal we might apprehend and then call local law enforcement to pick up. We do this the right way to make certain the guy spends the rest of his life behind bars."

Drake kept his gaze pinned to the house, but his thoughts wandered. He wished he could pace, but he couldn't give away their location. So he sat. Quietly. Waiting for Londyn to arrive. Time ticked slowly past. Everything was playing out in slow motion. Gave him time to think. Lots of time.

About Natalie and the moment they just shared. A moment he wanted to experience again and again. He wanted to keep seeing her. Maybe he'd fallen half in love with her. Maybe all the way in love. The feelings were too new to classify, but it was different from anything he'd experienced. So, was it love?

If thinking about not seeing someone again put a huge ache in your heart, it probably was. He really needed to get someone else's opinion. He couldn't ask Erik about it. First off, Natalie was with them. But even if she weren't, Erik hadn't had any serious relationships since his high school sweetheart.

And his other brothers? They'd all recently gotten married or engaged. Yeah, maybe he could talk to them, but they'd probably razz him. Sierra was the best sibling to talk to. If she were there, he'd take her aside and tell her everything. She'd be shocked that he consulted her, but once she got over that, she'd give him good advice. That he knew for certain.

So his best move was to do nothing and let some time pass. Forget the blazing emotions that Natalie's touch ignited and gain perspective. Certainly not make a decision sitting here at the beach with the memory of holding her fresh in his mind.

His phone buzzed in his pocket, and he grabbed it. "It's Londyn."

Natalie's eyes widened, and he answered.

"I'm here with SWAT," she said. "Parked near your vehicle. We'll be breaching the house and need you to fall back to your vehicle."

"Understood," Drake said, though he wanted to be able to see the arrest.

"Move now."

"Roger that. We're on the move." He hung up. "SWAT team is here. We need to fall back to our SUV. Erik first. Natalie next. I'll take the rear." He motioned for them to move ahead of him, and they crept through the gritty sand.

Drake used the time to pray for everyone's safety. Even Gentry's. Death would be too good for the guy. Drake wanted to see him prosecuted and serve the rest of his time behind bars.

They reached their vehicle and greeted Londyn with a

wave and thumbs up. She signaled for the SWAT vehicle to move forward and followed with another plainclothes detective, both wearing a Kevlar vest.

Drake opened the passenger door and looked at Natalie. "I need you to wait in the SUV. It's safer."

He thought she might argue, but she slid in. He left the door open a crack so he could communicate with her if needed then watched the law enforcement advance through his NVGs. Envy crept over him. He had to swallow it down to keep from pacing. If God wanted Drake in on the action, he would be. Best Drake could do now was keep Natalie safe.

"You want to be part of the takedown as much as I do." Erik stared down the road. "An arrest like this one will go down in history. I'd love to be part of it. And I wouldn't mind releasing this adrenaline."

"Yeah," Drake said, the same jittery feeling inching over him. "I'm gonna get the binoculars to take a better look."

He went to the back of the vehicle and ditched his NVGs to grab the night vision binoculars. He opened the driver's door and climbed up to rest his arm on the roof and stare at the house.

"SWAT's moving into place," he told Natalie and Erik. "Surrounding the house."

"I know half the guys on the team," Erik said. "Always wanted to be one of them."

"We did the right thing in forming the company for Aiden. But staying back is hard."

"I can't begin to understand you two," Natalie said. "I'm glad to be here instead of in the thick of a potential shoot-out."

"We have no reason to believe that Gentry has a gun," Erik said.

"Gotta think he does, though." Drake kept his binocs on

the house watching the men dressed in tactical gear move into position. No sign of movement in the house. "A guy wanted for multiple counts of murder would likely want protection."

"No matter," Erik said. "They have to approach the house assuming he's packing."

Drake zoomed in on the officers at the front door. The front guy held a battering ram. He lifted it and slammed it into the door.

"They're breaching now." Drake's heartbeat crept up. "And they're in."

The officers flooded into the building shouting words Drake couldn't make out, but he knew they were identifying themselves as police and telling anyone in the house to show their hands.

He held his breath and waited for gunshots or any sign of an altercation. Nothing. Just the rush of waves hitting the shore and blustery wind coursing in with the water.

"C'mon. C'mon. C'mon, Londyn," Drake whispered. "Report."

"This waiting business is almost enough to make you certifiable. If you weren't already, that is." Erik chuckled.

Drake didn't find it humorous. He tapped his foot and started counting. *One one thousand. Two one thousand. Three one thousand.*

He'd reached one hundred when his phone buzzed. He shoved the binoculars into Erik's hand and answered the call from Londyn.

"We have Gentry." She sounded short of breath. "Found him in the living room. Conked out and no resistance. Appears to be under the influence of drugs. I'm sending a picture to have Natalie positively ID him."

"Send away." He waited for his phone to ding, and then took a long look at the picture before sliding into the vehicle and holding out the phone to Natalie for a final confirmation. "This him?"

She stared at the screen for a second before nodding. "Yeah. Yeah. He looks out of it though."

"Londyn said he appears to be under the influence of something."

Natalie's eyebrows rose, wrinkling in a way he'd come to associate with her. "In the time I knew him, I had no reason to suspect he was doing drugs, but then it's clear there are a lot of things I didn't know about him."

Drake returned his attention to his call with Londyn. "Identity confirmed. I'd like to see him and the house."

Silence met his request.

"Come on, Londyn," Drake said. "This is going to be the arrest of your career. Make you a big shot in your agency, and you wouldn't have him if it wasn't for us."

"We would've eventually found the body shop."

"Yeah, but he could've been long gone by then. Just a minute. That's all I ask."

"Fine." She sighed. "Gentry is already out of here, but I'll open the curtains and give you five minutes to look in the windows. Five minutes only. Got that? It's the best I can do, and you have to be long gone by the time the feds arrive."

Drake left Natalie in Erik's care and hightailed it down the road to the beach house. He double-timed his approach and was winded when he reached the officer dressed in tactical gear and stationed at the door.

Drake identified himself.

"Boss says to meet her at the west side of the building." The officer handed over a pair of booties but didn't note Drake's name on the log.

Drake slipped the paper booties over his boots, wondering if Londyn would get in trouble for letting him look in the window. He couldn't believe she'd actually agreed to anything. Sure, he'd been instrumental in bringing Gentry to justice, but still. Drake was a civilian, and she could get in trouble for even letting him near the building. But she got it—she understood that he needed to see this through to the end.

He stepped up to a window overlooking the large living room where Londyn said Gentry had been found knocked out. He was now likely in the back of one of the police vehicles on his way to lockup. Or maybe to the ER for evaluation.

Drake peered through the wall of windows covered with checked curtains. Londyn stood in the wide open space with white slipcovered furniture. She spotted him and crossed the room to open the window. A familiar fragrance floated out of the house.

Drake looked at Londyn. "You recognize the smell?"

She nodded. "Either Gentry sprayed his wife's perfume, or she was here."

"You thinking she might be alive after all?"

Londyn shrugged. "We don't have any evidence either way."

"True, but what're the odds he didn't kill her?" Drake continued to look around the room. "A third of all women murdered in the U.S. are killed by their male partners."

"Just because he murdered other women doesn't mean he killed his wife. The type of murders we're investigating usually have far different motives." Londyn got out her notebook and pen. "Killing a partner is usually done in the heat of passion. It generally involves drugs or alcohol and is motivated by jealousy. Or, in the case of a separation or a breakup, by revenge."

"Question is, did they break up or did he kill her? Or was she in on the murders with him?" Drake glanced around the space for any additional lead. "We won't know until we find her or her body."

"No bodies here, but even if we find her prints and DNA in the house, we only know that she's been here. Maybe she left the prints here before she disappeared."

"My sister can age fingerprints."

"You're kidding, right?"

"No. She has a way to tell how long a print has been on a surface. Not sure how. I only listen to half of what she says." He chuckled, but Londyn didn't laugh.

"Won't she be in the hospital and on leave soon?"

"Her team can do it."

"No baby yet, though?"

He shook his head, finding it odd that he was talking about the birth of his nephew in a place where a serial killer was just arrested. "Will you keep the investigation open until you find Tracey?"

"I doubt that the task force will continue, but our agency will likely keep working it. If not for closure, for the bad publicity we'd get if we let it go." She shook her head. "You know policing can be all about optics these days."

Drake nodded. He wanted to be in on this arrest, but he didn't miss the negative public perception of law enforcement officers these days. "I'd like to offer our services to help locate her. No cost."

Londyn spun to look at him. "Seriously? You want to know what happened to her that badly?"

"Sure, I'd like her to get justice if she was murdered, but more so, I want Willow and the kids to have closure."

Londyn evaluated him with her practiced cop stare. "The girl got to you, huh?"

His conversation with Willow about her fear played in

his brain, and the protective instinct he never knew ran so deep reared up again.

He never thought he could be a father figure, but that was how he'd felt toward her. Like a father. And now that he looked at the warm emotions this young girl and her siblings gave him, he knew it beat an adrenaline rush any day of the week.

∾

Drake, Natalie, and Erik arrived at the new safe house at four in the morning. Natalie was exhausted, but she sat at the big pine dining table with all the brothers and their parents and put a fresh cinnamon roll with cream cheese glaze on her plate. The roll looked amazing, but she was almost too tired to lift it to her mouth. She didn't want to offend Peggy, so she tugged off a moist corner and popped it into her mouth. Goodness exploded her taste buds. The pungent cinnamon. The sweet cream cheese and dough. The gooey texture. *Wow.*

"Oh, my gosh." She licked her fingers and looked at Peggy. "These are amazing."

"Thanks. They're a family favorite."

"I'll bet they're hard to make too."

"Not really. I could teach you in an afternoon."

"Yes, please." Natalie smiled at the older woman, who smiled back, her eyes crinkling.

Drake frowned.

Right. Once Natalie got the children safely home, his job would be over, and if she took the children in, he wouldn't likely want to see her. He just didn't want that much responsibility.

"I should probably finish up and head to bed," Natalie

said. "I need to get up early and take the children back to Portland. Willow needs to return to school."

"I can't even imagine it." Peggy crossed her arms. "The poor kid. The media will be all over her. Don't you think she might be better off out of school for a while?"

"It'll all depend on where we place her and what her counselors have to say about it."

"My heart just breaks for all of them, but Willow especially. They're all such precious children, and I can't stand to think this might mess them up."

Natalie gritted her teeth for a moment. "I'll do my best to be sure that won't happen."

"Tomorrow is supposed to be a lovely day." Peggy's eyes brightened. "I don't suppose you'd consider letting them have a day at the beach before you take them back to the harsh reality waiting for them."

"Mom." Drake shot his mother a warning look. "You're interfering now."

"I'm sorry." Peggy met Natalie's gaze. "I don't mean to butt in, nor do I pretend to know what's best for them. You're the expert. But I just remembered how much fun our kids had at the beach and thought one more day where they didn't know about their parents wasn't such a bad thing."

"Let's do it," Natalie said, suddenly eager to give the kids one more peaceful and fun day before the world imploded around them.

22

_____

Drake held Sadie as she dug into the sand with her shovel. He wasn't sure this was a good idea, but everyone was having such fun in the sun and sand. His brothers had headed back to Portland, but Erik left Pong behind so Logan could play with him. Plus, the dog loved running on the beach. And their parents had stayed too. His mom insisted on cooking for all of them. In fact, after everyone went to bed, she'd prepared food for a picnic lunch. He'd woken up to the smell of fried chicken and the sight of her mixing a big bowl of potato salad in the kitchen. And a pan of gooey brownies cooled on the counter.

Logan had wanted a brownie for breakfast, and Drake's mom agreed to let him have it, something she would never have done when they were growing up. But Drake had to admit the smile she got from the little boy was worth it. Especially knowing that it might be the last day he smiled for some time.

Logan whooped, and Drake looked down the beach where the boy was running with Pong and Natalie, their feet splashing in the rolling waves. Wind peppered her face that was already red from the cold and wind, but she looked so alive. So vital. And so beautiful. No makeup or all those girly products or even fashionable clothes and her high heels. Just the boy jeans, white T-shirt, and navy blue hoodie that Drake's dad had bought.

As the day had progressed, she'd been so full of life. So enticing that he knew he needed to be with her. But what about these kids? Could he be with a woman who had three kids?

Three kids. Even three great kids like the Gentry trio would be hard to adjust to, a change so big he still didn't know if he could make it. The weight of the decision felt like a boulder tied around his neck, threatening to suffocate him.

Sadie swiveled in his arms and clapped sandy hands on his cheeks. "Potty. Gotta go. Now."

Drake jumped up and yelled to Natalie, but she didn't hear him over the rushing surf.

"Hurry!" Sadie said.

Hang waiting on Natalie. He turned and powered through the sand and burst into the house. "Mom. Bathroom, now."

She flew out of the kitchen, scooped the child from his arms, and charged down the hall. He'd depended on his mother for so many things over the years, but never to take a little girl to the bathroom. He would've done it, but no sense in putting himself in a precarious position with all the issues these days around potential sexual abuse of minors.

The front door opened, and Natalie stepped in with Willow and Logan. "Everything okay?"

"Potty break. Mom's got her."

"Ah." Natalie's soft smile and her bright eyes really got to him. "These two could stand to take restroom breaks too."

"I don't haveta go." Willow gnawed on her lip.

"You okay, kiddo?" Drake asked.

She stubbed her toe into the tile floor. "Had to bring my kite down to come in here."

"We can fly it again," Natalie told her.

She fired at testy look at Natalie. "But I had it really high."

If Drake's mom had seen that look, she would've called the child out, but Drake figured with all that was going on in Willow's life, he'd cut her some slack. As apparently did Natalie.

"I'll help you get the kite back up there." Drake patted himself on the chest. "I was the champion kite flyer in the family."

His dad snorted from the living room.

Drake spun. "Well, I was. You used to tell me that all the time."

Sadie toddled down the hall, and his mother stepped after her. "Your father told all of you kids that."

"Aw, man." Drake mocked offense in hopes of making Willow laugh. He would do just about anything to get that kid to smile. "You're up next, Willow, so we can get back out there. Maybe we can set a record height."

"You're gonna need me for that." Grinning, his dad got up.

"Wait for me. Promise?" Willow's eyes were alight with excitement.

Drake nodded, reveling in the fact that he put the joy on her face.

She charged across the room and down the hall toward the bathroom.

"You might as well grab the picnic basket while you're in here," his mom said.

"You're going to have lunch with us, aren't you?" Natalie asked.

"I thought I'd let you all enjoy yourself without the old people around." She gave Russ a pointed look.

His smile fell. "I have some things to catch up on in here."

"C'mon, Dad," Drake said. "Join us. Willow would love to have an expert like you teach her how to get her kite up into the sky."

"You're sure." He cast a wary look at Drake's mom.

"Oh, go ahead." His mother's reluctance deepened her tone.

Drake gave her a hug. "You can come too, Mom. It'll be fun."

"More like you're avoiding some feelings you need to deal with," she whispered in his ear.

Yeah, more like that.

Natalie tucked Willow into the guest bed on the first floor of her townhouse. The space served as Natalie's office and guest room, but children had never occupied it. She looked at Willow and marveled at everything that had happened in a few short days. The younger children were going with the flow for the most part, Logan wanting his dad at times, but Erik and Drake had stepped in. They weren't here tonight, though, when Logan didn't want to go to bed and asked for his dad.

Kirk might be in custody, but Natalie wasn't going to tell the children about their dad until he was officially charged. She'd seen time and time again in court when people were released on technicalities before charges were brought. True that none of those people were potential serial killers, but still, she wanted to be cautious with the children's fragile psyches.

"Sleep tight, sweetheart." Natalie pressed a kiss on Willow's forehead. So what if that wasn't allowed on the job? The child's expression said she was crying out for love and affection, and Natalie couldn't turn her back on Willow's pain.

Willow grabbed Natalie's hand. "My dad's not coming back for us, is he?"

"I don't know," Natalie answered honestly. "Get a good night's sleep, and maybe we'll know tomorrow."

She released Natalie's hand and clutched the personal alarm that Drake had given to her.

"Are you afraid of something?" Natalie asked.

"I like it better when Drake is with us."

"Because you like him?"

"Because he won't let bad things happen."

Nobody had that kind of power, but Natalie didn't say so. "How about I ask him to come over and spend the night on the couch?"

Natalie doubted he would, but it wouldn't hurt to ask. Now that they were safe, spending time with them wouldn't be his top priority.

Excitement. Adrenaline. A challenge. Those were what he would be seeking. Not caring for a young child's fears. Sure he'd bonded with the kids for the time they were together, but he'd made it perfectly clear right from the start that he wasn't ready to settle down and have a family. She had no one to blame but herself if she wanted to believe his growing to care for the Gentry children would change anything.

"It's okay." Willow held up the alarm. "I have this. If I need him, he'll come. He promised."

Drake would keep his promise if he could. He would do just about anything if he thought a child was in danger. Or even Natalie. But now that they were safe, she didn't know where she stood with him. They needed to talk once the children were settled.

She left the door open a crack and rested her forehead on the nearby wall. The children were all tucked in, peaceful now, but the morning would bring such hardship for them. She could feel the pain as if it were her own. It had pierced her tender emotions so often as a child, it wasn't hard to imagine. She didn't want to think about it, but she had to face facts. These precious children were going to be hurt. Big time.

Tears sprang to her eyes and rolled down her cheeks and onto her hallway floor. Her job inflicted havoc on her emotions. Always had. But to be effective, she couldn't dwell on the heartbreaking aspects. She had to look at the wins. Linger on the times where she helped children and their families. Where she made a difference. Not look at a child who was an emotional wreck, wondering what her future held.

Because of that fear? That fear Willow was facing—that Natalie understood all too well. It was hard to obliterate. For years she'd clung to the belief that finding Gina's killer would erase some of the pain. But it didn't. It just left a big gaping hole that needed to be filled. Right there next to the giant-sized hole she'd allowed Drake to put in her heart.

Her fault. He never claimed to be looking for anything, and he certainly wouldn't enter into a relationship with someone as staid and boring as her. Despite all of that, she'd fallen for him. For his confidence. His compassion. His strength, kindness, and humor. Even the way he called out and questioned things that he didn't agree with. He was an amazing mix of all of that, and a man with impeccable manners taught by parents any child would kill to have. He would be a great husband and father. *If* he decided he wanted to be one. A big, huge if.

But what Drake wanted or didn't want didn't matter. Natalie didn't matter. She'd get over Drake. Helping the children was the only thing of importance right now. If she chose not to take them in, she would have to locate a great family. Sure, they would be scarred by their father's actions no matter what, but she prayed that they would eventually be okay.

She lifted her head, and a bone aching fatigue settled in. She started down the hallway toward her kitchen to set the coffee to brew on a timer for the morning, and the doorbell rang.

Fear lodged in her throat, and her heart clipped into gear.

No, you're fine. Kirk's behind bars. And if he somehow escaped, Drake would be here to protect us.

Could it be Drake come to tell her that he wanted to pursue a relationship with her?

She hurried to the door and looked out the peephole.

What in the world?

She quickly unlocked the door and opened it wide as footsteps sounded in the hall by the bedroom.

"Mommy," Willow's voice came from behind. "Is that really you?"

Drake sat on his couch in front of a Mariner's baseball game, a discarded dinner plate sitting on the table, and looked at the clock. He should hit the hay. It was early, but he was bone-weary. Problem was, his brain wouldn't shut down. He kept thinking about Tracey Gentry. They'd hoped to find her in the house. Her unique scent had filled the space, but Gentry could have a mistress who he'd also given the same perfume to.

As he'd followed Londyn around the house, he'd kept his eyes out for blood or any hint that Tracey or a girlfriend had lost her life. Could be the reason Gentry was so high. He'd killed her and couldn't face it, as it was so different from killing the other women. But there'd been no blood or sign of a struggle.

His phone rang. Seeing Sierra's name, he swiped to answer. "Hey, sis."

"You still with Natalie?" she asked.

"Just dropped her and the kids off at her townhouse."

"Is she going to take the kids in?"

"She's thinking about it."

"That must be a deal breaker for you."

"What?" he asked as he was honestly confused about where she was going with this conversation.

"You wouldn't get involved with a woman who had kids. That's just not you."

"A guy can change, right?"

"Sure. And I figure someday you'll want kids of your own. But I can't see you in the insta-dad role."

"Yeah, me either." He sighed. "You calling just to bring me down more."

"Sorry. No. I wanted to tell you the DNA is in from Tracey Gentry's blouse."

"Tracey's blood? Or even Gentry's?"

"Actually, no. And I can't tell you who it belongs to. I've told you more than I should already."

He punched a fist into his pillow. "Come on, Sierra. This might be important to these kids to know what happened to their mother."

"Sorry." Her sincerity rang through the word. "Detective Archibald is still officer of record for Tracey's missing persons investigation. Call him. Maybe he'll give you what you need."

Drake fisted his hands. "If you weren't so pregnant, I might come down and yell at you."

She sighed. "You know I'm only thinking of our lab, right? If it was up to me, I'd be glad to tell you."

"I know. And don't feel bad. I'm just a grouch to begin with."

"You hungry?"

"Nah," he said looking at the plate and noticing the lingering smell of fried chicken. "I brought back Mom's fried chicken and potato salad from the beach."

"And you didn't share? Now look at who's being heartless." She laughed.

"Stop by. There's plenty for you and Reed."

"Don't think I won't. Gonna head out in thirty minutes or so."

"I'll expect you then." He ended the call and was cheered by the thought of a visit from his sister, even if it was for only long enough to pick up the food. He could give her a hug and think about becoming an uncle. Take his mind off other things. Other people. Natalie.

But not yet. He dialed the PPB detective division and asked for Archibald. Thankfully the guy was working the night shift and Drake waited for him to come on the line.

"Archibald," he answered, his voice booming.

"Drake Byrd of Nighthawk Security."

"Ah yes, the new agency embraced by celebrities." His sarcasm was rife in his tone.

Okay, so this was going to be a bigger challenge than Drake had first thought.

"What do you want?" the detective asked.

Drake explained their involvement in capturing Gentry and how they'd been trying to find Tracey. "I was hoping you could share the DNA results that my sister just gave you for Tracey's blouse."

"Like I'm going to tell a civilian that."

"Way I figure it, we work together, find the woman, and you can take all the glory. You're retiring soon, and what if this info was just the thing to nail Gentry's coffin too? You'd go down as the one who put him away. Would be a huge win for you. You'd be a legend in the office."

"I could just tell Detective Steele." His deadpan response didn't give Drake a lot of hope. "Same result."

Drake needed to do some fast talking. "Would it be or would she try to take credit for the task force?"

"She's not like that."

"You don't know how anyone is until a high profile situation like this presents itself." He felt bad the minute the remark came out. Londyn wasn't that kind of detective, but he had to use whatever he could to help Willow find closure.

"After all of your years on the force, you have to know that," Drake added for good measure.

"Ha!" Archibald spit through the phone. "You're right about that."

Good. The guy was coming around. Drake just had to go in for the kill. "I can be sure the media knows all about your role when they interview you."

"Might not interview me."

Ah, yes. He was biting. "I have several contacts I can call who'll be glad to talk to you. Once one media outlet picks it up, the others are bound to follow."

He hemmed and hawed for a moment before he cleared his throat. "We have a deal, but don't you dare renege on me or I'll make you wish you hadn't."

"You have my word."

"Fine. The blood belonged to a Laura Zimmer."

"What?" Drake tried to process the news, but his brain couldn't even comprehend it. "Are you sure? Laura Zimmer?"

"Why?"

If this guy didn't recognize this name, he must really be phoning it in, as Erik had said. "That's The Clipper's last victim."

"Oh, yeah! Our deal is off. Keep this to yourself. I'll be forwarding this report on to that pushy FBI agent who took the blouse."

Drake couldn't stop Archibald from taking action, so he ended the call and phoned Natalie. He had to tell her that Tracey Gentry might've been at Laura's murder. Maybe she'd suspected Kirk of having an affair and followed him. Then she'd seen him kill Laura and had taken off. If she was still alive, it would explain why she'd run from Kirk and gone to ground.

Or maybe—and unthinkable to Drake—the woman was helping her husband murder other innocent women or even more shocking, she was the killer.

23

"You're alive." Willow flung her arms around Tracey Gentry's waist.

Natalie ignored her ringing phone to study the woman standing before her. She wore a knit gray mini-dress that clung to all of her curves and accentuated her voluptuous body, but it was her face that commanded Natalie's attention. Her lips were puffy and large, looking like she had way too much filler injected in them. Her beauty was long gone, and she looked almost clown-like. Willow didn't seem to notice, but then she'd seen her mother looking like this before.

Tracey smiled down on her daughter and stroked her hair. "Of course I'm alive, sweetie."

"Dad said he thought a bad man took you."

"Dad was wrong."

Willow peered up at her mother. "Where is he?"

"I don't know, but I'm sure he'll be here in the morning." She brushed Willow's hair back, her shimmering violet-blue nails catching the light.

Natalie wondered what that particular color was called and if it was in Kirk's trays of polish.

Tracey kissed Willow's head. "Right now, you need to go back to bed so you're not tired when he comes home."

Willow eyed her mother. "You'll be here when I wake up?"

"Absolutely."

"Pinkie promise." Willow held out her little finger.

Tracey locked fingers. "Promise. Now scoot."

Willow spun and raced toward Natalie, stopping to give her a hug too. "She came back. She really came back."

"Yes, she did." Natalie looked at Tracey. The woman's eyes were narrowed into tiny slits, and she was scowling. Maybe she thought Natalie had gotten too close to her children. "Now do as your mom said. Off you go."

Willow flashed Natalie the first radiant smile she'd seen since Natalie took her from her father.

Natalie waited for Willow to jet into the room before she turned back to Tracey. "How did you find us?"

"Kirk told me the kids were with you, and I had him do his IT magic on the internet to locate your address."

"Kirk?" Natalie had to work hard not to let her jaw drop. "You talked to him?"

"He tracked me down, and brought me up to speed on what you've been doing." Tracey put her hands on very curvaceous hips. "You had no right to take my children."

"You'd rather I'd left them with Kirk?" Natalie did let her jaw fall this time. "He's a serial killer."

"The last place I would want them would be with him. He's far too controlling." Tracey puckered her lips together. "I can finally be free of him and resume my career out in the open this time."

Career? "I thought you were a stay-at-home mother."

"That's what everyone thought. Even Kirk." Venom spewed out with the words. "He had no earthly idea. It was so simple to dupe him, especially while he was on active duty. He was deployed so often that I could pretty much do anything I wanted. But then he decided to separate from the military."

She sighed, and her large lips fluttered with the expulsion of air. "I had to hide everything from him."

"You still haven't said what you did."

"Have you ever heard of Dion Holistic cosmetics?"

"Sure."

She exaggerated a model pose. "You're looking at Dion herself. I started the company years ago and built a following."

"Come on, now." Natalie nearly scoffed at the thought. "The Nighthawk Security team did a deep dive on your background and didn't find anything related to that."

"Because I made sure to hide it. Kirk would've beaten me senseless if he found out. No wife of his was going to work. You don't know how many times he told me that. But I would've gone stir crazy if all I did was change diapers." She let out another long sigh.

"So I started with beauty and clothing tips online. Of course I used a false name. When it took off, I started charging to join my channel and got paid advertising. Then someone suggested I make my own line of cosmetics. So I did, and I got funds from an investor. It took off. I figured if I made enough money, I could take the kids and finally leave my husband."

"You wanted to leave him?" Natalie leaned against the wall. She was tired and wanted to sit, but she wasn't going to invite Tracey into her house. Something was very off about this woman, and Natalie didn't trust her around the children. Far easier to get rid of her from here than the living room.

"He was a bully and abuser. Not physical. At least he only hit me a few times. But he told me how ugly I was.

What a horrible mother I was. How I failed at just about everything. How I was getting old. Ugly."

"Is that why you had the plastic surgery?"

"Yes, and this happened." She stabbed her fingers into her lips. "I'll get it fixed, but I only want the best of the best working on my body from now on. No more mistakes. He was so stingy he wouldn't cough up the money for it, and I didn't have enough for the high-priced doctors. After this surgery, I couldn't record any videos to make more either. I was forced to re-release old ones, and followers started to get mad. End their subscriptions. People. They're so fickle. So I had to do something drastic. Find some money."

"And to do that you had to leave Kirk?"

"No, you fool," she snapped. "I had a revenue source, but Kirk found out how I got the money, and he threatened to go to the police if I didn't stop."

"How *did* you get the money?" Natalie's phone rang again, and she reached for it.

"No!" Tracey shouted. "If you want to hear my story, you'll give me your full attention."

Natalie lifted her hands. "I'm all yours. Tell me how you came up with the cash."

Tracey's anger evaporated, and she smiled, her lips thinning out to almost normal levels. "Let's just say a couple of my supporters invested in my business."

"And now you have the money?"

"Ha! I wish." She flashed up a hand. "But I'll soon have what I need."

"So, what do you want to do now?" Natalie asked. She wanted the woman to think she might have a choice so she wouldn't be as difficult to manage. "Obviously, I can't turn the children over to you until I review the situation with my supervisor in the morning."

Tracey stomped her foot. "You cannot keep my children from me."

"I am required by law to do so." Natalie pushed off the wall and lifted her shoulders. "Hopefully I'll have it all straightened out tomorrow."

"But they're my children."

"Who you abandoned for over a month."

"I didn't abandon them." She jutted out her chin. "They had their father, and I had to go. Because of him and his abusive ways."

"Or because you wanted to fix your cosmetic surgery issue."

"Well, both, but..." She took a long breath, her gaze traveling around the hallway as if looking for answers mounted on the walls. She jerked back her shoulders and stomped her foot again. "I won't stand for it. And I won't wait until morning. I'm going to take the children now, and you can't stop me."

Natalie grabbed her phone to dial Drake and took a stance in front of the guest room door, which was cracked open. *No. Oh no.*

Had Willow been listening? Natalie should've checked after Willow went back to bed. Natalie had listened at enough doors as a kid and knew better.

What a horrible way for Willow to hear about her parents? Natalie had been so careful around them for days but this conversation undid all her caution in minutes. She'd just been so shocked by Tracey's appearance that she hadn't been thinking straight.

But now her head was clear.

Tracey intended to take the children and Natalie couldn't let her do so. No matter what Tracey did to her.

"Step out of my way," Tracey demanded.

Natalie planted her feet in front of the door. "No."

Tracey reached into her purse. When her hand came out, she was brandishing a switchblade that glinted in the overhead light. "Then prepare to become The Clipper's fifth victim."

~

Drake tried calling Natalie again. Still no answer. Had she gone to bed when the kids did? Possible, but his gut said something was wrong.

His phone suddenly pealed out an alarm. *Willow.* The device he'd given her. Was it a false alarm? Or was she in danger?

Drake could ask if Natalie picked up her phone. He had to assume there was something wrong. His brothers would too when the alarm sounded on their phones, and they'd be gearing up and ready to roll. Drake's vest lay on the dresser where he'd ditched it after their op, too tired to put it away properly.

His negligence might come in handy now. As might the assault rifle, which he grabbed as he raced for the door. By the time he reached the hallway, Erik was out of his condo and headed Drake's way.

He had his vest on too. "Willow in trouble?"

On the way to the elevator, Drake explained about calling Natalie and not being able to get through. "My gut says something's wrong, and she can't answer. And Willow is afraid. Or maybe Willow's in danger too."

Erik boarded the elevator after Drake and tapped the button for floor six. "I don't get it. Gentry's in custody so what could've happened?"

Drake wished he knew.

The elevator stopped at three. Looking alert but just woken, Brendan and Clay got on, and Drake relayed the information again. Then on the sixth floor where they all parked, Aiden waited in the hallway for them, and Drake told the story again. He couldn't begin to say how thankful he was for his brothers' instant response. They didn't ask any additional questions but marched toward the parking garage.

"I'll drive." Aiden took the keys from Drake. "You're shaking."

Drake wanted to deny his unease, but he didn't want to waste any more time, so he got out additional vests from the back of the SUV and tossed them to his brothers. The rasping of Velcro was the only sound in the garage save the whistling wind. Drake next handed out comms units so they could communicate at the townhouse. Finishing first, he grabbed a few extra ammo clips and slid into the passenger seat. Aiden got behind the wheel and the others took the backseat.

They all felt the sense of urgency, and the tension was palpable in the vehicle.

Aiden raced down the ramp at a speed that might make others nervous, but Drake was used to tactical driving. He knew how to get to Natalie's townhouse, but he entered the address in the navigation system for Aiden to make it simple. Besides, the GPS would tell them the quickest route at this time of night.

"Tell us about her townhouse," Clay said from behind Drake.

He swiveled to face his brother and noted that Erik had his attention on his phone. He was likely looking for the best satellite photo of the complex. "It's a two-story end unit with three bedrooms and a garage on the left. The main entry is to a long hall. The steps are to the left. A guest bedroom immediately to the right when you enter the town-house. The kitchen's in the back right and is open to the living room. Powder room under the stairs and two beds with attached baths upstairs."

"Where do you want to make entry?" Clay asked.

"Locks are all buttoned up tight. I made sure of that when I dropped Natalie and the kids off, so it'll be a challenge. Living room has a sliding patio door and a wall of windows, but the back is fenced and there's no gate. I want to make sure Natalie is okay, but we need to check on the kids first. They're sleeping in the front bedroom."

"Assuming Willow's awake, if we breach that window, we'll likely scare her," Brendan said. "She might react and unintentionally out us to whoever's causing Natalie not to respond."

"I'll do a quick check through the window to be sure we're clear to enter, and then turn on my flashlight so she can see my face." As Drake visualized the scenario, he ground his teeth.

"You want me on overwatch?" Brendan filled the role as the team sniper and often took the high ground for ops like this one.

"Got the townhouse up on sat view." Erik looked up. "No place to take a stand."

"Yeah, the complex is too densely built for that." Drake looked at his brothers. "Erik, you're with me. Aiden standby in the vehicle in case we need a fast getaway. Brendan and Clay, take the kids to the SUV. Then come back and take a stand in the front and back."

"Be careful on the rear of the townhouse," Erik said. "There's a green space behind the complex, and our subject could skate."

They fell silent, and Drake listened to the GPS voice calmly give Aiden the next direction. Drake was glad he'd given the computer charge of directions. One less thing on his mind. The closer they came to Natalie's townhouse, the more worried he'd become.

If he'd wondered if Natalie was important to him, there was no question now. He couldn't lose her. That would be unfathomable. He'd only known her for a few days, but he couldn't imagine life without her. If she chose to adopt the children, then he would make the best of it. And if they eventually got married, he would help raise them to the best of his ability.

Wow! Had he gone to thinking about marriage? Not something he should fill his head with right now.

He drew his gun and checked the clip, then shoved the extra clips into his vest pockets. Next, he cleared his brain and envisioned the task ahead. They had no room for errors. A woman and three children depended on them to take the right actions. Their strike would be speedy, but also had to be precise.

"Where's the best place to park?" Aiden asked.

"All the spots nearest the townhouse are reserved for owners," Drake said.

"Visitor lot is just after the entrance," Erik reported. "I don't think we should park there though. Too long of a walk while wearing tactical vests and openly carrying. Might spook a neighbor who could try to intervene."

"Agreed," Drake said. "Go ahead and double park until the kids are out. Then move the vehicle to the lot, and I'll let you know what we need from there."

"Roger that." Aiden turned into the lot and drove straight to the end of the main road where Natalie's town-house was located on a cul-de-sac.

"Only one way out," Drake said. "Not a great situation for a fast getaway, but we'll have to deal with it."

They passed several units to arrive at the right address.

"Go time." Aiden shifted into park.

Drake was out of the vehicle before it stopped rocking. He ran his gaze over the area, looking for people and at vehicles. No one about, and he didn't recognize the cars.

He turned to his brothers. "Ready?"

Each of them nodded, and he set off, Erik behind him, Clay and Brendan taking up the rear. They stacked next to the window, and Drake peeked through the open curtains, where he saw Willow by the door that was cracked open. A sliver of light illuminated the room enough for Drake to make everything out. She had Curious George clutched to her chest. Sadie and Logan slept in the queen-sized bed.

Drake turned on his flashlight, and Willow spun. He pointed the beam to his face and gave her a thumbs up. She bolted across the room and slid the window open.

"It's my mom. She's gone crazy. She has a knife pointed at Natalie." Willow's words tumbled over each other in the rush to get out.

It felt as if someone was sitting on Drake's chest, and he couldn't breathe, but he had to hold it together for Natalie and these kids.

"Where are they?" he managed to get out.

"In the living room. Natalie's sitting on the couch and Mom is standing by her. Yelling at her. I think she's going to kill her." Willow started crying.

"Okay, honey. Stand back. I'm going to cut the screen and come in."

She complied and hugged George tightly to her chest. Anger raged in Drake's body. This kid. This poor kid. She'd experienced too much. He dug out his pocket knife, sliced through the screen, and ripped the material free. Turning, he nodded at Erik then climbed into the room. He took Willow by the hand and got out of Erik's way and knelt by her. "We'll take care of this and everything will be fine."

Willow threw herself at him, and he held her warm little body close. "It'll be okay, honey. I promise."

She leaned back. "Don't kill my mom. Please."

Oh, man. No child should have to say something like that? Sadly, he couldn't make any promises.

"I'll do my very best." He forced a smile for her. "Clay and Brendan are right outside, and they're going to take you and Sadie and Logan to our vehicle."

"But we're okay in here." Her eyes narrowed. "Mom would never hurt us, would she?"

He honestly didn't know, but wouldn't tell her that. "If you go to the SUV, I won't have to worry about you."

She chewed on that lip. "Okay."

"I need you to be brave and help with Logan and Sadie if they get scared. Can you do that for me?"

She nodded, but her lower lip trembled.

"Great. Go ahead and climb out and Clay will take your hand." Drake stood and motioned for Erik to follow him. At the door he glanced back to be sure Willow was exiting. Clay reached in and lifted her over the sill then climbed in for the other kids.

Good. Good. Now Drake could concentrate on the woman who meant more to him than he could ever imagine and save her from a lunatic with a knife.

24

Tracey moved closer, her knife shining in the overhead light. Natalie swallowed her shock over Tracey claiming to be The Clipper and frantically looked around the room. She'd managed to stall Tracey by puffing up her ego, but Natalie was running out of things to say to build this killer's ego.

Think, Natalie. Think.

"The nail polish," Natalie blurted out. "How did you decide on the colors you used? And why do it at all?"

Tracey cast a well-duh look at Natalie. "Every woman should look her best at all times. I had to help them for their funerals."

That made no sense. "Why only do their nails? Why not do the makeup, too?"

She pursed her lips and looked like a puckering fish. "Makeup requires perfection. It would take too much time. I couldn't risk getting caught."

"And the color choices?" Natalie caught sight of the large brass candlestick she'd bought last month. Solid and heavy. She could defend herself with it. She just needed to get closer. She moved a few inches.

"That was easy." Tracey shifted on her sky-high heels but

didn't seem to notice Natalie's movements. "*Angelic* for your sister. She made everyone think she was a devout Christian, but she was as two-faced as they come. She was going to steal my clients. I couldn't lose any money, and I had to stop her before she did."

"How did you know that she was planning such a thing?" Natalie asked, as her sister would never have stolen anything from anyone.

"She told me she was branching out on her own."

"But that doesn't mean she'd steal your clients." Natalie scooted a few more inches.

"Of course it did. Any business she started would compete with mine. I couldn't afford for her to interfere. I just couldn't." Panic flitted through Tracey's deep blue eyes, which were so reminiscent of Sadie's that it put an ache in Natalie's heart.

This woman feared business competition? That had to be the lamest reason for committing murder that Natalie had ever heard. "And the other colors?"

"*Chameleon,* for Veronika. She was more two-faced than your sister. She once managed my website and took care of uploading my videos. She wanted to start her own online channel too, under the name of Onyx and was going to promote another line of cosmetics. I was afraid I would lose a lot of clients to her, even if her product was inferior." Tracey planted her hand on her hip and glared at Natalie.

"And *Bewitching* for Rebecca?" Natalie asked.

"Ah yes, Rebecca. She was a very special lady. Older, but she liked to look her best all the time. She could afford to— she was loaded, one of my best customers. I friended her online then visited in person to sell her new products. She paid me with cash from a safe filled with money. I needed that money. And I took it." She laughed, a maniacal kind of laugh, her gaze flitting around, not landing anywhere. She seemed to be losing focus.

"And Laura?" Natalie asked.

"*Vixen*." Her focus returned, and she stared at Natalie. "I met her like I met the others—after they commented on my videos. Laura left nasty comments about a few of my products, so I decided to interact with her to stop her from leaving more of them. I wanted to simply unsubscribe her, but I knew she would find a way to get back at me. So we engaged. I learned she had a boatload of money too. I needed it. She didn't deserve it. So I took it." She shrugged as if killing this woman and stealing her money was of no consequence.

"And what role did Kirk play in this?" Natalie scooted again. A couple more feet and she could reach the candlestick.

"Kirk, a role? No. No. It was all me." She pulled her shoulders back. "He doesn't have the courage to go after something bigger and better for us. The fool caught me doing Rebecca in. I thought he would go to the police, but he didn't have the nerve to do that either. He simply ordered me to quit. Like he ordered me not to work. Not to dress flashy. Not to wear makeup. But I was done with his ordering me to do anything. So I left him—just walked out."

"But you said you talked to him, and he told you about the children."

"Oh, I did. He couldn't stay away. Hunted me down. Asked me to run away with him. He'd never planned to turn me in so he prepared for a getaway. For all of us. But I liked being in charge for once. And no matter how hard he begged, I wouldn't go with him so I slipped some drugs in his drink and left. He just didn't understand. I *need* the money. I must have it."

"Couldn't he have gotten a loan?" Natalie saw someone

step into the hallway. Drake? Could it be? Or was she hallucinating in her fear and longing?

She blinked a few times. The man who'd sworn to protect her stood strong and powerful in his vest, his gun aimed ahead, his brother Erik backing him up. Drake held a finger to his lips, telling her to remain quiet and not alert Tracey to his arrival. Natalie had no idea how he knew she needed help, but here he was.

Thank you. Thank you. Thank you.

"That's what he said. Finally. But that would leave me under his control again. I couldn't have that. Wouldn't have that."

"Did you know he started polishing Willow's nails?" Natalie tried not to look at Drake, but she had to glance at him to see if he was coming closer. He was stealthy and silent, and he was nearly to the living room.

"Gross, right?" She shuddered. "He said it was a way to remember me. If I'd known that sooner I would've turned him in as The Clipper. I mean, I knew he kept the polish. He thought he could control me that way, but I was careful. I didn't leave any prints or DNA on them. I could tell a convincing story to implicate the fool."

She waved her knife. "Enough of this talking. I'm ready to take the kids and leave."

She took a bottle of polish from her pocket, a glossy deep magenta, and grinned. Even with Drake and Erik nearly reaching Tracey, the sight of the polish nearly paralyzed Natalie.

"*Passionate*," Tracey said, her tone giddy. "I figured you would try to keep the kids from me and force me to act. I chose it for you because Kirk told me how zealous you were in making sure the kids had a good home. He really respected you." She rolled her eyes. "But your looks. You're pretty enough. If you'd put on some makeup and style your hair, you just might be beautiful."

Drake reached Tracey and snaked an arm around her neck, hauling her backward. She screamed and clawed at him with her free hand. Tried to stab him with the knife. Erik lunged ahead and knocked it to the floor.

Natalie felt every muscle in her body turn to liquid, and she thought she might slide to the floor like a pile of slime.

Drake eased Tracey to the wall and pressed her upper body against it.

"What's the meaning of this?" she demanded.

"You confessed to being The Clipper," Drake said. "That's the meaning of this."

"I did no such thing," she snapped. "Now unhand me."

"Three witnesses heard your confession." Erik tugged her arms behind her back and secured her wrists with zip ties. "I've got her. Go."

Drake hurried across the room to Natalie.

She smiled up at him. "You came."

He knelt down next to her and took her trembling hands. She drank in the sight of him and worked hard to slow her breathing back to normal.

"Willow used her personal alarm," he said. "The kids are in the SUV with Aiden. Willow's freaked out though. She heard her mother and saw her with the knife."

Natalie sighed. "I thought she might have, and I wanted to break it to her gently. But maybe hearing it straight from her mother will help Willow accept the situation better."

"She's still going to have a very hard time."

"What will happen to Kirk now?"

"Good question. He'll serve time for covering up the murders, especially since it allowed Tracey to kill another person." He took a long breath and let it out. "I'm so glad I gave Willow the alarm. I don't know what would've happened otherwise."

His voice quivered, and it hurt to see such a strong man taken down by Tracey's actions. She squeezed his hands. "But you did. You got here in time."

"When I thought I might lose you..." His voice cracked, and his Adam's apple bobbed. "I want to be with you. Kids or no kids. I don't care. I'll make anything work if you'll have me." He looked deep into her eyes, and his passion warmed her to the depths of her very being. "This isn't exactly the most romantic time to say this, but I think I've fallen in love with you." He shook his head. "I know I have."

"I figured the same thing out," she said. "And I also figured out that I can't take the children. I just don't have the time to devote to them. They need a stay-at-home mom to help them overcome the trauma. And that's what I'm going to recommend to my supervisor in the morning."

His eyes widened. "You're going to work tomorrow after all of this?"

"I have to. The children need to go to authorized care, and I need to find out if I have a job."

"If we can help ensure that in any way, let me know." He sat back on his haunches and looked at his brother and their suspect. "Take Tracey down the hall. I have something I need to do without either of you present."

Natalie had no idea what he had planned, but the grin Drake shared with Erik gave her an idea, and her heart rate started kicking up in anticipation.

Erik pulled Tracey away from the wall.

"Hey," she complained. "Not so rough."

Erik ignored her, leading her down the hall.

The moment they were gone Drake drew Natalie to her feet. He looked into her eyes and lowered his head. He was moving too slowly. Way too slowly. She cupped the back of his head and drew his lips down to hers. They were warm and wonderful. Insistent. She slid her hands down his neck and pulled him even closer. He deepened the kiss and seemed to revel in her touch, which fired her desire even more. She could hardly believe he returned her feelings.

She drew back. Reluctantly. But she had to. Kissing, though wonderful, was meaningless unless they were going to move forward.

"I didn't ask," he said slightly breathless. "Would you go out with me? I mean not just on a date, but something serious. Is it too soon to talk serious?" He leaned back and dropped his hands. "It is. I'm sorry. I..."

She grabbed his hands. "I'm not saying no. I was just thinking about what it might mean to my work. But I need to stop thinking about that and begin to consider having a life outside of the job."

"I think that's a good idea for both of us."

"You do? Since when?"

He reversed hands and gripped hers in earnest. "Since I learned something from you. We have to go through difficult times to get to where we are. I need to stop feeling bad for you and what you've experienced. You were right. It was God's plan for you. You have the right attitude. God doesn't give us the stress or the problem. He gives us the strength to go through the situation and emerge whole on the other side. That's where we are now. On the other side, and I'm thankful we've come through it together."

She nodded, but her thoughts wandered. "I'm still so worried about Willow. She doesn't know God. Doesn't have the inner strength. At least I had God on my side when I was young."

Drake let out a long breath. "Can you specify a Christian home when you place the kids?"

Natalie shook her head. "But I can try to find homes whose values will be good for them."

"Well, come on." He dropped one of her hands but held tightly to the other. "We don't have to figure this all out tonight."

She looked up at him. "Can I ask a big favor?"

"Anything. I'm yours to command."

"Can they spend the night at your place? I don't want Willow to have to come back in here after the scene with her mom."

"Of course. Or, if you think it's better to have a house, I can ask Mom if you all can stay there tonight."

"Your condo will be just fine. Unless you'd rather not have us on your doorstep."

"No. No." He circled his arm around her shoulders. "You're welcome to come home with me anytime."

Natalie had enjoyed being with Drake at his condo when she'd visited before, but tonight the warmth in her heart was greater. How could it not be when she was willing to admit she had feelings for him, and they were going to pursue them together? She couldn't wait for that date he'd suggested, but before she could fully embrace her happiness, she had to take care of the Gentry children.

She looked at Willow, who was sitting on the couch with one of Peggy's famous chocolate chip cookies and a big glass of milk. But she was just holding the cookie. Her eyes were red and swollen from crying, and her chin still trembled.

Natalie left Drake in the kitchen, where he was brewing a pot of coffee, to sit next to Willow. "Not hungry?"

Willow shook her head and set the cookie on the plate and glass on the table next to it.

"Do you want to talk about your mom and dad?" Natalie asked softly.

Willow shrugged and curled her arms around her waist.

Natalie scooted closer. "It must be good to know your mom is alive."

Willow gnawed on her lip. "Maybe. I don't know. She's a bad person. Really bad."

"No." Natalie waited for Willow to look at her before going on. "She's not bad. There's no such thing as bad people. Just flawed people whose actions are bad. She's still your mom. She loves you, which is why she came to my place, to get you and Sadie and Logan."

"Really? You mean that?"

"I do. It seems like she has some mental health issues that are causing her to do what she's doing. She should get the help she needs in prison."

Willow's eyes brightened. "And then she'll come home?"

Natalie didn't want to have to explain, but Willow had to know the truth. "No, sweetie. She won't ever come home. She'll have to stay in prison."

Willow gasped.

Natalie tried to take the child's hand, but she jerked back. Natalie worked hard to convey her sympathy in her expression. "I'm sorry to have to tell you that, but you need to know so you can move forward in your life. A life I know will be amazing if you let us help you through this stress."

Willow's chin quivered, and she sucked in a breath and let it out. "What about my dad?"

"I don't know many details about that, but he will go to prison too because he covered up what your mom did. I don't know how long he'll be there."

She bit her lip. "What happens to us?"

"I'll find you a home where you can stay until your dad is able to care for you again." Natalie wasn't sure that he would ever be able to be a good father, but it was a possibility at this point.

"No! I don't want to." Willow's expressive eyes implored Natalie. "Can't we stay with you? Or with Drake?"

"We aren't in a place to take care of three children right now."

"Please." Willow grabbed Natalie's hand. "I'll be really good. I won't make a mess. And I'll help with the little kids."

Natalie wanted to cave, to take on these children. To keep them under her wing and raise them. But she couldn't. It might work out for a short while, but things would gradually fall apart. Natalie wasn't prepared to be a parent. She'd seen it happen and knew where it would lead, no matter her effort to be the best parent possible. No matter good intentions, if a person didn't have the right resources, the situation would collapse, and the children would end up more emotionally damaged than before.

She firmed her shoulders. "I'm sorry, sweetie, but I can't."

Willow jumped up and ran to Drake. She put her arms around him. "Please, can we stay with you? Please."

Muscles in Drake's face tightened, and his eyes filled with anguish. He was suffering, too, and Natalie wished he didn't have to go through this. But then, as he'd pointed out not more than an hour before, God would bring Drake through. Didn't mean the trial wouldn't be painful. Just meant, with God in his life, the situation would be easier.

Drake gently released Willow's arms, knelt in front of her, and put his hands on her shoulders. "If I really thought it was best for you all to live with me, I would take you in a heartbeat. But I'm not ready to be a dad yet, and you need someone who is and knows what he's doing."

"Nuh-uh." She crossed her arms. "I need you or Natalie. Or my dad."

Natalie joined them. "I know you think this now, but one day you'll understand." Natalie tried to smooth Willow's hair back from her face, but she jerked away.

She pouted. "I want to go to bed now."

"Good idea." Natalie forced a smile. "Things will look brighter in the morning."

Willow glared at her. "I don't need anyone to tuck me and George in. We're good."

She spun and raced from the room.

Tears pricked at Natalie's eyes, and for once, she didn't try to stop them.

"Oh, honey." Drake gently gripped her arms. "Don't cry."

"I don't want to, but..." A sob took her voice. "Sometimes it's just so hard to see a child starting down the same difficult path you lived. Even if you know that God will bring good from the situation, you know the child is hurting. Sure, hurting is part of growing up, but not this kind of hurt."

"We have to find the very best place for them." He drew her into his arms, and the warmth of his body, of his care for her, helped ease the pain that she would normally be facing alone.

She felt so safe, so secure and cared for, that she could believe everything was going to be okay. She just needed to lean on the Byrd family's support and trust in God's all-knowing plan.

Natalie left the children with Drake at his condo and went home to shower and change for work. As she marched into her office, head held high to try to stem her unease, she heard her co-workers' whispers and saw the challenging looks they gave from their cubicles. She put her things down in her cubby and went straight to her supervisor's office.

Melinda Blankenship sat at her desk, pen in hand, perusing a report. In her late fifties, her gray hair was cut into a bob, and stress wrinkles on her face left her looking ten years older than her age. Thankfully, her thick dark-framed glasses hid many of the wrinkles.

"About time you showed your face." She scowled and gestured at the chair in front of her cluttered desk. "Sit."

"Just so you know right up front, the children are fine."

"And the dad?" Melinda arched a busy eyebrow. "Did he turn out to be The Clipper?"

"No, he—"

"I knew it." She pounded a fist on the desk. "I knew you overreacted."

"Actually, I didn't." Natalie lifted her chin. "The mother is The Clipper, and the dad knew about it and covered it up, allowing her to go on killing. They'll both be serving time, and the children will need placements."

Melinda gasped. "The mother? A serial killer?" She shook her head. "Not many female serial killers, are there?"

"I looked it up last night when I couldn't sleep, and there are more than you might think." Natalie didn't want to talk about the parents anymore. She wanted to get straight to work and do her job the best she could. If she had a job. "I'd like to get started on placing the children."

"No," Melinda stated firmly.

So, Natalie was fired. She'd expected that. But she wouldn't go without a fight. She opened her mouth to speak.

Melinda lifted a hand. "Save your argument. You're too close to the situation to make an informed placement. This is going to be high-profile. I'll place them myself."

"But I'm—"

"Lucky these parents turned out to be unfit and you were removing the children for their own safety." She shook her head. "I'll be suggesting we take disciplinary actions and give you some time off to get your head on straight."

Wait. What? She wasn't fired. That meant she could at least track what happened to the children. *If* she was in the office not lounging at home on some enforced time off. "I don't need a break."

"Either you take unpaid time off or you're fired. You're a good worker, Natalie. Dedicated. Honest. Hardworking. And that's the only reason I'm not booting you right now. So take the leave or be fired. It's as simple as that."

Nothing was as simple as that. Natalie didn't want time on her hands right now. She wanted to throw herself into her work so she didn't have time to think about the Gentry children, but on the bright side maybe she could spend the time with Drake.

"Just in case it turned out that you were right, I arranged emergency placement for the children and have a strong lead on a long-term one. Have them in the office by lunchtime." She locked gazes, her message clear. This was not negotiable.

"Can you tell me where they will be going?"

"No." Melinda crossed her arms.

Her supervisor's signal told Natalie not to bother delving deeper. She'd done all she could. It was time to move on. "When can I come back to work?"

"A month off should allow you to recoup and for all of this to blow over, but we'll play it by ear." Melinda stood. "Enjoy the time."

Enjoy it? Sure, she now had more time to get to know Drake, but she wouldn't know what happened to the Gentry children, and that would eat away at her very being. Eat away at her for one very long month at the very least.

25

Sunny and seventy degrees with no humidity, the weather was perfect for a barbecue, and Drake was stoked for everyone in the family to meet Natalie at his parents' house. He'd only been away from her for a day, but it had felt like a lifetime. She'd been quiet ever since he'd picked her up, an unusual thing for her. Or at least he thought it was unusual. He couldn't be sure, considering they'd known each other for less than a week.

With the depth of his feelings for her, how could that even be possible?

He glanced across his pickup. She wore denim shorts and a soft pink top that should clash with the reddish hints in her hair but looked great. Not that he spent a lot of time looking at her clothing when her legs were the big attraction.

She turned and caught him watching. A soft smile formed on her face.

"You okay?" he asked. "You've been pretty quiet."

"I was thinking about the Gentry children." She frowned and recounted what happened at work the prior day.

"Not knowing has got to be hard."

"I understand why Melinda did it. I'm way too attached to the children to be impartial. But she could tell me where they are. It's as if she's afraid I'll kidnap them again."

Drake squeezed out his frustration on the gear shift. "I wish I could've kept my promise to find them a forever home."

She rested her hand over his. "I know your heart was in the right place, but I also knew you couldn't really do anything so I didn't get my hopes up."

"Still, I'm sorry."

"No, *I'm* sorry." She took a long breath. "We're headed to your family's barbeque, and I don't want to ruin the day. From this moment forward, I'm going to think positively about the children and be happy."

He smiled at her. "I love how you can find the positive. I hope the longer I'm with you, the more that rubs off on me."

Her smile widened, and she took hold of his hand. Her skin was soft and warm, and he wished they were heading somewhere private so he could hold her instead of into his family's big and blustery gathering. He couldn't seem to get enough of touching her and knowing she was right by his side.

How did he go from the footloose and fancy-free guy to this in the span of a few days?

He didn't know, and he didn't care. He was happy, and for the first time in his life, he felt a deep and abiding contentment that he'd been searching for and didn't know it.

He let go of her hand to turn onto his parents' street. Seeing the formal two-story house, he hoped the Gentry kids had been placed in a home like this with parents like his. He'd come to appreciate his parents and his siblings more, and he also hoped when the newness of all these feelings wore off that he wouldn't lose that appreciation.

He pulled up to the beige house with black trim with five windows on the second story and four on the main floor and nestled in tall evergreen and maple trees. An addition had been built on the left side after Clay was born to up the number of bedrooms.

He parked behind other family vehicles.

Natalie removed her hand to unbuckle her seatbelt. "I knew there would be a lot of people here, but look at all of these cars."

"Nervous?" he asked.

"Yes and no. I know the majority of people, but we haven't been together since you and I became a thing."

"They're all good with it so don't worry." He slid out and hurried around to open her door. He circled his arm around her back and started up the brick walkway. He didn't bother knocking but ushered Natalie in and stepped in behind her. His mom's sixth sense was on alert, and she was in the hallway to greet them.

"Natalie." His mom scooped her into a warm hug. "I'm so glad you came and that you're going to be part of our family."

"Now, Mom, you're getting a little ahead of yourself there," Drake said. "We're not talking about the future yet."

His mom released Natalie and hugged him. "I know. But I also know the look of contentment and love in your eyes, and you will be. Trust me."

"You're going to scare Natalie away," he whispered.

His mom stepped back and waved his warning away. "If the full force of all your brothers didn't cause her to run, nothing will."

Natalie laughed. "She's probably right."

"I saw Reed's vehicle out front," Drake said, changing the subject before his mother said anything else. "So no baby yet, then."

His mother frowned. "Now don't go spoiling my day by bringing that up. And don't bug your sister. She's just as disappointed that she's gone beyond her due date."

"Elvis is a stubborn little guy, just like his mama." Drake laughed.

"Takes one to know one." His mother turned to Natalie. "Everyone's on the deck. I'm just finishing up the potato salad, and the burgers are almost done. Have Drake introduce you to the people you don't know, and we'll eat soon."

"Can I help?" Natalie asked.

"Thank you, but no. After the crazy week you've had, I want you to just sit back and enjoy yourself. Besides, I have my own little army to help tote things." She looked up at Drake. "Isn't that right, son?"

"Absolutely." He gave his mother a smile and an extra hug.

She pulled back, her concerned gaze digging deep. "Two hugs in a matter of minutes. Is something wrong?"

"Nope. I just appreciate you is all."

She swatted a hand at him. "Go on now. I don't need fussing over."

"But you do more often than we give it."

She waved her hand again, seeming embarrassed. "Now go on out and introduce Natalie so I can get that potato salad ready."

He took Natalie's hand and headed down the hall and through the kitchen to two large French doors standing open. His siblings and significant others, plus Brendan's nearly five-year-old step-daughter Karlie sat in plush chairs on the deck.

Drake glanced at Natalie. "You ready to meet everyone?"

She smiled up at him, and his heart somersaulted. God had blessed them with such glorious weather to gather, and this was just the beginning of an amazing life together with this woman at his side and the family spread out before him, welcoming and supporting her. He couldn't imagine being more blessed.

~

Natalie relaxed in the cushy chair, her thoughts full of so many things as the family members joked around her. The Byrd house was just the kind Natalie had longed for when she was a kid. She'd seen similar houses on TV, and she'd wanted forever parents to go with the house, parents who would love her and Gina to the moon and back. She knew her dreams could come true. Good families like she wanted to be a part of were real, and she'd believed it could happen. Until her dad had taken off. Then she realized that idyllic life would never come true for her. She would always live the life of cheap apartments and a sullen mom, and she had to make the best of it.

But today, it felt as if God had flung doors open wide, not only offering her a spectacular man but the forever parents to go with him. And these amazing brothers and sisters and their significant others. Even little Karlie, who couldn't be any more precocious and adorable.

And yet, the Gentry children were clinging to Natalie's thoughts and heart, and she had to work hard not to let it get her down. If only she knew where they were. What they were doing. If they were okay. Adjusting.

"Lunch is ready." Peggy carried a giant bowl of potato salad to the table.

"Help me up, Reed," Sierra said. "If this baby doesn't want to be born yet, I might as well feed him."

Reed gently tugged her out of the chair, and she pressed a hand to her back as she lumbered to the table. Natalie couldn't imagine being pregnant. She hadn't even talked to Drake about potential children. Sure, they'd only started dating, but being together in close confines almost twenty-four hours a day was like going on a hundred dates, and it felt as if they'd known each other for a long time.

"You look so serious." He leaned close. "What're you thinking about?"

"Children," she whispered back. "Now that you're ready to get into a serious relationship, I wondered if you'd thought about that."

"I want at least three. Maybe more, depending on how the first three go."

"Oh." She sat back in surprise.

"Is that a deal breaker?"

"No. I mean, I've honestly never thought in terms of numbers of kids, just knew that if I ever married, I would want the chance to raise kids the opposite of how I was raised."

He took her hand. "You're going to be an amazing mother."

"And you'll be a great dad. Though I might have to rein in your love of adventure so you don't put the children in too many risky situations." She grinned at him.

He laughed. "That would be good."

"Come on, Natalie," his mother said. "Since you're our newest member of the family, you're up next."

Drake didn't object to his mother's comment, just got up without letting go of Natalie's hand and brought her to her feet with him. A long folding table butted up to the house was filled with burger fixings, fresh fruit, baked beans in a Crock-Pot, and a giant bowl of potato salad. And at the end of the table were all the ingredients to make s'mores. A fire pit surrounded by colorful Adirondack chairs sat in the yard.

"Nana, can I eat too?" Karlie tugged on Peggy's hand. "I'm really hungry."

"Karlie," her mother, Jenna, warned. "Wait your turn."

"Aw." Her lower lip slid out.

"It happens to be your turn next." Peggy smiled at the little girl, who wore a sundress and white sandals. "Let's get in line behind Natalie, and I'll help you fix your plate."

"Do you like Natalie?" Karlie asked.

"Karlie!" Jenna leaned forward as if preparing to get out of her chair to come after the little tike.

"What? I just wanna know cause I like her. She said really nice stuff about my dress."

"It is a pretty dress, and I do like Natalie. A lot." Peggy grabbed a plate. "She loves children, so I know she will become a good friend to you."

Karlie cast Natalie a questioning look. "Is she gonna marry Unca Drake?"

Jenna gasped. "Sweetheart, just get your food and forget all the questions."

"Do you like potato salad?" Peggy asked the child.

"It's yucky."

Jenna looked like she might say something, but Brendan took her hand, and she held her tongue.

"Okay, how about baked beans?"

"Yummy."

As Natalie filled her own plate, she listened to Karlie weigh in on the different foods. Natalie reached the end of the table, where Russ stood wearing a black apron that said *Grill Sergeant* in big white letters.

"We've got cheddar cheese, jalapeno, or Swiss." He held his large stainless steel spatula at the ready. "Or you can have a plain burger, though I only recommend that for people with dairy issues."

"Jalapeno, please." She held out her plate.

"Yep," he said looking at Drake. "She's a keeper."

Natalie felt ridiculously proud of her decision to have the spicy burger. "I'm a big fan of hot things."

"Odd that you chose Drake then," Erik said and laughed at his own joke.

The others laughed with him, including Drake, telling her that he was secure in his looks where *Hand-Me-Dunn* might've come out for her. But come to think of it, *Hand-Me-Dunn* hadn't made an appearance at all today, not even when Natalie had stepped onto the deck and could've felt just a little bit inferior as she remembered her family's rusty charcoal grill on the tiny apartment patio slab and the ancient lawn chairs they'd never been able to replace. That was, when they had a patio. She'd endured times when they'd lived in their car. In fact, Natalie could only remember them grilling food once, and they sure wouldn't have had any company.

Drake got a Swiss cheeseburger, and she followed him to a long table, where they sat across from Sierra and Reed. Jenna, Brendan, and Karlie soon joined them. Another table and folding chairs had been set up at one end to accommodate all fourteen people in the group.

"Sit on my lap, little bit," Brendan said to Karlie. "So we can save a chair for the big people."

She cast him the most stunning smile, her expression filled with adoration, as she climbed up on his lap. She looked at Natalie. "This is my daddy."

"I know," Natalie said. "And it looks like he's a great dad."

Karlie gave a serious nod. "He doesn't make fun of me."

Jenna frowned but didn't explain.

Drake leaned close to Natalie. "She has juvenile idiopathic arthritis, and her father used to make her feel bad about being sick."

Shocked, Natalie looked at the precious child. Natalie

knew parents could be cruel. She'd seen it over and over. She just didn't expect to see it here. She offered a prayer for the child's health and one of thanks that she now had a father who cared for her.

She dug into her burger. "Oh, wow. This is really good."

"Shh, Dad might hear you, and his head will get even bigger." Aiden set down his plate and pulled out a chair for his wife, Harper.

"I can hear all of you," Russ said. "And I know my burgers are the best. Peg tells me every time I make them."

"Did you ever stop to think she does that so you'll keep making them and she gets a break from cooking?" Clay asked from his place in line behind his fiancée, Toni.

"But I..." Russ clutched his hand to his chest and mocked an offended look. "Say it isn't so, Peg."

She gave him a big kiss on the cheek. "It isn't so, honey. Your burgers could win awards."

"Agreed." Harper held hers up. "Best ever."

"And you've had burgers from all over the world, right?" Aiden asked.

She nodded. "I've even had one in Hamburg. Yours is still better."

Russ puffed out his chest and smiled while Peggy put her arm around him and looked at the table. Clay and Toni sat, leaving a place next to them for Erik, who was grabbing a burger, Pong at his side. The end chairs remained open for Peggy and Russ.

Natalie's heart overflowed with happiness. This was her dream come true. The family she'd always wanted.

Please, she prayed. *Don't let this slip away from me. And please, please, please let the Gentry children be placed with an amazing family like this one. A forever family.*

Sierra suddenly pushed her chair back, her eyes wide. "My water just broke."

Reed jumped to his feet, his chair tipping over behind him. "We should leave now."

Sierra nodded and stood.

Peggy rushed over and gave Sierra a hug. "Go. Go. If you're like me, you won't have a very long labor at all. We'll clean up here and get to the hospital as soon as we can."

Sierra smiled at her mom. "I can't believe it's finally time." The smile faded as she clutched her belly and moaned. "Oh, yeah. It's time."

"Let's go." Sounding panicked, Reed took her arm and led her to the door to a chorus of best wishes.

The guys resumed eating, and Peggy shook her head. "I knew nothing much could stop you from eating, but now I've seen it all."

"Hey," Drake said, "we're going to be at the hospital for hours. We need to fortify."

"He's right," Peggy said. "Everyone eat up before we go."

Natalie started eating again, but as she pictured the upcoming scene at the hospital, she suddenly felt awkward. Did she go with the family? She barely knew Sierra, and this was such a personal time.

As if Drake read her mind, he bumped her shoulder and lowered his voice so only she could hear. "Will you come with me to the hospital? I know we're all new to you, but I'd like you there."

"Of course," she said.

He rested his hand over hers for a moment and looked into her eyes as if he knew she needed reassurance.

"Can I watch the baby come out?" Karlie asked.

Laughter burst from the others, and she looked crestfallen.

"Sorry, honey." Jenna ran a hand over Karlie's hair. "We'll go in to see the baby as soon as Sierra says it's okay, but he'll be born and wrapped in a blanket by then."

"Okay." And just like that—like a child could do—she moved on and scooped up a bite of baked beans. "I like Nana's beans."

"Thank you, sweetie." Peggy stood by the table holding her plate as if she might have to dump it and run.

As if taking a cue from her, everyone put their attention to eating, and they were all soon cleaning up. The guys knew exactly what to do. Jenna, Harper, and Toni seemed to be well versed too. Even Pong seemed to know what to do and laid down under the table and out of the way.

"Hey, Natalie," Russ said. "Mind getting me a container to put the leftover burgers in?"

"Glad to." By the time she made it to the kitchen, Drake had gotten out a big glass container with a red plastic cover and held it out to her. Their hands touched, and she smiled at him. He fired her a sweltering look, and she suddenly wished this newfound family was already on their way to the hospital so she could have a few minutes alone with Drake.

"Don't let Mom catch you slacking off." Clay winked at her.

She rushed out with the container and held it out as Russ plopped the burgers in. "I never have this many left. Guys just didn't eat their usual quota. Maybe I should bring them to the hospital. I know they're all gonna be hungry in an hour or so."

Natalie wasn't sure what to say to that.

"Yeah, you're right. Not a good idea." He took the cover from her hand and snapped it on the container. "Let's get out of here."

She turned to find the tables bare and everyone inside. She and Russ crowded into the space with them.

"Okay, too many cooks in the kitchen," Peggy

announced. "Dad and I'll go ahead while you all finish here."

Russ removed his apron, and Peggy grabbed her purse from a built-in desk on the far wall.

"Mom's right," Drake announced. "Too many cooks. Natalie and I'll head out too."

No one argued, so she took Drake's hand and followed his parents from the house. They set off for the hospital, where Natalie knew she would find out what it was like to truly be a member of this amazing family.

In the waiting room five hours later, Drake watched his mom give Reed a hug, then the expectant father all but fled toward the hall. Malone had joined them and caught up to him. She was dressed in high fashion, as usual. She wore a leather jacket and crisp white blouse with designer jeans and knee-high leather boots. She didn't say a word but grabbed her brother up in a hug. He sighed, gave her a tense smile, and rushed away.

Each time Reed updated them on Sierra's progress—everything was going according to her birth plan, and Elvis would be born soon—Drake could feel the guy's anxiety. Drake had never seen Reed so amped and terrified.

In this situation, Drake would likely feel the same way. Maybe worse.

"Please, Peg." His dad stood. "Tell me I wasn't such a basket case when our boys were born."

"Not by the time we had Drake and Erik, but before that? Yeah, you were." She chuckled.

His dad planted his hands on his waist. "Not possible."

"Mom doesn't lie," Drake said.

"No, but she *does* exaggerate."

She circled an arm around her husband's waist. "This isn't one of those times, dear."

He shook his head.

The others shared a knowing look. Sure, they hadn't seen their dad at the time, but as Drake had said, their mom would never lie, so they knew it was true.

"Okay, back to charades," his mom announced. "Who's up?"

"Me. Prepare to be dazzled by my acting skills." Malone grinned and grabbed a card from the game box.

They laughed and resumed the game, and Drake participated, but he held tightly to Natalie's hand as they played and just sat back to admire his amazing family with a strong belief and reliance on God. And now he had a girlfriend too. She fit in like she'd been here for years. Sure, she seemed a bit tentative at times, which was why he held tightly to her hand. Or maybe he did it to convince himself that they were really going to pursue a relationship together.

Many rounds later, Reed barreled into the waiting room. "Eight pounds, thirteen ounces. Big healthy boy."

"That's a Byrd for you." Their mom grinned. "Big and strapping from birth."

"I'm a dad," Reed said, looking baffled. "For real. A dad."

"Congrats, big brother." Malone hugged him as congratulations were shouted all around.

"Okay, so I'll come back and tell you when you can see him." He bolted away.

Drake hugged Natalie, but he wasn't sure why. Maybe it was because it was such a special moment, and he figured that was a good way to express his joy.

"This is so exciting," Natalie whispered and pulled back, her face glowing. "I see the tough side of babies coming into this world with challenges the child doesn't even know he will face. But here, with this big loving family, it's just the opposite. Thank you for letting me be a part of the special day."

"I'm the one who's blessed to have you here." He sat back and snaked his arm around her shoulders. feeling so contented that he figured his face held the same big dopey look that Reed's had before he bolted.

The family talked about the birth and speculated on the baby's coloring. Would he have dark hair like Reed or be blond like Sierra? After growing a little more comfortable with kids, Drake was looking forward to meeting the little guy.

Reed came back, the same big smile brimming on his face, glowing from ear to ear. "You can come in now. I begged for permission to let you all in at the same time, but get rowdy and you'll be bounced."

Their mom and dad went first, and then the guys filled in behind in birth order. They were so accustomed to the lineup that, even if they didn't like it, it felt normal.

When Drake laid eyes on Sierra smiling down on the baby wrapped in a blue blanket, their parents' faces enamored and eyes glistening, tears stung his eyes too. He'd never felt so emotional before. So overwhelmed. Birth was an amazing thing. So amazing, and he'd never really understood that.

Natalie's hand slipped into his, and she grinned up at him, her eyes brimming too.

Drake squeezed her hand, swallowed, and tried his hardest for a level voice as he looked back at his sister. "Do we have a name?"

"You would be the one to ask." Sierra wrinkled her nose at him. "And we do. Meet Asher John Rice. John after Reed and Malone's dad."

"Thank you. That's so special," Malone said, not even trying to hide the tears rolling down her cheeks.

"My pleasure." Sierra gave Malone's hand a squeeze. "And we chose Asher because we like it and, hey, why not start with an A? Just in case."

Drake groaned along with his brothers.

"Oh, sweetheart." Her mother kissed Sierra's cheek. "That's a lovely name. Sounds like a judge or lawyer."

"Now, Mom," Sierra warned. "It's a little too soon to decide on his career."

"Besides," Reed said. "No son of mine is going to be a lawyer."

"Hey, now." Malone socked Reed in the arm. "What's wrong with lawyers?"

"What's not?" Drake asked.

The others exploded in laughter, and Malone grinned.

Karlie looked confused. "Can I see the baby?"

Brendan lifted her up and took her to the head of the bed. Jenna joined them, and Brendan put his arm around his wife, the warmth of contentment on her face.

Karlie patted Asher's head. "I like Asher." She swiveled to look at her mother. "Can we get a baby just like him?"

Jenna's peace evaporated, and she gaped at her daughter.

Brendan didn't freak out at all. "We'll for sure get a baby someday, but right now, I don't want to share my attention with anyone but you and your mom."

"Aw," Peggy said. "That's my son."

Drake had to agree that Brendan had a stellar way of answering Karlie's question.

Karlie smiled at Brendan. "I don't want to share you either. You're the bestest."

Sierra yawned.

"Okay, everyone," Peggy announced. "Sierra and Asher need their rest. Let's head back to the house for s'mores."

"S'mores, yay!" Karlie clapped her hands.

Everyone took their turn to wish Sierra and Reed well

then exited the room. His mother's phone rang, and she took the call while the others strolled toward the exit.

They were nearly at the elevators when she caught up to them. "Your dad and I'll meet you all back at the house. We have a stop to make."

"Now?" Drake asked, baffled by his mother's behavior. She would never leave the family on Sunday. Especially on such a big day.

"It's a surprise." She gave him a secretive grin. "One I know you'll enjoy."

26

_____

Natalie clicked on her seatbelt in Drake's truck. "Any idea where your parents went?"

He shook his head. "I'm totally baffled."

"Maybe she wanted to get some sparkling cider or something to celebrate Asher's birth."

"Nah, she's a planner. I'm sure she already has that in the fridge."

"She's an amazing woman and mother."

Drake nodded. "We are most blessed. As you will be someday, if I have anything to say about it."

"You know it's too soon to think about something like that."

"Is it?" He glanced at her. "What difference does time make when it feels so right?"

"We need to make sure we're compatible. If we agree on the big things in life, and if we don't, decide if we can live with the differences."

"I know you're right," he said.

"And you have to really know you're ready to settle down. And I have to be certain I can believe in happily ever after. That our emotions, which have been running high, aren't clouding our judgment."

He locked eyes on her for the briefest of moments then looked back at the road. "I know what I want, and I hope to show you that happily ever after does exist. Things won't be perfect, but we'll work through all the problems."

"How can you be so certain?"

"Because I know that once I commit to you for life, I will do everything in my power to make sure I don't do anything to ruin that commitment. And I know you're the same way. You honor your commitments."

"Yeah, I do. But I've never had one this important before."

"We'll go slowly then. Whatever you need. If you need to back off from my family, we can do that starting right now. I can take you home if you want."

"No, oh, no. That would be rude, but also I have to see this surprise." She grinned at him, thankful that he caught her lighthearted mood again.

A mood he kept as they left the truck to join his family in the backyard again and helped his brothers gather the s'mores items and bring it all out on trays to the fire pit.

Natalie chose a bright red chair, and Drake took the navy one next to her. The others settled around the pit, Karlie standing at the ready with a roasting stick. Erik knelt by the fire pit and started laying kindling in the middle.

"You planning on burning down the neighborhood," Drake asked.

"Karlie said she wanted a big fire, right kid?" He grinned up at her.

"I do." She jumped up and down and clapped her hands. "Daddy said I get to roast my own mellows today."

Brendan grabbed the stick. "Big girls are careful with the pointy end."

"I'm a big girl."

"I know, and that's how I know you'll be careful."

She let him hold the stick and flung her arms around his neck. "I love you, Daddy."

"I love you too, little bit." Brendan let out a sigh of contentment, and Jenna placed her hand on his arm and smiled at him.

An overwhelming urge to have her own child hit Natalie, something that had never happened before. Maybe it was because she was embarking on a serious relationship with an amazing man, and that had never happened before either.

Erik struck a match, the kindling caught fire, crackling and flames sparking. Karlie jumped down and stood with her hand on Brendan's arm. She looked like she wanted to dance again but was holding back because she wanted to be a big girl.

The power of a single parental comment always struck Natalie. She knew firsthand how they could help and how they could hurt.

What kind of parents were the Gentry children experiencing right now?

Oh, Father, please. I know I keep asking when I should trust You. But give them a good home together.

Drake leaned close to her. "You okay?"

"Just thinking about what great parents Brendan and Jenna are. Your parents too."

"And so you're worried about the Gentry kids."

He really had come to know her. "Yeah."

"I've been thinking about them too. Especially Willow."

"I know I should be trusting God. I know worry is a sin. I just don't know how to turn it off right now."

"Wouldn't it be great if we could just turn it off like a

light switch and flip on another one for trusting God? Or turn off our doubts?"

"Yeah," she said, staring into the now blazing fire.

"Is it time?" Karlie asked. "Can I have a mellow?"

"We should wait for Nana and Papa to get back," Jenna said.

"I don't want to wait." She stared at the fire.

"A big girl would wait," Brendan said.

Karlie pouted.

"Anyone know where they went?" Clay asked.

The others shook their heads.

"Must be pretty important if Mom skipped out on even a minute of Sunday family time," Aiden said.

"Maybe it has something to do with Asher," Harper suggested.

"I think Mom would have that all covered," Clay said.

"Not if it's a personalized item that she couldn't get until she knew the name," Jenna said.

"Right. Good thought."

"Mommy, you're waiting," Karlie said. "Means you're a big girl too."

Laughter rang around the fire pit, and little Karlie looked confused again.

"I wish I had other kids to play with," she said. "'Cause I don't know why you keep laughing."

"Your wish is fulfilled," Peggy said from the patio doors.

Natalie swiveled to look at her. She held Sadie Gentry, and Logan held onto Russ's hand. Willow stood next to them.

"Let's go meet everyone you don't know." Peggy led the children out to the fire pit.

"We're going to make s'mores," Karlie announced. "I can share my fork with you."

Logan went straight toward her, but Pong caught his

attention, and he stopped to smother the dog in a hug. "We get to be in your family. I'm going to love you."

Natalie gaped at them. "I don't understand."

"We're going to live with Nana and Papa," Willow announced.

"You're what?" Natalie looked between Russ and Peggy.

"It was all Drake's idea. We often talked about fostering kids. Even got approved, but we didn't step out and do it. Then Drake said that these little sweeties might be split up, and we knew it was time to quit talking and take action."

Natalie jumped up. "I'm not dreaming, am I?"

"Want me to pinch you?" Drake grinned at her.

"No, but I want to hug your parents." She swept Peggy into a tight hug. "My heart is so full from your generosity. I am so blessed to know you."

"I'm the one who's blessed." Peggy leaned back. "They're amazing kids that God has given us a chance to help raise for as long as they're with us. Nothing better than that."

"And since I'm retired now, I'll be around more, so that will help," Russ added.

Natalie approached him for a hug, and he accepted a quick one. "Now let's get some marshmallows going."

He grabbed the package from the tray and ripped it open. Sadie, Logan, and Karlie ran to him.

Willow hung back and looked up at Natalie. "Are you going to be part of this family?"

Natalie thought about her answer. "I hope to."

"I'm glad. I cried when they said you couldn't be our caseworker anymore. But this will be even better, right?"

"Right." Natalie knelt and hugged Willow, giving her the kind of emotion-filled hug she'd been wanting to offer for days.

Willow starting crying, her little body sobbing, and Natalie's heart creased from this child's visceral pain, which she would continue to feel for some time. But Natalie knew the child was in good hands now. The best hands. God's and Russ and Peggy Byrd's capable hands.

She let the child cry herself out, and when she settled down, Natalie leaned back. "Want to go make that s'more now?"

Willow nodded, her expression still serious.

Drake moved closer to her. "I'll bet I can make a more perfect marshmallow than you."

"Nah." Willow's eyes brightened. "I'm pretty good at it."

"Oh, game on, girl. Game on." He headed for the forks, and Willow raced past him, excitement on her face.

"By the way, we can take that fishing trip anytime you want," he said, as she passed. "I have just the pole for you to use."

"I wanna go." Willow's voice was tight. "But no worms. You promise?"

"I promise."

A smile spread across her freckled face, a genuine, gloriously happy smile.

Thank you. Thank you. Thank you.

Natalie knew in her heart that with the Byrd family at Willow's side, this girl was going to be okay. Not unscathed by the events but okay. Drake was a big part of that. She wanted to hug him right now for his kindness but just stood back and watched him joke with Willow as they poked their marshmallows into the fire.

"Hey, I want in on this action." Erik shoved Drake out of the way, and Pong gave a sharp yelp.

Willow giggled.

"It's okay, boy," Logan said. "We're all having fun. I like fun."

Aiden and Harper had taken Logan in hand and helped

him make his s'more, and Sadie sat on Toni's lap while Clay fixed one for her.

Peggy and Russ stepped over to Natalie.

"You have an amazing family," Natalie said. "And I know the Gentry children will do the best that can be expected in your hands."

"Thank you. I hope so. I got permission to homeschool Willow for a while. At least until everything dies down in the media. We'll evaluate from there."

"That will be good for her," Natalie said.

"And then we'll see about adoption if that's a possibility."

Natalie swung to look at her. "You want to adopt them?"

"We're taking it one step at a time," Russ said. "We want what's best for them."

"But you know I already think of them as ours," Peggy said. "So letting them go might be hard."

"Whatever happens, I know you are the right couple to care for these very fragile children," Natalie said with oomph.

They fell silent and watched the adults and children interact. Drake and Willow sat in the grass eating their s'mores and talking. When he'd finished his, he escorted her and Logan inside to wash up, carrying a very messy Sadie with them. When they came out, the children took off toward an old swing set and fort.

"Would be good to build a new one of those," Drake said to his dad. "We could help you and crank it out in one weekend."

Russ nodded. "Gonna get my tape measure now and start the plans."

Peggy gave her husband a glowing smile. "I'll go with you and grab the cider for a toast to Sierra, Reed, and baby Asher."

The couple walked away, and Natalie let out a contented sigh.

"That a good sigh or bad?" Drake asked.

"Good. Very good."

He took both of her hands and smiled at her. "Big day, huh?"

She looked up at him. "Did you know about this?"

"Just that I'd mentioned it to Mom. I didn't really think she'd act on it, but now that she has, I couldn't be happier."

"Yeah, me either."

"I think in the future we should consider adopting them if Mom and Dad can't."

His bombshell should shock her, but it didn't. It felt right.

"You know, when our emotions aren't running so high and we're not fearing for their future. Because now"—he stopped to look at his parents, who were stepping out the door—"with my mom and dad in the picture, they're set for a good long time, and their future is looking bright."

She twined her arms around his neck. His hands came around her waist, and he hauled her closer.

"I'm going to kiss you now, and if you object because everyone is watching, tell me and I'll stop."

She slid her fingers into his hair and drew his head down. Their lips met in an explosion of emotions, and her heart soared. She tried to deepen the kiss, but he pulled back.

"I guess you didn't mind." He grinned.

"Nah, they're going to have to get used to it."

He cupped the side of her face, his touch like a warming balm. "You look happy."

"I am, and I was just thinking I'm like the children in more ways than I ever knew. I didn't experience great parents growing up, and I never got the amazing family until now, but I did. Finally. And seeing all of you. Seeing your priorities, your love for one another, I know you'll do your best to make our relationship work, and we'll have just as bright of a future as the kids."

"No question about it. That's what we Byrds do." He grinned at her. "We flock together."

～

Thank you so much for reading NIGHT MOVES, Book four in my Nighthawk Security series.

I'd like to invite you to learn more about the books in the series and my other books by signing up for my newsletter and connecting with me on social media or even send me a messsage. I also hold monthly giveaways that I'd like to share with you, and I'd love to hear from you.

You'll also receive a **FREE** excerpt of my upcoming book and learn about my monthly giveaways when you sign up. So stop by this page and join in.
www.susansleeman.com/sign-up/

Now read on for a sneak peek at the next book in the Nighthawk Security series.

~

NIGHT WATCH - BOOK 5

Everything points to suicide or accidental death
Underwater crime scene investigator, Kennedy Walker is
shocked when her mother dies and the police rule her
death a suicide or an accidental overdose. Her scientist-
mother was on the verge of a scientific breakthrough, and
Kennedy knows her mother would never end her life, but
the detective won't listen. Kennedy moves back to her home
town and commits to finding her mother's killer and
finishing her work.

And she must prove them wrong.
Kennedy digs deeper, garnering the killer's focus, and he
puts her in his cross-hairs. She can't give up on such an

important project, so she swallows down her unease over the tumultuous breakup with Erik Byrd in college and hires Nighthawk Security, not only to protect her, but to help find her mother's killer. It takes only one look for both of them to know their feelings for each other haven't gone away. With so many people counting on her to complete the project, giving in to old feelings is a distraction neither she or Erik can afford, and they both need to keep watch. Especially in the darkest hours of the night, when the killer comes out to play.

Pre-order Night Watch from your favorite bookseller!

NIGHT PREY - BOOK 6

She lived for upholding the law...
Defense attorney, Malone Rice, doesn't want to go to her

fifteen year class reunion. Attending means running into her former high school flame, now Portland police detective, Liam Murphy. But when the committee decides to honor her for her pro-bono work with homeless teens, she knows it would be churlish not to attend. She will have to go and make the best of it.

But now the law won't save her.

As expected, Liam attends the reunion, but what Malone doesn't expect—could never expect—is that Liam would find her standing over their classmate's dead body. Or that she would still have feelings for the once bad-boy of their high school. Liam's struggling too, between arresting Malone for murder and his age-old attraction to her. He walks a tightrope, until evidence surfaces that the real killer's still out there, and Malone becomes his prey. Can Liam overcome his feelings to focus and uncover the truth before the killer strikes again and Malone ends up dead?

Pre-order Night Prey from your favorite bookseller!

NIGHTHAWK SECURITY SERIES
Protecting others when unspeakable danger lurks.

Keep reading for more information on the additional books in the Nighthawk Security Series where the Cold Harbor and Truth Seekers teams work side-by-side with Nighthawk Security.

A woman plagued by a stalker. Children of a murderer. A woman whose mother died under suspicious circumstances.

All in danger. Lives on the line. Needing protection.

Enter the brothers of Nighthawk Security. The five Byrd brothers with years of former military and law enforcement experience coming together to offer protection and investigation services. Their goal—protecting others when unspeakable danger lurks.

Book 1 Night Fall – November, 2020
Book 2 – Night Vision – December, 2020
Book 3 - Night Hawk – January, 2021
Book 4 –Night Moves – July, 2021
Book 5 – Night Watch – August, 2021
Book 6 – Night Prey – October, 2021

For More Details Visit -
www.susansleeman.com/books/nighthawk-security/

THE TRUTH SEEKERS

People are rarely who they seem

A twin who never knew her sister existed, a mother whose child is not her own, a woman whose father is anything but her father. All searching. All seeking. All needing help and hope.

Meet the unsung heroes of the Veritas Center. The Truth Seekers – a team, that includes experts in forensic anthropology, DNA, trace evidence, ballistics, cybercrimes, and toxicology. Committed to restoring hope and families by solving one mystery at a time, none of them are prepared for when the mystery comes calling close to home and threatens to destroy the only life they've known.

For More Details Visit -
www.susansleeman.com/books/truth-seekers/

BOOKS IN THE COLD HARBOR SERIES

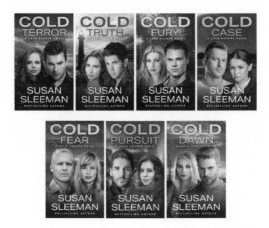

Blackwell Tactical – this law enforcement training facility and protection services agency is made up of former military and law enforcement heroes whose injuries keep them from the line of duty. When trouble strikes, there's no better team to have on your side, and they would give everything, even their lives, to protect innocents.

For More Details Visit -
www.susansleeman.com/books/cold-harbor/

HOMELAND HEROES SERIES

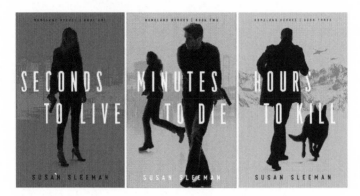

When the clock is ticking on criminal activity conducted on or facilitated by the Internet there is no better team to call other than the RED team, a division of the HSI—Homeland Security's Investigation Unit. RED team includes FBI and DHS Agents, and US Marshal's Service Deputies.

For More Details Visit -

www.susansleeman.com/books/homeland-heroes/

WHITE KNIGHTS SERIES

Join the White Knights as they investigate stories plucked from today's news headlines. The FBI Critical Incident Response Team includes experts in crisis management, explosives, ballistics/weapons, negotiating/criminal profiling, cyber crimes, and forensics. All team members are former military and they stand ready to deploy within four hours, anytime and anywhere to mitigate the highest-priority threats facing our nation.

www.susansleeman.com/books/white-knights/

ABOUT SUSAN

SUSAN SLEEMAN is a bestselling and award-winning author of more than 40 inspirational/Christian and clean read romantic suspense books. In addition to writing, Susan also hosts the website, TheSuspenseZone.com.

Susan currently lives in Oregon, but has had the pleasure of living in nine states. Her husband is a retired church music director and they have two beautiful daughters, a very special son-in-law, and an adorable grandson.

For more information visit:
www.susansleeman.com

44459076R00189